Acknowledgements

I stumbled across the premise of this story quite by accident. I wanted to try my hand at a capturing a period and remembered vaguely reading a story about a socialite in England, who flew planes for the Air Transport Auxiliary (ATA), during the Second World War. I recalled reading the article about her with fascination and decided to find out more; it was then that I came across the American equivalent of the ATA...The Womens Service Airforce Pilots or WASP

The more I researched about the WASP the more interested I became, and the more determined to ensure that I did their story justice within the confines of my own little tale. I spent hours on a fantastic website resource Wings Across America, reading articles and documents as well as reading and listening to interviews with the WASP themselves. To say I became a little obsessed would be correct!

Many of the situations that occur during the book have been based upon real life experiences of these remarkable women and whilst I have tried to be as accurate as I can, there are occasions where I have used artistic license, it is a work of fiction after all and not a historical textbook.

I have many people to thank, so thank you to those that read this story in its original guise and my everlasting gratitude goes to those that subsequently became my guinea pigs - Angela, Karin, Jennifer, Jenny H, Margaret, Lesley D and Lesley P thank you!

Particular thanks go to Fiona whose ideas, questions, and feedback were invaluable.

Finally, all my love and appreciation goes to my wife for her encouragement and patience (particularly when editing and proofreading various drafts).

Silver Wings

by

H.P. Munro

Copyright@2013, H.P. Munro.

All rights reserved. No part of this book may be reproduced or transmitted in any form by any means electrical or mechanical, including photocopy without permission in writing from the author.

All characters within this work are fictitious. Any resemblance to real persons living or dead is purely coincidental.

For Jane

Contents

Acknowledgements 3
Contents 6
Prologue 7
Chapter One 15
Chapter Two 25
Chapter Three 36
Chapter Four 51
Chapter Five 69
Chapter Six 88
Chapter Seven 112
Chapter Eight 136
Chapter Nine 152
Chapter Ten 159
Chapter Eleven 174
Chapter Twelve 181
Chapter Thirteen 199
Chapter Fourteen 223
Chapter Fifteen 226
Epilogue 236
Entry In May 2012 Airforce Magazine 246
About the Author 249
Other Titles by Author 250

Prologue

<u>March 8th 2010 – Washington, DC.</u>

Joanne Parsons yawned widely, her jaw popping at the action. She rolled her shoulder, careful not to inflict any further damage to it, silently cursing the injury that was preventing her from flying. Not being able to do what she loved to do was making her even more cranky than normal.

"Aren't you excited?" Jennifer asked pushing her tray along the shelf, frowning at the breakfast options available, finally settling on a bowl of oatmeal.

Grabbing a bowl of fresh fruit Joanne shot her a look of disgust, "No…why would I be excited?" She turned and started to walk briskly towards a table.

Jennifer gave the server a grateful smile as she scooted behind Joanne, "Did you not read the pack they gave us? These women flew for the military thirty years before women officially graduated from flight training. Why wouldn't you be excited by that?"

Tossing her tray down onto the table and flopping down onto a seat, Joanne picked up a fork and started to pick at her fruit, "Because they're old, they're going to be like, what, ninety? What am I going to talk to a ninety year old about?" She stabbed a piece of pineapple and put it in her mouth. Then, waving her fork in the air, she continued, "She'll be old and probably senile and…" she leaned forward conspiratorially towards Jennifer. "And, she'll probably smell of pee," she nodded leaning back as if her case was now at rest.

Looking at her colleague in shock Jennifer shook her head slowly, "There are so many bits of what you just said that are wrong, that I don't know where to even begin."

Shrugging Joanne continued to separate out the fruit in her bowl with her fork, "You know I'm right. Two days babysitting a pee smelly old woman is not why I joined the Air Force."

Unable to respond Jennifer just sat with her jaw slack while Joanne ate her breakfast.

"What?" Joanne asked innocently, noticing Jennifer's expression.

"You are going to burn in hell," Jennifer shook her head quickly, gathering her tray and standing up. She had known Joanne a long time and was used to her brusqueness but her response to what Jennifer regarded as an honor, surprised even Jennifer.

"Yeah? Well be sure to save me a space," Joanne quipped not looking up from her plate. Jennifer spun round, glared at the woman and letting out a small growl felt her entire body tensing with frustration.

"Just because you can't fly right now, doesn't mean you have to be a complete bitch about everything," Jennifer seethed. "I regard this as a privilege and you should too!" she added, before storming out of the canteen.

"Privilege my ass," Joanne muttered under her breath, rolling her injured shoulder slowly.

***

Checking the flight arrivals board from California, Joanne frowned, the flight that she was there to meet had landed a half hour before and a number of people had come out of the arrivals entrance. She, however, was still there holding up a board like a damn chauffeur and was starting to lose the small amount of patience that she had with this assignment.

"Probably died on the flight or too busy changing her diaper to get her ass out here," she grumbled aloud to herself, halting as she felt a tap on her shoulder.

Joanne turned round, her head recoiling slightly in surprise at the elderly Hispanic woman standing close to her. Deep brown eyes were studying the young woman in uniform carefully.

"I'm who you're waiting for. You'll be Parsons?"

"I…um…yeah. Where'd you? How did you?" Joanne spluttered as she cast a look back towards the arrivals gate. She was sure that this woman had not passed her.

"Abuela!... I said to wait!" running, pulling two suitcases behind her was a dark-haired woman in her thirties, her brown eyes similar to the older woman's. As she watched the woman approach, an unexpected flicker of attraction sparked in Joanne and she started to think that the assignment might not be as boring as she had anticipated.

"Hi," she said breathlessly to Joanne. "I'm sorry, we came in with the pilots, they heard they had a WASP on board so they wanted to show her the cockpit and talk to her, and of course my grandmother couldn't resist."

"Flying these days, it's like playing a God-damned computer game. All those dials and buttons, there's no finesse to it anymore!" the older woman started to shuffle off at a surprising pace for her age, the tip of her walking cane tapping against the tiled floor as she walked. "Well come on, can't wait all day…I could die anytime," she shouted over her shoulder.

"Is she always like that?" Joanne asked.

"Oh no, she's on her best behavior today," the young woman replied, setting off in pursuit of her grandmother. Joanne paused before tossing the piece of cardboard with 'Rivera' written on it into the trash and setting off after her charge.

***

"So have you been to Washington before?" Joanne asked awkwardly in her stilted attempt at small talk. She was never great with people when she first met them; the fact that the woman sitting next to her was stunning compounded this feeling.

Staring out of the window from the rear of the car at the passing scenery, Lily smiled in recollection, "Many a time, Ellie here studied nearby so we visited often." Leaning forward, Lily checked the insignia on the shoulder of the young woman's uniform. "So First Lieutenant Parsons, how old are you?"

"Abuela?" Ellie gasped. "I'm sorry, she can be…direct." The woman apologized turning in her seat to glare at her grandmother.

"It's my age. I don't have time to waste with niceties anymore," Lily grumbled from the back, taking several attempts to propel herself forward to poke her head between the headrests of the two front seats.

"Ma'am, you should put your seatbelt on," Joanne said, glancing over her shoulder.

"Psh," she waved her hand dismissively. "Just you drive carefully, so how old are you?" Lily repeated her question, ignoring the ongoing glare from her granddaughter.

"I'm twenty-eight ma'am," Joanne replied.

"Enough with the ma'am. You make me feel old. It's Lily," the elderly woman huffed. "Twenty-eight eh?" she gave a small smile as she recalled her own life. "I moved back to Florida when I was twenty eight, New York wasn't the place for two young children so Florida it was. You married?"

"No ma…Lily," she corrected. "I'm not married."

"Boyfriend?"

"Nope," Joanne answered, risking a glance towards Ellie, who had turned to watch her response.

Something in her tone and the glance towards Ellie made Lily narrow her eyes before asking, "Girlfriend?" Lily's eyebrow rose as she noticed Joanne's grip on the steering wheel tighten.

"Abeula, seriously," Ellie growled. "You can't ask that, she's military." She flashed another apologetic look at Joanne.

"Stupid God-dammed policy. As if who you love means you can't serve your country," Lily sighed and sat back in the seat. "I don't understand your generation, twenty eight and single. You're a good looking girl," she said tapping Joanne on the shoulder. "My Ellie here is a good looking girl but she's single too. She's too fussy to find the right person," she added, watching Joanne's reaction closely, a small sly smile appeared on her face as the young officer's eyebrow raised at the use of the pronoun. "You can't go through life without a little love in it girls. Life is over in the blink of an eye and love is precious, you have to hold onto it tightly." Lily stared out of the window lost in her memories. Moments later the car filled with the sound of gentle snores from the backseat.

Joanne turned to Ellie who was smirking at her sleeping grandmother.

"So where did you study?" she whispered trying not to waken Lily.

"It's okay you can speak normally, she sleeps through anything. I studied medicine at Hopkins."

"Impressive," Joanne replied, flipping the indicator and turning towards the hotel where Lily and her granddaughter would be staying.

Ellie shrugged modestly, "My grandma always said that I was to leave the world a better place than it was when I entered it."

Pulling the car to a halt outside the hotel, Joanne released her seat belt, "That's a big ask."

"She also said that small victories were still victories," Ellie responded, opening her door and stepping out.

Walking into the foyer Joanne pulled Lily's case behind her. "There's a breakfast reception tomorrow with dignitaries and similar folk, followed by a trip to the war memorial and then to the ceremony itself and tonight, if you feel up for it, there is a dinner with some of the other WASP attendees. They've brought in a whole host of memorabilia and photographs from the Sweetwater Museum and have set them up in one of the conference rooms here," she completed her speech learned from half listening to Jennifer as she had repeatedly read out the two-day itinerary to her.

"Give me ten minutes to go freshen up then I want to go see the display," Lily said as they waited for Ellie to collect their room keys.

Ellie walked over catching the last part of her grandmother's announcement, "Abuela, are you sure you don't want to rest? It was a long flight." She had promised her mother that she would not let the matriarch of their family overdo it.

Lily scowled at the younger woman, "It's bad enough that your mother is so worried that I'm about to up and die that she has you escort me Ellie, but don't you start to play doctor with me. I am fine, and I would like to go see the display before dinner where I'll be so busy trying to remember people's names that I won't have time."

Joanne fought the smirk that was threatening at the elderly woman's crusty demeanor.

"What you smiling at fly girl? You wait there and give me ten minutes to go change my diaper and I'll be back down."

Joanne's eyes shot open in surprise.

"You don't wear a diaper Abuela," Ellie said horrified.

"I know that, but at the airport Parsons here seemed to be under the misconception that I do," Lily replied with a wide smile on her face as she hobbled off towards the lift leaving Joanne opening and closing her mouth at Ellie unable to create an adequate sound.

Ellie smiled and reached out a hand to Joanne's shoulder, "Don't worry, two days and you never have to see her again, I get to fly home with her!"

Joanne laughed, "She's feisty. I'll give her that."

"Oh yes," Ellie chuckled.

The sound of her laugh generated a warm feeling in Joanne's chest; so much so that she immediately decided that she had to hear it again.

Ellie studied the patterns on the carpet before looking towards the elevator where her grandmother was waiting impatiently pressing the call button repeatedly with her cane. She chewed her lip nervously before turning to Joanne, "About earlier. I'm sorry if she made you uncomfortable in the car. She seems to think that her role in life is to find me a partner or embarrass me in the process."

"That's okay. She does seem intent on finding you someone."

"I'm the only single one in the family, she says that she needs to make sure I have love before she goes," Ellie sighed, looking affectionately towards her grandmother.

"Sounds like my mother," Joanne said sympathetically.

"I doubt she can be as bad as Lily over there," Ellie grinned.

Joanne mirrored her grin, "Oh I'm fairly sure I could hold my own with some appalling stories of her set ups." Her grin turned into a shy smile, "Maybe later when your grandmother is settled, we could meet in the bar and swap war stories."

"Okay," Ellie licked her lips nervously. The ding of the elevator door caught her attention. "I should go," she said, pointing towards her grandmother. She paused as if to say something else then shook her head slightly before walking away pulling the suitcases behind her. She entered the elevator and caught a final glimpse of Joanne before the doors closed.

"She's cute," Lily said, studying the floor numbers, her eyes wide with fake innocence.

"You're a nightmare," Ellie growled.

"Did you get a date at least?"

"I'm meeting her for drinks later," Ellie replied, rolling her eyes. "You don't even know if she's gay."

It was Lily's turn to roll her eyes. "Have I taught you nothing?" she asked, slapping Ellie's forearm lightly. "Trust me…she's gay. But if you're not sure I bet if you asked nicely, she'd tell."

Ellie laughed loudly, grateful that they had reached their floor, "Come you, let's get you into your room and sorted before you cause more trouble."

Chapter One

<u>April 1943 – New York City</u>

It was the drop of water on her face that finally woke Lily from her sleep. Opening one eye she glared up at her roommate, standing with a brown envelope in one hand and a glass of water in the other.

"I swear you could sleep through a hurricane girl," Eva said grinning wildly. She placed the glass of water down on the nightstand and waved the envelope in Lily's face, "It came, it's finally here." She held the envelope in front of Lily's face as she flopped onto the bed beside her.

Drowsily Lily noticed that Eva was still dressed in her nightgown, her thick black hair remained coiled around rollers, which meant Lily hadn't overslept.

"What time is it?" she asked sleepily, rubbing her eyes with the heels of her hands as she sat up.

"It's midday," Eva replied, rustling the envelope impatiently.

Lily let out a frustrated whine, "Eva, I could have had two more hours sleep, before I needed to get up. I didn't get in until eight this morning."

"And? Me and Eli got in at nine. You want sympathy you are lookin' at the wrong woman," Eva scowled. "So you gonna open this or not?"

Lily took the envelope from Eva's hands and stared at the typed address, recalling that the other time she received an official letter from the army it was to tell her of her husband's death.

"It's for you. How many Lily McAllister's you think live here?" Eva said impatiently, nodding encouragingly towards the envelope. "If you don't open it, I will."

She reached out to grab the envelope earning a slap to her hand.

"I'll open it, just not with you sitting there staring at me," Lily replied, clutching the envelope to her chest protectively.

Eva let out a dramatic sigh as she stood. "Fine, I'll put the coffee on," she narrowed her eyes giving Lily one last look before disappearing out of the bedroom. "You got five minutes missy before my little black behind comes back in there and makes you open it," Eva called from the hallway.

Still smiling at her friend's words Lily pulled back the bedclothes and padded over to her dressing table. She propped the envelope up against the mirror and studied her reflection, the rags she had placed in her hair when she arrived home earlier were now arranged haphazardly on her head. She reached up and methodically began to pull them from her hair revealing soft curls. She concentrated on the task, deliberately ignoring the envelope before her, until her dark brown locks were free of their bedtime constraints and she could no longer postpone the inevitable. She was considering letting Eva carry out her threat to open it for her when her friend reappeared in the doorway carrying two cups of coffee. She crossed the room and set the coffee cups down on the nightstand, then returned to stand behind Lily.

Sensing Lily's nervousness Eva sighed. "Are you as good as your daddy says you are?" she asked, looking at Lily's reflection in the mirror.

Lily dropped her eyes to gaze at her hands toying with the last of her rags, her brown skin reddened at Eva's question. Finally, she raised her eyes to find Eva still waiting on a response. She nodded quickly as if worried she would be accused of bragging.

"If your daddy thinks you are good enough, why on God's great Earth would you be worrying about the opinion of that dead husband of yours, a man that lied almost every time he opened that mouth of his?"

"I don't need a lecture on how stupid I was Eva," Lily warned.

Eva tilted her head to the side and her expression softened, "I didn't say you were stupid honey, what would be stupid is to let Henry's words dictate to you now. Open the letter and you'll know whether you're good enough."

Taking a deep breath Lily picked up the envelope and slipped her fingernail beneath the seal. She slid the folded letter out and with a final glance up at the mirror at Eva, who was smiling at her encouragingly while clutching her hands to her chest, she opened the paper up and started to read its contents.

Eva waited an excruciating couple of seconds before taking a step forward, trying to see beyond Lily to the paper.

"Well?"

Lily turned and gathered Eva into her arms, "They want to see me."

Both women started to dance around yelling in celebration.

"Is it over?" a male voice yelled from outside the room.

"Is what over?" Eva asked testily, as the owner of the voice appeared in the doorway, scratching absently at his overnight growth of beard.

"The war. Is it over?" he asked again as he pulled his suspenders onto his shoulders with a snap.

Lily shook her head, "Sorry Eli. No, it's not the end of the war."

Eli gave a disappointed shake of his head, "Then what the hell has got you two hollering so early in the day."

"It's Lily," Eva said proudly, her arm still around Lily's waist. "She's got an interview to go fly planes."

***

Headquarters

Army Air Forces Flying Training Command

    Fort Worth, Texas

    April 1943

    Dear Mrs McAllister,

    It will be convenient with this headquarters for you to be granted an interview any day, Monday through Saturday, between 9:00 a.m. and 4:00 p.m.

    This office is located in the Texas and Pacific Building, Room 1001. It is suggested that you bring your logbook and pilot's license at time of interview.

    Yours very truly,

    Jacqueline Cochran,

    Director

    Women's Flying Training

Lily looked at the piece of paper again. Re-reading the words, a slow smile spread across her face. She folded the letter along its already worn crease lines, the damage betraying the number of times she had opened it to check that the content had not changed. She placed the letter back in the purse on her lap and watched the landscape change as she departed New York and traveled towards Texas. She let the noise of the train lull her as it beat its rhythm along the rail tracks, while half-listening to the chatter of the uniformed men sharing her carriage. *Finally*, she thought as the scenery swept by, *finally I'm going to be doing something useful.*

***

Sitting stiffly outside the office waiting to be called, Lily was dressed in her Sunday best. Her light blue suit, despite her best attempts to steam it in the bathroom at her hotel, was slightly crinkled from being in her small suitcase during her journey to Texas, her gloved hands toyed nervously with the handle on her purse.

"Mrs McAllister?" a woman said, looking up from the paper in her hand towards where Lily was sitting.

"Rivera," Lily corrected. "It's Mrs Rivera," she smiled as she stood up and shook the woman's outstretched hand.

The woman looked down at the paper and frowned, "I'm sorry…administrative error…come in." She opened the office door and allowed Lily to enter first.

"So…tell me why you want to join the Women's Airforce Service Pilots?" the tall lean woman asked, as she sat down behind a large wooden desk, indicating Lily towards the chair opposite.

Lily swept her hand to arrange her skirt before she sat perched on the seat, her knees pressed tightly together, she swallowed nervously her hands still clutching the handle of her purse. She was thankful that she was wearing gloves despite the Texas heat, that way the director would not be able to see how white her knuckles were from her anxious grip. She reached a cautious hand up to her pillbox hat to check that it was still in place.

"I have been flying since I was able to walk and I want to serve my country Miss Cochran," Lily answered, her voice unwavering despite the nerves. She gave each finger of her glove a gentle tug and slipped them off, before laying them neatly in her lap.

The director smiled and nodded in understanding, "You are married?" she asked gently, nodding towards the gold ring on Lily's finger. In these times, it always felt a dangerous question to ask. However asking questions was the point of these interviews.

"Widowed," Lily responded, her jaw tightened slightly as she answered, "earlier this year."

Deciding to move back onto safer ground Jackie looked at the credentials she had in front of her. "You have logged over two thousand hours in the air?" she looked up in surprise towards the young woman in front of her.

Lily gave her a slow smile. "Like I said I've been flying since I could walk," she laughed. "My Dad co-owns a fixed base in Miami, so I've been around planes my whole life. I would have logged more but my air time was limited while I was away at school and then I got married."

Jackie laughed, "You have a degree in music I see."

"I majored in violin and was playing with the New York Philharmonic when I heard about what you were doing." Lily could feel herself start to relax; her heart rate had slowed as her nerves started to disappear. "Miss Cochran," she said growing in confidence, "I would relish the opportunity to use the talent that I was born within this service."

Nodding, the older woman smiled, "I trust we're talking about your flying abilities and not your musical acumen?"

Lily frowned thinking she had made a mistake. Her nerves started to make an unwelcome reappearance.

"Yes, sorry. I meant flying," she corrected, feeling flustered.

"Relax Mrs Rivera. I'm teasing," Jackie laughed, her face almost immediately turning somber. "I am surprised that we haven't seen someone with your experience before now, we're on our ninth intake you know?" Her tone held just a hint of challenge in it.

"I'm aware of that. When I heard last year of what you were doing I wrote to my husband," a touch of red appeared on Lily's caramel skin as she recalled the memory. "He forbade me to join."

"I am sorry for your loss, but I am glad that you reconsidered," Jackie said kindly, smiling empathetically. "If you could ensure that you show my secretary your pilot's license, log book and papers, we'll be in contact." She stood up and stretched her hand out over the desk, "Thank you again for taking the time to come Mrs. Rivera. It's been a pleasure meeting you."

Feeling disappointed that her interview had been so short, Lily stood up to shake the older woman's hand. As she turned to leave she opened her mouth to plead her case further but closed it again as she lost confidence, before quietly uttering her thanks.

"Thank you Miss Cochran."

Lily left the office and walked over towards the secretary's desk, pulling out her papers for verification. As she walked, she noticed that another woman now occupied the seat that she been sitting in. However, in stark contrast to Lily's stiff demeanor today, this woman was relaxed, her body language oozing the confidence that Lily so desperately desired. Even her hair, swept up into a fashionable victory roll at the front, fell into relaxed waves of blonde curls, unlike Lily's own tightly pinned brown locks. As Lily waited for her papers to be verified her eyes met with the blue eyes of the woman sitting waiting, they shared a smile of acknowledgement that both were here for the same reason. The blonde woman glanced towards where the secretary was jotting down information from Lily's license, raising her eyebrows conspiratorially towards Lily in recognition of the hoops that they were currently jumping through.

"Miss Richmond?" Jacqueline Cochran asked exiting her office in the same manner she had done only fifteen minutes previously to ask Lily to enter.

The blonde woman stood, smoothed her suit over her trim frame, and gave one last smile towards Lily who returned it with a smile of support and a slight nod. Lily watched as the blonde woman entered the office and closed the door, only snapping back to the moment when her papers were waved in front of her face. She retrieved them, thanked the secretary, and left the building squinting into the Texas sun as she pulled her gloves on. She released a long slow breath, "And now we wait." She gave a half laugh as her stomach reminded her loudly that her nerves had made her forgo breakfast. Now that the tension had finally eased she set off in search of some lunch.

***

Helen Richmond walked into the office feeling her bravado from the outer office slip in the presence of the famous female aviator. "Miss Cochran, it is an honor and privilege to meet you," she gushed. "I have long been an admirer of you... I mean of your achievements," she corrected quickly.

"Well, thank you! Please come in and have a seat," Jackie motioned to the seat opposite, smiling at her new interviewee. "I see that you have a varied amount of experience," Jackie said her smile growing wider. "You've been based in Hollywood for a while doing stunt work, do you know Pancho?" she asked, referring to fellow aviator and one time stunt pilot Pancho Barnes.

Smiling, Helen nodded, "Our time didn't coincide but I have met her, she is a force of nature."

Jackie smiled an acknowledgment, "That she is." Her smile wavered as she turned to the one issue that troubled her with Helen's application, she hesitated uncertain whether to voice her reservation. The dilemma lasted seconds before she went ahead. "I am concerned that we won't be able to satisfy your taste for risk and adventure Miss Richmond. We transfer aircraft and participate in training and we're military trained," Jackie cautioned.

Taking a deep breath Helen answered with as much passion as she could muster, "I have no desire towards risk or adventure Miss Cochran, I only wish to perform my duty, had it not been for family matters I would have been here last November pounding on your door."

Jackie nodded, "I met your father in Washington before the war started. He was a remarkable man as well as a great General and his death was a loss to our nation."

Helen swallowed hoping that she managed to hide her grief, despite the passage of time she still struggled to accept her father's death.

"Thank you Ma'am, I appreciate that."

Placing her palms on the desk Jackie pushed herself out of her chair. "Thank you for coming, I have enjoyed our chat," she held her hand out for Helen to shake. "Provide my secretary with your logbook info on your way out and we will be in touch."

Helen rose and shook the tall woman's hand, "Thank you for meeting with me, I can assure you Miss Cochran that if you let me, I will give you all that I have."

"Of that I'm in no doubt Miss Richmond, no doubt at all."

Walking back into the main office Helen smiled absently at the woman now sitting waiting to go in, her mind flashing back to her earlier exchange with the woman with dark soulful eyes and caramel skin that had been interviewed before her. It had been a while since she had shown an interest in any woman and their brief exchange had both calmed her pre-interview nerves while creating an altogether different flutter in her stomach. She was intrigued to see the name of the woman who had sparked such a response in her. She handed her papers over and furtively looked over the secretary's shoulder to look at the list. She smiled to herself as she spotted the name on the line above her own,

Liliana McAllister, she thought, *I sincerely hope the song is correct and that we do meet again.*

Chapter Two

<u>July 1943 – Sweetwater, Texas</u>

Lily stood across the street facing a large square building; it was nowhere near as tall as the buildings that she was accustomed to in New York but here in Sweetwater, Texas, the hotel was an imposing building in the small town's skyline.

Her purse hung loosely from her wrist as she tightened her grip on the handles of her suitcase and violin case. Taking a deep breath, and forcing her shoulders back, she walked towards the Bluebonnet Hotel. Entering, she felt the cool drafts of the ceiling fans take the edge off the searing Texan heat. She approached the empty desk and hit the service bell. A small grey-haired woman appeared.

"Welcome to Sweetwater," she said in a lazy drawl.

"Thank you. I have a room booked for the night, Riviera?" Lily said putting her suitcase down at her feet and switching her violin case into her left hand.

The small woman appraised the young woman standing in the foyer, her lips pursed as she narrowed her eyes. "You one of those fly girls?" she asked.

A small smile crept onto Lily's face, the pride at being called a 'fly girl' and the excitement about what she was about to undertake unable to hide itself, "Yes Ma'am...yes I am."

The receptionist sucked air through her teeth. "Thought so, can spot you lot a mile off with a squint. Well here's hoping I don't see you in a couple of weeks crying your heart out cause you got washed out," she added as she pulled together paperwork for Lily to complete. She passed the form over with a pen and gave Lily another once over before turning to collect a room key from the rack behind her.

Lily stood contemplating the woman's words. She had never even thought about the possibility of being kicked out of the program. A feeling of self-doubt, which her acceptance and enthusiasm had kept at bay, started to seep in. She took the pen and filled in her details.

"Room sixteen. Dinners at six. Doors lock at nine. No bringing men back to the room," the older woman recited absently as she took the paper and pen from Lily and handed her the key. She took a look at Lily's luggage. "And don't be playing that fiddle."

Lily flashed a smile and, taking the key, picked up her bags before heading up the stairs towards her room for the night.

***

It was still dark when Lily awoke the next morning; her excitement robbing her of sleep that she suspected she would be lamenting later. The months since her interview with Miss Cochran had passed slowly for her. After the initial wave of activity, that included her medical and written test, it became a waiting game until she was informed of her acceptance onto the program and instructed to head to Sweetwater.

She was grateful for Henry's insurance payment that meant she could pay for her travel to Texas and hotel stay while retaining their apartment in New York. She would be earning far less as a WASP than she could earn with her violin and that was before she paid for her room and board on the base. She smiled as she thought of Eva who was now no doubt claiming the larger bedroom in her absence. She had thought that she would never smile again when she received the telegram telling her of Henry's death and the subsequent events that unfolded. Had it not been for Eva's friendship and dogged determination to move into the home that Lily had shared with her husband. That prediction may have proved correct. The move had benefited both of them since, although small, Lily's apartment in Greenwich was more comfortable than Eva's in Harlem.

Standing and stretching out her stiff muscles, she grumbled that her body clock was still assuming she was keeping her usual pattern. After her hours with the orchestra, she would play with various nightclub bands, often arriving home as others started their day. Her nerves about the day she was about to face were starting to return along with concerns about her abilities. All of her insecurities seemed to come out in the dark. She could hear Henry's voice telling her that she was only playing with the orchestra as there weren't enough male violin players because of the war; her stomach started its familiar roil.

She walked over to her violin case and opened it carefully. She reached in and caressed the smooth wood with her fingertips before lifting the violin reverently from its case, leaving the bow nestled in its slot. Placing the instrument beneath her chin her fingers started to dance silently across the strings, her empty right hand mimicking her smooth bowing action as she soothed herself with the only thing, other than flying, that she knew could calm any anxiety she felt. When she finished she felt better, stronger and more assured, she walked to the window, drew back the curtains and looked up at the night sky. From nowhere, Eva's words about letting Henry still influence her emotions came to her.

She squared her shoulders and said defiantly towards the heavens, "Damn you to hell Henry McAllister, you will not dictate my life any longer!"

She nodded confidently towards the stars before slipping back into her bed and trying to reclaim any sleep that might come her way.

***

By zero seven hundred hours Lily was up and ready to join the muster point outside the hotel as her acceptance letter had instructed her. She paid her bill and walked out into the morning;

the sun had started to warm the air but had not yet cast its glare down on the town. Instead, a cool breeze blew which caused dust from the road to dance along the sidewalk.

She saw a group of women standing on the corner by the hotel and wandered close to them. Surreptitiously she took in what she assumed were her classmates. She counted around twenty women all dressed in their best clothes, their hair perfectly pinned, their makeup carefully applied. It was as if they were auditioning for a beauty pageant rather than joining the WASP, Lily mused then inwardly laughed as she thought about the care and attention she had given to her own appearance that morning. She hung back from joining the chatter, preferring instead to observe, when she noticed a tall red-haired woman turn and put her hand up to her eyes to shield her vision.

"What the hell?" the woman exclaimed.

The rest of the gathering turned to where she was looking and watched as what looked suspiciously like a cattle truck pulled up outside the hotel.

The door opened and out jumped a woman dressed in beige pants and a white shirt; rolled up sleeves revealed deep tanned forearms. Stepping towards the group, she removed the aviator sunglasses she was wearing and looked around the women standing nervously outside the hotel. Twirling her glasses in her hand, she gave them a reassuring smile.

"Good morning class 44-1. I'm Emily Foster your Establishment Officer. Let's get you to your new home."

She walked round to the rear of the truck and waited for the women to follow. She smirked as they struggled in their heels to get themselves and their belongings into what was a converted cattle truck and shook her head knowingly; their grooming regime and fashion tastes would change dramatically over the next couple of days.

"All in and comfortable?" Foster asked, before slipping her sunglasses back on and slamming shut the tailgate of the truck without waiting for a reply.

The nervous chatter that had been building outside the hotel momentarily stopped as the women started to comprehend what they had signed up to. Sitting in their dresses and suits on the hard wooden bench that lined the interior of the dusty truck, they bumped around on the uneven road surface trying not to breathe the potentially intoxicating exhaust fumes.

***

Helen stretched languidly across the bed, popping joints and extending muscles tired from the days spent travelling east from California to Texas on her motorcycle, as well as the unexpected end to her evening.

It had been late when she arrived in Sweetwater and she had only stepped into the local USO as the Blue Bonnet Hotel, where she had a room for the night, had stopped serving food. The last thing she expected was to see a familiar face in the sea of uniformed men and women. However, it had been a pleasant surprise after a long few days when Peggy had approached her fresh from the dance floor, a wide grin on her face and her blonde bangs plastered to her forehead with perspiration.

"Hell's Bells! Aren't you a sight for sore eyes?" Peggy had said, pulling her into a tight embrace. "Have you joined the WASP?" she asked, holding Helen at arm's length and inspecting her.

"I have indeed; I didn't know you'd joined up," Helen replied while wracking her brain to think when she had seen Peggy last. Theirs was more a casual acquaintance than deep friendship, often seeing each other at the clubs in LA; she hadn't even realized that Peggy had her pilot's license. Had Helen known that they had more in common than their mutual preference for women she may have made more of an effort to get to know her better. "I'm not sure I even knew you flew," Helen added as an afterthought.

"I'm a woman of mystery," Peggy replied waggling her eyebrows. "Got my license in college but hadn't flown much since," she admitted with a rueful grin. "But hey, I'm flying plenty now. I'm two months in and loving it all. Well, apart from the early mornings and PT. You want to grab a drink and catch up?" she pulled Helen towards an empty table and motioned for the waitress.

After receiving their drinks, Peggy observed Helen over the top of her glass. "I heard what happened with your father, I'm sorry…"

Helen interrupted her with a wave of her hand, "So how has your training been so far?"

Peggy let her off the hook and allowed the change the subject, "It's been good but I hope that you're ready for a vow of chastity here 'cause it's slim pickings."

They caught up on the gossip about mutual friends and danced together, taking advantage of the fact that no one batted an eyelid at the two women lindy hopping together. It was only when they took a break in their dancing that Helen noticed Peggy looking down at her lasciviously; her blue eyes were practically undressing Helen where she stood. Looking around quickly to make sure that no one else saw the look, Helen whispered towards her friend, "What are you doing?"

"It's been two months Hell's Bells! I'm ready to climb the walls. I am surrounded, literally surrounded, by women but I can't touch. Please!" Peggy whined, her full lips pulled into a sumptuous pout.

Seeing the look of hesitancy on Helen's face Peggy tried another angle, "Think of it as doing your duty for your country. I'm not asking you to marry me. I just need you to scratch an itch."

She leaned in towards Helen and breathed sensuously in her ear, "I promise that I will worship every inch of that gorgeous body of yours and return it to you when I'm done, almost unscathed." She leaned in closer and whispered breathily, "Well almost unscathed."

Feeling an itch of her own and with Peggy's celibacy warning ringing in her ears, Helen grabbed Peggy's hand and pulled her from the USO towards the hotel.

***

Helen rolled across the now empty bed, smiling as she thought about the previous night. She had been grateful that the old woman who had checked her into her room, although paranoid about men being brought back, did not flinch as the two giggling women had returned and had taken the stairs two at a time in their haste to get to Helen's room.

Exhaling a deep, satisfied, sigh Helen lifted her head to check the time. Her eyes widened in horror as she realized that, thanks to Peggy's visit, she had forgotten to set her alarm to get up and she was in danger of being late for her arrival time at the WASP training base. Leaping from the bed before running around her room throwing things into her bag, she stopped suddenly when she caught sight of herself in the mirror. Her lips were swollen and her hair was sticking up in a thousand different directions thanks to Peggy running her hands through it. She rolled her eyes and forgetting her packing for the moment, switched her attention to disguising the fact that she had spent the evening being ravished by a tall enthusiastic blonde-haired woman.

"Well, this is going to be interesting," she said to her reflection, unable to stop the large grin on her face, her dimples appearing deep into her cheeks, and her blue eyes sparkling with merriment.

***

Lily, thanks to her hesitancy, had been the last to enter the truck so had managed to snag the prime position beside the tailgate, which meant that although already caked in dust, she had managed to get some fresh air in between belches of black smoke from the exhaust. She looked back into the gloomy interior of the truck and quickly scanned the faces of those women not standing to hang their heads out of the small glassless windows in an attempt to stave off the oppressive heat within the truck. She felt a pang of disappointment at not seeing the blonde-haired woman who had followed her into the interview room. She was wondering how she had been accepted and someone like that confident woman had not succeeded when her thoughts were disturbed by the roar of an engine loud enough that it managed to drown out the dull throb of the truck's engine. She turned with the other women to look out the open back of the truck.

Gaining on them, in a thunderous roar, was a red motorcycle. As it blazed past them, Lily just managed to get a glimpse of blonde curls dancing in the wind.

"Oh my giddy aunt, wooooooweeee!" a small brunette woman shouted as the motorcycle overtook them. "Did you see that?" she asked in a honeyed southern accent as she brought her head back into the truck and looked around the other woman. "She was going like a bat out of hell with a rattlesnake up her ass!"

There was an explosion of laughter at the brunette's colorful description.

As the truck finally turned off the road, all the women stood up to look out of the windows. The sense of excitement started to return as they caught sight of airplanes stretched out almost as far as the eye could see; the silver metal catching the morning sun blinded them momentarily. For a brief moment, Lily considered hanging out of the back of the truck to take in the sight, but opted for a more decorous position and turned to the small window for a better view of the planes. She gripped the metal frame of the window, resting her chin on her knuckles as she gasped at the rows of shining planes. The red-haired woman, who had caught Lily's attention outside the hotel, was standing next to her. She nudged Lily and smiled.

"Aren't they beautiful?" she remarked as the truck continued into the base.

Lily smiled in response and took a deep breath, the smell around the base instantly transporting her back to Miami.

"Can you smell it?" she asked as she turned to the redhead their eyes sparkled with exhilaration.

"The smell of the planes?" the woman asked a broad grin on her face. "Yeah, I can smell it."

She nudged Lily's shoulder with her own and both turned their attention back to the sight of the planes. They could hear the sound of engines above them. Every woman hunched down to better her view before looking towards the sky in the hope of seeing the source of the glorious noise. The truck pulled up and Lily stood at the rear. Holding onto the edge as she hung her upper body out, her free hand shielded her eyes as she searched the sky for planes.

Foster rounded the truck and laughed seeing the new cadets' eagerness as they scanned the sky. Prodding each other in excitement and babbling animatedly their arms pointed enthusiastically out of the truck at sights around the base.

She loosened off the catch and opened the tailgate allowing it to fall down with a bang that stopped any chatter or movement. The cadets froze looking towards where the blonde woman stood visible though only from the hips up.

"Okay. Everybody out and line-up," she barked.

Lily crouched down and put her hand behind her to steady herself before jumping down, the dust puffed up around her feet as she landed ruining her keenly polished patent leather shoes. She turned and collected her belongings. Placing them beside the wheel of the truck, she made sure her violin was stowed safely before turning and holding a hand up to help the next woman down. The red-haired woman smiled gratefully putting her hand in Lily's as she slipped down from the truck landing as gracefully as her high heels would allow. Lily remained helping others down before collecting her suitcase and violin and falling into line.

Foster held a clipboard at her side as she surveyed the rag tag line of women in front of her, "Welcome to Avenger Field. For the next twenty three weeks this is your world, your time will be spent either in ground school, in the air on the exercise field or in bed and believe me you're gonna want your beds," she smiled at the few nervous laughs. "You will be allocated six to a bay, reveille is at zero six hundred hours, curfew is twenty one hundred, and Taps will sound at twenty two hundred hours. Although you are civilians, we train like the military."

Foster caught sight in her peripheral vision of a blonde woman in slacks and a soft brown leather jacket joining the end of the line-up.

"You will be on time!" she said pointedly. "We march everywhere. Your bunks will be inspected at weekends. You will be provided with clothing for flying. Hanging in your bay lockers are your zoot suits, you will wear these for training, they come in three sizes big, bigger and way too big. You'll have to make do. When not in your zoot suits, well, we don't have a uniform as yet, but our informal dress is what you see me wearing. You can buy this down at the general store in Sweetwater, we will take you there tomorrow to get you kitted out." She brought the clipboard up and rested it on her hip, "Let's get you into your bays and we will continue with your orientation, you will have one hour to sort yourself out then you will report in your zoots for a medical with the nurse and a tour of the base. When I call your name, step forward."

She pushed her sunglasses onto the top of her head and squinted at the white paper on the clipboard, "Barthelmess, Bisset, Brickford, Call, Carter and Clark...you're in Bay One Section Ttwo."

The six women stepped forward looking at each other and shared nervous smiles.

"Stand over there," Foster pointed and the women gathered together.

"Daly, Edmunds, Eggleston, Fisher, Gee and Hill. Bay Two Section Two. Stand there."

The women repeated the actions of their classmates and stood where told.

"Jenkins, Jones, Keene, Littleton, Mackie and Marnoch. Bay Three Section Two. Over there."

Foster didn't even bother to look up this time but continued with her roll call.

"Richards, Richmond, Rivera, Rosecroft, Simpson and Stott, Bay Four Section Two."

Lily joined the small group eyeing up each other nervously; to her right was the tall red-haired woman she had been sitting next to on the truck and two blonde women that had not been with them on the ride from the hotel. She turned her head and peeked to her left where the small brunette woman who had yelled on the truck stood grinning and beyond her were the blonde curls that had shot passed them earlier at an alarming speed; curls that were shorter than when she had first seen them after her interview.

They followed Foster as she walked them towards the barracks, pointing out the relevant bays as they walked. The numbers dropped as each bay unit peeled off to their new abode until finally it was only Lily and her bay mates left, "Home sweet home girls!"

Foster grinned as she held out her arm towards the small hut.

Chapter Three

The six women entered the whitewashed barracks and stood surveying their surroundings, sound in the knowledge that their exact movements were no doubt being mirrored elsewhere in the other bays. They looked at the six Army issue cots, each with a tall locker beside them and a chair plus three desks lined up against the wall. Helen wandered into the bay opening a door at the rear. "There's one john, a bath and a shower in here," she called over her shoulder.

"Is that it?" the tall redhead frowned. "The mirror isn't even full length!" she remarked looking at the small mirror on the wall.

"I have a feeling that we're not gonna care about the mirror," the small brunette remarked as she held up one of the zoot suits. The garment drowned her tiny frame and her ironic remark received a loud laugh from each woman in response.

Lily put her suitcase and violin down.

"Should we introduce ourselves?" one of the women asked, pausing before going on to do exactly that. "My name is Marjorie Richards, Portland Oregon," she announced placing her suitcase down onto one of the beds to claim it.

"Lucy Simpson, I'm Marjorie's sister so I'm also from Portland," Lucy smiled nervously.

"Adrienne Rosecroft," the tall redhead smiled as she sat down onto one of the beds and bounced once to check the comfort. "Boston."

"Adele Stott," said the small brunette, hanging the zoot suit back up. "Tennessee."

Helen grinned, "Helen Richmond, latterly of California." She raised her eyebrows looking towards Lily waiting for the woman she had seen on the day of her interview to introduce herself.

"Lily Mc..Rivera," Lily corrected herself. "Lily Rivera, Florida originally, New York recently."

"So now we know who we are, we should get ourselves dressed in these rather fetching overalls and get ready to fly," Adrienne smiled as she stood up and took the zoot suit out of the locker beside her.

Lily turned and placed her bags onto the cot behind her, she gave Helen a small smile as the blonde did the same onto the bed beside her. Lily let a long breath leave her body as she unpacked her case into what storage space she had. She was here, she was a WASP, and soon she would fly.

***

Helen pulled on her zoot suit, she smiled as she watched from the corner of her eye as the other women undressed and got ready, each trying to protect their modesty as they dressed. Had she been a betting woman she'd lay money on the fact that in a couple of days time they would probably be wandering around naked and not give two hoots who saw what. She sat on her cot, pushed up her sleeves over her elbows and leaned down to roll the legs of the overalls, which were currently covering her feet, up to a suitable length.

"What the hell do we wear on our feet?"

Helen raised her head towards Adrienne who was standing in her overalls, looking down at her bare feet waggling her toes, the nails of which were painted a bright shade of red.

Lily looked up as she pulled the zip on her suit up and reached around to grab the belt to pull it in at the waist in an attempt to make the men's overalls more sympathetic to her womanly curves.

"Wear whatever you're comfortable walking in I guess," she responded, straining her neck, as she twisted unable to snag one-half of the belt.

Helen stood up and knelt on Lily's cot, "Here, let me."

She reached around Lily's waist and grabbed the illusive piece of cloth pulling it back and handing it to Lily.

"Thanks."

Lily gave her a quick smile as she tied the belt into a tight knot. Helen looked up from her position on Lily's bed finding herself drawn again towards those dark eyes that she'd first seen on the day of her interview and that had calmed her last minute jitters.

"You're welcome," she smiled, dimples appeared deep into her cheeks, and she edged her way backwards off Lily's bed before reaching down to smooth the two crevices in the blankets that her knees had created.

Standing up straight, she shook her arms to allow the fabric to drop back down over her hands.

"Could you?" she asked hopefully towards Lily, holding her arms up, her hands completely obscured by the fabric flailing loosely over them.

Lily laughed at the woman waving her arms, the material flapping around her head. She stepped around her bed to stand in front of Helen, took one arm down, and started to roll the material up until she could see the blonde woman's hands. She repeated the action with Helen's other arm. This time, however, she completed the task slowly, not wanting to end the contact.

"There," she said with a shy smile. She could feel the heat in her cheeks as she pondered briefly her reluctance to halt the connection with Helen, immediately resigning it to the need for some small form of physical comfort while she became accustomed to her new and unsettling environment.

Helen oblivious to Lily's embarrassment inspected her newly adjusted outfit and placed her hands onto her hips giving Lily a quick twirl, "How'd I look?"

Lily chuckled. "Wonderful, what about me?" she asked, flourishing her hands up and down her sides feeling more like her normal self for the first time in a long time.

"Marvelous," Helen replied, a small smile playing on her lips.

A disembodied yell of "Cadets!" halted any further conversation.

Adele stood up from her bed and looked out of the window at the front of their bunkhouse.

"Everyone else is going out, we should git goin'," she opened the door and stepped out leaving the door open for the others to follow.

Helen motioned to Lily to go first and then followed behind. They left the bay and joined the assembled women, lined up in pairs, outside. Lily stood next to Helen; both stood ramrod straight their eyes fixed upon an indeterminate point in front of them.

"What in the name of Roosevelt have you got on your feet?" Foster yelled as she halted her walk down the ranks at their unit.

Lily froze. Thinking that the shout was aimed at her, she looked down quickly towards the saddle shoes she had changed into. However, as she looked down she saw where Foster was directing her query. Adrienne stood in front of her, her overalls, rolled up at the feet, revealing bright red platform heels. Lily bit at her lip to stop laughter from spilling out.

"I'm wearing what's comfortable," Adrienne replied innocently.

"You think you'll be able to fly in those?" Foster asked her tone full of challenge. "You planning on being an HP in heels?"

Adrienne regarded her footwear and smiled. "I can do anything in these," she replied her tone full of suggestion. "Ma'am," she added.

"What's your name cadet?"

"Adrienne Rosecroft, ma'am."

The Establishment Officer shook her head. "Okay Rosecroft, step out," she motioned with her arm towards her and Adrienne fell out of the line up and walked towards the officer,

"HP?" Lily whispered out the side of her mouth.

"Hot Pilot," Helen whispered in response.

Foster scanned the footwear of the other cadets, seeing Helen wearing a pair of men's lace up boots she nodded.

"You!" she shouted, pointing towards Helen. "Step out."

Helen shot Lily a quick look of panic, thinking she was about to be chewed out for talking in line. Lily gave her an apologetic look thinking the same and risked a whispered apology as she passed. She stepped out and stood beside Adrienne.

"You see that over there?" Foster pointed towards a small reflecting pool near to their barracks. "That's the wishing well, I want to see how comfortable those shoes are. When I say go you're going to run against…"

"Richmond," Helen offered.

"Richmond. There and back," Foster looked towards the two women expectantly.

Adrienne turned to look at Helen and raised an eyebrow towards her.

"Ready…Steady…Go!" Foster yelled.

Despite not knowing the two women racing, the women standing in line quickly picked sides and yelled supportively as they sprinted towards the pool. Thanks to her longer legs, and in spite of her ridiculous footwear, Adrienne had gained an advantage on Helen who skidded on the loose gravel. The tall redhead reached the pool first bending down quickly to tag the concrete surround before turning and tearing back towards Foster. As she reached the officer with a panting Helen shortly behind her, Adrienne slowed to a halt.

"Wellesley College track team," Adrienne smirked when she noticed Foster's raised brows.

Foster laughed, shaking her head. "Okay, you can wear them for tonight. Tomorrow when you're in Sweetwater, get something more suitable. Fall in."

The two women walked back to their places slightly out of breath. Adrienne waited until Foster was out of earshot before turning to smile at Helen.

"Thanks."

"No idea what you're talking about."

Adrienne shook her head giving Helen a knowing smile, "You threw that race and you know it Richmond, so thank you."

She turned to face the front as they set off at a quick march pace.

***

Several hours later after being immunized against small pox, tetanus, and typhoid, given a dental identification survey and a visual acuity test, they were sitting crossed-legged on the floor of a classroom together, while being lectured on personal hygiene.

"You have got to be kidding me," Helen whispered, leaning forward to put her head between Lily and Adrienne's heads as she rubbed her still sore arm from the earlier injection. "They're seriously telling us about washing our bits and bobs!"

Lily tilted her head and never taking her eyes off the front of the room murmured a response, "I know! I mean I, for one, have never had a problem washing my bobs."

Helen laughed turning it into a cough as one of the medical officers glared their way. She sat back and schooled her face into an interested expression; soon however, she found her attention wandering and drawn to the captivating woman in front of her.

Lily seemed to be growing in confidence as the day wore on. Her dark hair was pinned in a more relaxed style than the day of her interview; long lashes framed the dark brown eyes that held Helen captive anytime they were directed at her. Full lips that seemed to give Lily an almost continual sensual pout were currently pursed in concentration as she gave her attention to the speaker at the front of the room. Her long slender fingers absently beat a tattoo against her shin as she listened intently. As the speaker changed, Helen realized she had not heard a word spoken and reluctantly she returned her attention to the officers, however despite her best intentions her eyes continued to observe Lily.

Thirty minutes later, they were shuffling into the mess hall lining up with their metal mess trays waiting for lunch to be slopped onto their tray.

"Excuse me, what kind of meat is this?" Lucy asked the woman dishing out the food.

"Cooked. Now move on fly girl," came the curt reply.

Lucy looked down at the undistinguishable meat and screwed her face up moving on to receive her portion of potatoes. She slipped onto the bench beside her other bunkmates. "Do you have any idea what kind of meat this is?" she asked as she slid her tray onto the table.

Adrienne poked around the food with her fork. "The cadets that wash out?" she replied drolly. "What the hell are these?" she asked poking around at the white substance on her plate.

Adele looked over and smiled.

"Why those are grits," she answered. Seeing that her response had not cleared the matter up for Adrienne she looked at her in surprise. "Ain't you ever eaten grits afore?"

The redhead took a small amount onto her fork and lifted it towards her mouth. "Are you sure I should be eating them?" she asked before taking a small amount into her mouth. She swallowed the grits then shrugged. "They don't taste of much," she remarked.

"They taste o' grits!" Adele laughed. "If you don't want 'em I'll have 'em," she said grinning as Adrienne lifted her tray and scraped the offending item onto her tray.

They ate in relative silence each woman silently assessing what their lives were going to be like from the brief view of life at Avenger Field that they had seen so far. After lunch, they were shown around the base taking in the administration buildings, the hangars including the ready room where their flight leathers and parachutes were packed and stored, and the observation deck, which gave them a three hundred and sixty view around the base and the runways.

Following their orientation tour, they were standing in formation in one of the hangars when their commanding officer joined them.

He stood in front of them his hands crossed at his back. "Welcome to Avenger Field. My name is Captain Hardy. I'm your base commander. Ladies you may be good civilian pilots. I believe amongst you that we have a lot of air hours and experience. Some of you will be used to crop dusting and I believe one amongst you was flying stunt planes in Hollywood, but this is army flying and by the end of your twenty-three weeks some of you will have returned home."

The women looked at each other trying to work out who flew stunt planes in Hollywood, trying to ignore the shadow of failure that hovered over each, and every, one of them. They returned their attention back towards the red-haired officer who was now striding up and down their lines.

"You will be taken through army check flights by my instructors at each stage of your training. Fail any of these and you will be washed from the program. You will be expected to learn about the principles of flight and the mechanics of engines. You will learn navigation, weather, instrument flying and communications. Fail any of these and you will be washed from the program."

He finished his speech with a rousing, "Are we going to make army pilots of you?"

He received an emphatic, "Sir. Yes. Sir."

Satisfied, he nodded towards Foster then left them to continue their tour of the facilities.

The rest of their afternoon was spent filling out forms and being drilled on the rules and regulations that would be in place during their stay. Finally, after their evening meal they were enjoying their recreation time before they would return to their bay for lights out. The women were huddled in small groups; some reading the small gazettes produced by the WASP that filled them in on the activities around the base, others huddled around the radio listening for news from the war and enjoying the music programs.

Lily sat beside Helen who was cussing under her breath as she tried to sew her WASP patch carrying the image of the Disney designed mascot Fifinella onto her A-2 leather flying jacket. She yelped and pulled her finger up into her mouth as she pricked herself for around the tenth time. Lily rolled her eyes and reached over pulling the jacket from Helen's lap, the blonde woman furrowed her brows as she sucked on her injured finger, "Wha ou doin?"

"Saving you from certain death," Lily replied, picking up the needle and starting to sew the patch.

"I pricked my finger, how am I going to die from that?" Helen asked looking at her finger as the blood started to bubble again from the small hole.

Lily stilled her hands and looked up towards Helen who was still looking quizzically at her bleeding finger, "Because, if I have to watch you butchering this patch any longer, I may be forced to kill you!"

Helen's eyes widened and her lips tugged into a smile as she popped her bleeding finger back into her mouth, "Fankyou."

Twenty minutes later and Lily had unpicked Helen's handiwork and attached the patch neatly.

"All done. I think I may head back to the bunk," she smiled wearily; now that the excitement from the day had calmed down she felt a tiredness start to overwhelm her.

Helen accepted her jacket and stood up shrugging it onto her slender shoulders, "I'll come back too, I don't know about you but I'm ready to trip over my eye lids."

Lily nodded silently and gathered her things together. As they prepared to leave the other occupants of Bay Four noticed their departure and by silent agreement rose to leave.

They practically fell over themselves apologizing for getting in the way as they each tried to get ready for bed, waiting patiently to brush their teeth while someone used the toilet, moving aside to allow each access to the mirror. Finally, they were all dressed in their pajamas and one by one slipped into their small army bunks pulling the sheets and blankets over them.

Helen lay in her cot and stared up at the ceiling processing all that had happened during the day when she heard a snort behind her.

"It's eight o'clock."

She turned onto her stomach and looked over the small walking space between their beds towards Marjorie who was lying on her front her elbows propped on her pillow while she looked at her watch, "I'm in bed and it's eight o'clock!"

Soon all the Bay Four residents had turned onto their front and were looking at each other in amusement.

"I don't think I've ever been in my bed at eight o'clock," Adrienne mused. "At least not alone," she added which received a burst of laughter from the other women. She turned onto her side and rested her head onto her hand.

"We have two hours before lights out. How about we find out a bit more about each other. Adele?" Adrienne looked over towards the small brunette, "We know you're from Tennessee. Are you married?"

Adele gave a shy smile, "Engaged. My fiancé is over in England at the moment…we're gonna get married when he gets back."

Adrienne smiled, "What's his name?"

"Mathew," Adele couldn't help the grin that spread across her face as she thought about her sweetheart. "Mathew Winchester the

Third. I've known him since we weren't much more off the ground than a cricket's belly."

The women smiled as Adele shuffled under blankets to get comfortable.

"Okay, now for the good stuff," Adrienne grinned rolling back onto her front. She narrowed her eyes and looked across at Adele, "First time?"

"We were fifteen in my daddy's barn, was over before I even got started," Adele pursed her lips together at the memory.

Adrienne's eyebrows shot up and she rose up onto her knees. "Oh God Adele, sorry no… I meant first time flying! How you knew you wanted to…," she stuttered in embarrassment. "I meant first time flying solo."

The other women roared with laughter as both Adrienne and Adele blushed at the misunderstanding.

"I don't know, I love flying but I'm more interested in hearing about the barn," Marjorie smiled mischievously.

Adele's color darkened even further in embarrassment, "Believe me the flying was better! I was sixteen when I first flew solo; I became obsessed when I was little. My grandma died when I was six and someone told me she was up in the sky. Ever since, I wanted to go up into the sky to be close to her. My Pa, he had an old beat up 75 Kaydet for crop dusting an' I learnt in that." Adele chewed on her lips and, taking a deep breath, put a smile back onto her face, "An' that's that! How 'bout you Adrienne? You married and when was your first?"

Adrienne's fingers automatically went to her neck where a simple wedding band hung around her neck, "Nope, not married." She gave a forced smile feeling the simple act of speaking the words aloud choke in her throat. She had made the decision to lie about her marriage to Ben when she knew that she would be training in Texas; a state that regarded her marriage illegal thanks to the color of Ben's skin. Her mind flittered to her husband who, to her great pride, was part of the 99th Pursuit Squadron; a small group of black men trained to fly, and was to the best of her knowledge now in Europe somewhere.

"Not married," she repeated sadly. "As for flying, when I was sixteen my father was hosting a benefit dinner for one of his charities and one of the guests was Amelia Earhart. I heard her talk about flying and I was hooked. I begged him for lessons and within a month I had my license," she laughed as a barrage of questions about her meeting Amelia Earhart were fired her way. Patiently she answered her star stuck bay mate's questions, until finally they ran out of queries. Adrienne turned in her bed to face towards the woman in the bed next to her, "Marjorie?"

Marjorie raised her head up from her pillow. "I'm married to Daniel; he's a doctor and is out in the Pacific and my first..." she looked over towards her sister. "Well I guess our first flying," she clarified with a sly smile. "When we were kids we stayed near a base and we would both run out anytime we heard a plane going over. There was just something about the sound of the engine."

She and Lucy shared a grin as Lucy took over the story.

"We both got onto the Civilian Pilot Training Program while at college and got our licenses through that, so I guess compared to the Addies here," she smiled towards Adrienne and Adele, "we're late bloomers."

Adrienne groaned and picked up her pillow and tossed it in Lucy's direction. "You just know that name is going to stick!" she grimaced towards Adele who laughed in response.

Lucy laughed and tossed the pillow back, "I'm married to Peter; he's also a doctor and is serving with Daniel in the Pacific."

"Please tell me that your other first times aren't as linked as your husbands and flying experience," Adrienne grinned as she tucked her pillow back under her arm and turned her attention towards Lily. "So, our two quiet ones! What're your stories?"

Lily's eyes widened. "I, um, I'm not married," she said hesitantly. "And my first time was when I was twelve. Flying that is," she added as she noted the raised eyebrows from Adrienne. "My dad owns a base so I grew up around planes, he took me up on his lap when I was four and I was hooked," she smiled fondly as she thought about her father and the others at the base in Florida. "And up until a few weeks ago I played violin for the New York Philharmonic. Just in case you were worried by the violin case. It's not for show, I can actually play it."

Helen frowned during Lily's speech, as she listened she looked closely at Lily's left hand which bore the telltale indent on her ring finger. She could have sworn that Lily had been wearing a wedding ring when she had seen her at the interview and the paper work that she had seen, when completing her own, had her name listed as McAllister.

"So, hey, Richmond just you," Adrienne called, stopping Helen's musings.

"Oh yeah, um, not married, never will," Helen nodded to emphasize her words. "I was about seven when my father took me and my brother to see a barnstormer near where he was based." She took a deep breath as her mind flashed up the image of her father and brother's smiles that day, "We basically lived on Army Air Corp bases our entire life without blinking twice at a plane and then after that one afternoon that was it for us, we both talked nonstop about planes and flying. We drove my father insane!" She giggled and shook her head at the recollection. "My father refused to teach us but agreed to my brother getting lessons when he turned sixteen. I tagged along and begged the instructor to teach me. I worked after school washing planes and doing any bit of work they would throw my way just to get them to teach me, I got my license after around a year. I wanted to fly so I did chores for money and saved every dime I got until I could afford to buy an old wreck of a 1929 Travel Air, got the old girl going, and then started off barn storming and offering rides," she shrugged as she finished her introduction, realizing she had shared more than she intended. "I worked my way across the country until I hit water. I stopped in Hollywood and have been flying stunt planes there ever since." She focused her gaze on her pillow, "Then my father was killed in the Pacific last year and I wanted to do, no, I needed to do something."

Lily reached over and gave Helen's arm a sympathetic rub. The blonde looked up and smiled gratefully.

Eager to break the atmosphere that had settled in their small bay, Adele turned onto her side and looked at Helen, "And the other first time?"

Helen hooted with laughter, "Definitely not for first night discussion."

The sadness evaporated from Helen and conversation started to flow seamlessly between the six women. They were shocked when, in the middle of an in-depth discussion about the films that Helen had flown in, the lights suddenly went out in their bay and they could hear the sound of a bugle playing the mournful tones of Taps.

"Well ladies I guess that is that," Adele murmured in the darkness. "I s'pose I'll be seein' y'all in the morning."

They muttered good nights to each other and settled down for their first night's sleep in strange surroundings.

Chapter Four

Helen heard the first notes from the bugle playing reveille. It had only started the repeat when she was out of her cot and in the bathroom to brush her teeth. She used her flannel to wipe the remnants of sleep from her face and freshen up before returning to the living quarters. Her bay mates were in various states of consciousness; apart from Lily who was still blissfully asleep on her front, with one arm and leg draped over the side of the bed, brushing the floor.

Helen went to her locker and pulled out a white shirt and shorts. She changed quickly, pulling her zoot suit onto her lower half and secured it with the canvas belt, leaving the body and arms flapping at her backside.

Adrienne mumbled a good morning as she padded past her towards the bathroom, wash bag in hand with Marjorie, Lucy and Adele following like goslings behind their mother.

Making her bed and tucking the blankets into the corners Helen fell naturally into a long forgotten habit. She realized the benefit of being a military baby, she had been conditioned to be up, 'As soon as the bugle player wets his lips' as her father drummed into her. She ran a hand through her short blonde curls and surveyed her handiwork.

Yup, she thought. *The General would be proud*. She smiled to herself as she raised her eyes from her neatly made bed towards the explosion of blankets and limbs in the bed next to her. Guiltily she allowed her eyes to trail up Lily's exposed leg, appreciating the tanned shapely calf and view of her thigh thanks to Lily's shorts having ridden up during her sleep. She smiled as Lily continued to sleep deeply, soft, snores coming from the pillow that her face was partly submerged in.

"Lily," she called walking around her cot to stand beside Lily's bed. "Lily, wake up."

She gingerly tapped the sleeping woman's shoulder.

Getting no response she shook her gently, "Lily, it's time to get up."

She chewed on her lip wondering what tactic to take next in order to wake the woman who would seemingly sleep through a tornado. She was about to give Lily another shake when Adrienne returned.

"What gives?" she asked noticing Helen hovering above Lily's bed.

"I can't wake her," Helen replied indicating down towards the still sleeping Lily.

Adrienne deposited her wash bag on her bed.

"Let me try, my brother Cameron would never get up when we were at home. So I'm pretty good at this."

As she walked back over she hooked Adele's pillow from her vacated bed, swung it above her head and smacked Lily square on the head.

"What the…!" Lily yelled as she sprang up on her arms blinking her eyes, desperately trying to focus. She looked up towards a wide-eyed Helen who simply raised a hand and pointed behind her. Turning, her eyes focused on Adrienne who was standing still holding the pillow, a smug smile on her face.

"Told you, never failed me yet. Morning, sleeping beauty," she added, tossing the pillow back onto Adele's unmade bed and sauntering back towards her own area to get ready.

"That's no way to wake someone," Lily grumbled pulling herself up into sitting position facing Helen and stretching out the kinks that the small sprung bed had put into her back and shoulders.

Helen felt her face flush as Lily's stretching accentuated her breasts. Standing, Lily sleepily pulled the legs of her bed shorts down from where her sleeping position had pushed them.

"Morning Helen," she mumbled, her mouth dropped open as she took in the neat bed beside her.

"You're dressed and your bed is made!" Lily said astonished, rubbing at her still sleepy eyes with the heel of her hand.

"How long did I sleep in?"

"Not too long." Helen replied. "You go freshen up and I'll take care of your bed," she offered, reaching down to the floor to retrieve the blankets from Lily's bed.

Lily flashed a grateful smile. "Thank you, I'm not much of a morning person," she admitted, pulling her things from her locker and passing the others as they left the bathroom. By the time she'd returned from the bathroom washed and dressed, Bay Four was ready for the day; Helen was just finishing mopping the floor, wringing out the mop into the bucket which Adele took outside and poured into the dirt. As she returned they heard Foster's voice ringing out along the bays.

"Fall in."

Quickly putting her wash bag back in her locker Lily pulled her shoes on and ran along with the rest of the bay to line up outside, zipping her zoot suit as she ran.

***

"Someone from Bay Two washed out," Adele said as she placed her mess tray down and sat beside her bay mates.

"Already?" Marjorie asked surprised. "But we've not even been near a plane."

Adele shrugged as she tucked into her breakfast, "Something showed up in the eye test."

The other women looked at each other in silence each thinking the same thing - *Now it was real.*

Lily looked over at Helen and gave her a hesitant smile, "Thank you again for earlier."

Helen raised her attention from her oatmeal, "You're welcome. So when you say you're not a morning person. You mean you're *really* not a morning person."

Laughing Lily shook her head, "Not that early, no. Being a musician you keep odd hours, it's more likely getting in at dawn, not usually getting up," she smiled broadly. "So you're a morning person then?"

Helen scrunched her face up. "I never thought I was, but growing up on bases with my father means I'm conditioned to either sleep or wake depending on what the bugle is playing," she grinned.

"Ladies!" Foster's voice captured the mess hall's attention. "This morning you will be allowed to go into Sweetwater, the General Store should be able to cater for all your clothing and shoe," she looked pointedly at Adrienne, "requirements. On the notice boards there is a list of the items you will need, remember your ration books."

Foster raised her voice over the low rumble of the women starting to talk excitedly amongst themselves.

"The truck will be leaving at nine am, those of you that drove yourself here are permitted to take your own vehicle into town. You should be back on base by twelve noon."

Foster took a breath to sustain her voice for the final set of instructions, "Your first class today is navigation you will be lined up outside the mess hall ready to go to Ground School in thirty minutes, remember to clean your trays away."

***

"It's eight forty five an' ma head is thumping!" Adele groaned as they returned to the bay to change out of their zoot suits and into civilian clothing for their trip into town.

"Navigation class at seven thirty in the morning will do that to you," Lucy commiserated, pulling her arms from her overalls.

Marjorie pulled her suitcase out from under her bed. "I'm not sure I know which way is up or down anymore," she shrugged, opening the latches to select something to wear. "I'm driving into town if anyone wants a lift," she added absently as she rummaged through her suitcase.

Adrienne's head shot up. "Oh God yes," she replied. "My ass still hasn't recovered from the ride here," she moaned as she slipped on her blouse.

"Me too!" Adele added waving a hand in the air.

"That would be lovely," Lily smiled gratefully, buttoning up the small buttons on her floral print dress.

Helen sat on the edge of her cot as she pulled on a pair of blue pants, "Thanks for the offer, but I'm going to take my motorcycle."

"It was you!" Adrienne exclaimed. "You passed us yesterday like a... Adele, how did you describe it?" she asked turning to the smaller woman.

"Like a bat out of hell with a rattlesnake up her ass," Adele grinned.

Blushing slightly as she fastened the button on her trousers Helen smiled, "That would be me."

As the others returned their attention to getting ready, Lily perched on her bed. With her hands tucked under her thighs and her shoulders nearly touching her ears, she quietly asked a question of Helen. "What does it feel like?"

Helen grinned, "As close to flying without leaving the ground, I'll take you out on it sometime." She nodded encouragingly towards Lily, whose eyes widened in excitement.

"I'd like that."

"We all set ladies?" Marjorie asked slipping her shoes on. "We have shopping to do."

***

They wandered slowly around the small general store assessing the range of goods on offer that could be of use for their 'informal' uniform.

"Anything we don't got, we can order fer ye," the owner drawled in a smooth Texan tone before smiling at the throng of young women edging round his small shop.

"Aren't you going to get a spare shirt?" Marjorie asked Adele as they picked up the white shirts that formed part of the uniform. "Otherwise you're going to be constantly doing laundry," she remarked, lifting another shirt in her size.

Adele's cheeks flushed as she ducked her head slightly towards Marjorie, "I just plain can't afford it," she admitted. "I'm gonna have hands like an ol' woman by the time we graduate."

She laughed as they walked to collect their whipcord slacks. Adrienne moved into the space they created and checked the sizes of the shirts before tucking five of them under her arm. Aware of being behind the others she moved briskly to catch up with them in selecting her pants.

The store was throbbing with activity as what seemed like the whole of their intake shopped for clothing essentials. Lily had selected her items and was now standing at the desk with them neatly piled. As the assistant rang up the purchases of the other women, she was trying to not take it personally, that despite standing patiently, she hadn't been served when Helen bounced up, her arms full of her soon to be bought clothing.

"Did you get everything?" she asked.

"Yeah I think so, you?" Lily asked, still trying to attract the shopkeeper's attention.

"Well what I don't have, I'll just have to live without," Helen grinned. "How come you've not been served?" she asked. Helen was aware that Lily has been waiting for some time as her eyes would often, subconsciously be drawn to her, almost tracking her movements.

"I've no…" Lily was interrupted as the shopkeeper appeared.

"Can I help you?" he smiled at Helen.

"My friend is in front of me," Helen gave him a good-natured smile and nodded towards Lily.

The shopkeeper coughed slightly, glancing at Lily before addressing Helen. "We don't serve her sort here," he stated simply.

Both Helen and Lily's eyes widened, Lily opened her mouth but before she could say anything Helen had dumped her clothing on the desk and was squaring up to the shopkeeper, "You have something against her because she's a woman? Or 'cause she's from Florida?"

She stood with her hands on her hips, her face hardened with fury.

The shopkeeper flushed as he pointed towards a sign behind the counter stating in stark black lettering 'No Mexicans'.

"What's going on?" Adrienne asked, sauntering up to the desk with her pile of items.

"He won't serve me," Lily said quietly trying to maintain control over her anger at the situation. Adele wandered up with Marjorie and Lucy in tow and the Bay Four women formed a protective circle around their wronged bay mate.

"How much do you make off us Avenger girls?" Helen asked narrowing her eyes. "'Cause I will guarantee that unless you apologize to my friend here and serve her, the WASP won't spend a dime in your store again."

The impact of her words saw the rest of the women dump their items onto the counter and glare at him.

The man looked at the gathering of angry women across from him; the full rank of the Bay Four six having been quickly reinforced by others in the class yet to pay for their provisions.

Calculating the impact his next action, he plastered a smile on his face, "I'm sorry about the mix up, let me work out how much you owe." He held out his hands for Lily to pass the clothing across, and then proceeded to tally the items on a bill pad.

Adele stood on her tiptoes and peeked over Lily's shoulder, "That's real nice of you sir, to not charge for those pants."

The shopkeeper jerked his head up to look at the small face peering at him from behind the dark haired woman.

"As a good will gesture n'all," she added, giving him a toothy grin.

He scowled begrudgingly as he removed the cost of Lily's slacks from her bill. Lily handed over the money and relevant pages from her ration book, trying not to laugh at the look on the man's face as she did so. She took her items now neatly wrapped in brown paper, tied with string, and leaned across the counter, "For the record, my grandfather was Cuban, not Mexican and my father was born here and fought in the Great War for the country he loves." She gave him a final look of disgust before turning and leaving.

Still seething from the treatment that she had received, Lily closed her eyes and rested her head on the back of the seat as she waited for the others in Marjorie's white Plymouth Convertible.

"You okay?" Helen tossed her clothing package into the car, swung her legs over the side of the car and dropped onto the back seat beside Lily.

"Just angry. I had hoped that with everything that's going on in the world that things might be different," she wiped a heated tear from underneath her sunglasses resting on her cheek. "I'm just *so* mad," she growled angrily.

"Things will change," Helen rubbed her arm comfortingly. "And until they do, you've got us," she smiled.

Lily felt her skin tingle where Helen had touched her. She placed her hand over her forearm and frowned slightly, unsure of why her body had reacted that way. The frown disappeared as she caught sight behind Helen's head of the others leaving the shop. "Thank you," she smiled gratefully.

"I'll see you back at the base," Helen grinned, before hopping back out of the car. Lily pulled Helen's and her own packages onto her knee to make a space for Addison and Adele for the journey back. She turned at a loud engine roar as Helen pulled up beside the convertible.

"You want to blow off some steam?" the blonde-haired woman shouted over the noise of the engine.

Lily didn't need to be asked twice; before Helen could change her mind Lily had ripped open her package and pulled out a pair of pants. She jumped out of the car and pulled the slacks on to protect her bare legs from the dust, grit, and heat from the motorcycle itself. Pulling her dress over the pants, not caring how ridiculous she looked, she smiled over towards her friends.

"Gimme your scarf Adrienne."

Adrienne unwound the red scarf from her neck and handed it across to Lily who tied it around her head to stop her hair from whipping in the wind. She threw her leg over the motorcycle and wound her arms around Helen's slender waist.

"Hold on tight," Helen yelled over her shoulder.

Lily nodded and tightened her hold bringing her body closer to Helen so that her nostrils filled with the smell of leather from her jacket. "See you at the base!" Lily shouted as she lurched backwards as Helen pulled off, dust surrounding their departure.

"Only if she don't kill you on the way," Adele remarked climbing into the car.

***

"You're right," Lily yelled in Helen's ear. "It's as exhilarating as flying."

She felt Helen's body shake with laughter and in response the blonde opened the throttle further, the bike lunged forward as its speed increased taking all possibility of conversation away. Lily took a deep breath in through her nose, loving the wind battering against her face, her clothes flapping against her skin, the throb of the bike beneath them. She felt alive!

The increase in speed caused Adrienne's scarf to whip from Lily's head, she turned to see the material dance into the distance, feeling her locks lash around in their newfound freedom. Turning back towards the front she pulled herself closer to Helen, she wasn't sure what she was enjoying more the thrill of the motorcycle or the physical contact with Helen, who for some inexplicable reason Lily felt drawn to. She loved the fact that she could feel Helen riding the bike, not just with her hands and feet but her entire body was at one with the machine.

Helen for her part was fighting trying to concentrate on riding and not focus on the arms gripped around her waist and the thighs pressed against her own. She was pleased that Lily had not tried to speak again as feeling her breath on her ear had almost caused her to lose control of the cycle. She tugged on the throttle again while they were on a straight bit of road, picking up the pace determined to make Lily forget about the incident in the shop.

They pulled into the base and Helen killed the engine, neither making a move to get off the bike.

"That was amazing, thank you," Lily smiled her ears still throbbing with the memory of the now quiet engine.

Helen reluctantly released the handlebars knowing that her movement would break the spell. "You're more than welcome," she smiled.

Lily released her grip of Helen and pushing her hands into the calfskin seat of the bike she propelled herself off, to stand on shaky legs.

"Adrienne is probably going to kill me for losing her scarf," Lily mused. "But you know what it was worth it."

***

They dressed in their beige slacks and white short-sleeved shirts taking pride in putting their uniform together, complete with their beige overseas hat. Adrienne looked down at her brown shoes.

"Still think the red shoes went better," she remarked. She sighed and picked up one of the white shirts she had bought. "Dammit, I must have picked up the wrong size," she frowned. "I got midget sized," she looked thoughtfully across to Adele. "Hey Adele, this is more your size. I'll swap you for three weeks mop duty," she held the shirt out towards the smaller woman.

Adele narrowed her eyes considering the offer, "Two weeks an' you've got yoursel' a deal."

Adrienne sucked air through her teeth and blew out a deep breath. "Two weeks it is then," she said grudgingly and tossed the shirt over onto Adele's bed. Adele picked up the shirt and grinned turning to hang it up in her locker.

Marjorie raised her eyebrows slightly at Adrienne who was smiling to herself as she put her hat onto her head. She gave Marjorie a small wink as she wandered over to the mirror to check her reflection.

***

Finally released from duty, they gathered in the recreation room. Relieved to be sitting down to free time after an hour of drill in the hot Texan sun, where they practiced their wheels, marching in formation and learning the marching songs that helped them ignore the heat and the discomfort of the activity. In addition to marching, they'd had a couple more hours of Ground School, which had fried their brains more than the afternoon sun beating down on their heads. They had wearily eaten dinner; Adrienne moaning that the afternoon's activity would no doubt have her, 'Burnt like a lobster' and that her feet hurt worse than if she had worn her heels.

The Bay Four girls sat scattered on the floor, books open as they helped each other make sense of what they'd learned during the day. After an hour, Lily packed her things up and arose saying she was going to play her violin while they were there so as not to disturb them.

Helen stretched her back, popping noises coming from her spine, she rolled her head around to release some of the tension acquired from sitting pouring over her notes. Checking the clock, she noted that there was still a quarter of an hour before they needed to be back in their bays for curfew.

"I'm done, I'm going to head back."

The others murmured their goodbyes barely lifting their eyes from their books.

As she entered the bay, she frowned at the empty room, although unwilling to admit it she had hoped that Lily would have been there. She rummaged through her case until she located a packet of cigarettes and a box of matches, taking the items she headed back out into the darkness of the night, which was still clinging to the oppressive heat from the day. She wandered around the base enjoying the relative peace, the quiet punctuated by sounds from the recreation room where all the current classes could gather. She lifted her head and blew smoke out into the night sky as she walked towards the flight line, inexplicably drawn towards the hangars where some of the planes were kept.

As she neared she could hear the sound of a violin, she walked towards where the haunting melody was playing, halting at the small door to the hangar. Highlighted by the shards of moonlight welcomed through the open aircraft doors stood Lily, her back to Helen as she swayed to music flowing from her fingers, which were dancing up and down the neck of her violin. Her movement accentuated the rise, fall, and flow of the music. Helen stood transfixed not just by the music but more by the sight of Lily.

Lily swept her bow across the strings for a final time; she stood still allowing the memory of the music to leave her body. She opened her eyes and jumped slightly as someone started to clap behind her. She turned lowering her violin and peered into the darkness only able to make out the red tip of a cigarette. She took a breath and relaxed as Helen stepped forward.

"Sorry I didn't mean to startle you," Helen apologized, throwing her cigarette onto the floor of the hangar before grinding her foot on it.

"It's okay," Lily smiled, leaning down to put her violin back in its case.

"That was beautiful."

Lily laughed, "Thank you, nothing like a bit of Bach to end the day."

Helen turned looking over to where a P47 'Thunderbolt' pursuit plane sat. "I can't wait to fly," she said wistfully walking towards the plane. Lily followed and they circled the machine touching it reverently. "What was it? The music I mean," Helen asked as she trailed her fingertips across one of the propellers.

"Sonata for Violin solo No. 1 in G minor. It's one of my favorites to play," Lily replied, mirroring Helen's actions. "So were you sneaking off to smoke?"

Laughing, Helen shook her head. "No not sneaking, although I don't make a habit of smoking. I only do it when I'm stressed," she confessed as she walked around the nose of the plane and climbed up onto the wing.

"You're stressed?" Lily asked surprised, following Helen she accepted her outstretched hand and scrambled onto the wing beside her.

"Aren't you?" Helen smiled sadly. "I'm terrified of not being good enough to graduate. I'm even more terrified of washing out before I even get to go up in one of the training planes, never mind one of these babies." She smiled patting the wing. She lay down, shivering slightly at the cold metal through her thin shirt. Lily lay down beside her and they both stared up into the dark rafters of the hangar.

"Can I ask you something?" Helen said quietly.

Lily hesitated before warily uttering, "Sure."

"Why did you say you weren't married?" Helen turned to face Lily a look of confusion on her face, she realized that Lily had stiffened at her question. "I'm sorry, it's none of my business, forget I said anything."

"No." Lily exhaled. "How did you know?"

"At your interview you were wearing a wedding ring and I saw your name on some papers and your family name was McAllister not Rivera, Liliana," she grinned as Lily rolled her eyes at hearing her full name. "Plus you almost said McAllister when you introduced yourself."

Lily turned, "You seem to be paying close attention to me Miss Richmond."

"You intrigue me," Helen answered honestly.

Lily felt her breath hitch slightly at Helen's admission, "I'm widowed, my husband Henry was killed earlier this year, his plane was shot up, he tried to land with a dead engine at full speed with no flaps, and still being shot at, he hit a grove of palm trees and firebombed," Lily recited with no emotion in her voice.

"Wait...McAllister? Henry McAllister?" Helen sat up, her eyes wide in surprise. "*The* Henry McAllister, Medal of Honor, cover of Life Magazine. That Henry McAllister was your husband?" she frowned wondering why Lily would choose to ignore being married to someone who had been heralded as an all-American hero and whose death had been mourned by a nation.

"That's him, my loving husband Henry," she gave a mirthless laugh. "We met through music. He played the clarinet, he was a sweet man then," she smiled sadly. "Do you know I taught him to fly, the first time I took him up he threw up, and then he becomes this hot shot pilot, claiming more victories than any other pilot and getting himself killed in the process," Lily said with a hint of anger in her voice.

"I, I don't understand," Helen shook her head looking down at Lily. "Why don't you use his name?"

Lily sat up, her finger playing nervously in her lap, "Three weeks after I got the telegram telling me my husband was dead, I get a blonde woman on my doorstep, Henry's mistress. Turns out my dear husband as well as being a condescending bully had been cheating on me the whole time we were married." Lily switched her focus from her fingers to the blue eyes looking at her full of concern and empathy. "People don't like to hear ill of the dead," she spat. "And while Henry may have died honorably, when he lived, he was the most dishonorable man I know." Lily took a breath releasing her fury, "So forgive me but I'd rather not have people put two and two together and have to stand there while they tell me I was lucky to have been married to such a hero and that they're sorry for my loss." She tore her eyes from Helen and laid back down returning her attention to the rafters; she felt her heartbeat slow down again as her anger dissipated leaving her with the usual emptiness that settled in her heart when she thought about her late husband.

Helen reached out and placed her hand on Lily's thigh. "I'm sorry for your loss, I mean in terms of losing the person you thought you were marrying and the life you had," she clarified.

Lily lifted her head slightly to look at the hand resting lightly on her leg, the heat from Helen's hand seemed to burn through the thick pant material, making Lily's skin feel on fire. She turned to Helen with a perplexed look.

Misinterpreting the look as one of concern about her disclosure, Helen was quick to appease her.

"I won't say anything to anyone," Helen gave a small smile, lifted her hand and ran it through her hair.

"Thank you," Lily watched as Helen dragged her fingertips through her soft curls, still feeling the heat on her thigh from the blonde's touch. She fell silent as she tried to rid herself of the confusing thoughts forming in her brain.

They lay in comfortable silence, each lost in their thoughts as they studied the rafters above, neither conscious of time passing. The silence was broken when Lily asked quietly. "So what about you? How come you said you'd never marry?"

Helen toyed with telling Lily the truth about her attraction to women. She felt guilty after Lily had been so open and honest, but she knew that it was too much of a risk to disclose her secret this early on in their fledgling friendship. She settled on telling the truth but omitting certain pertinent pieces of information.

"I've never met that someone that makes me feel like I'm flying," she smiled.

Lily pursed her lips and nodded. "You never know, it could happen," she shrugged.

"It could," Helen laughed, her smiled freezing as she heard an all too familiar sound. She breathed out a curse, furrowing her eyebrows at Lily's shocked expression. "That's Taps, we're out way beyond curfew."

A look of horror passed between them.

"We'll be washed out," Lily whispered.

"Not if no-one sees us we won't," Helen slid down the wing landing nimbly on the ground before turning and waiting for Lily to join her. Lily reached down for her violin case, clutching it to her chest as she took Helen's offered hand.

They snuck back towards the bays keeping to the shadows. Helen peaked around the corner of the final bay, swearing quietly under her breath as she saw the retreating figure of Foster shine a torch through each bay's window checking everything was in order.

"What is it?" Lily hissed.

"Ssh. Wait," Helen whispered back, she held her breath as Foster reached their bay, shining the torch in through the glass on the door. She let her breath out slowly as Foster lowered the torch and continued down the line of bunkhouses eventually stepping down at the end and gratefully heading towards her own bed.

Helen counted to ten to make sure that Foster was far enough out of sight and hearing distance.

"Okay, try not to make a noise," she whispered, leading Lily onto the wooden walkway of the bays. They tiptoed down until they reached Bay Four, turning the doorknob slowly they slipped in and Helen turned to close the door quietly behind them. She heard Lily snigger and turned back into the bay, their beds had been plumped with clothing to make it appear as if they were in bed asleep.

"You're so lucky I went to boarding school," Adrienne drawled in the dark. "That's two things you owe me Rivera, don't think I've forgotten about my scarf."

Chapter Five

<u>August 1943 – Avenger Field, Sweetwater, Texas</u>

Rosecroft, how'd you expect to pull a bomber out of a dive, if your weedy arms can't even haul your chin over a bar!" the PT instructor shouted as Adrienne attempted again to pull herself up, groaning at the effort, her legs flailing around as she fought to give herself more momentum.

"Sir. Yes. Sir," she yelled as again she felt her arms give, leaving her hanging uselessly from the bar.

Lily and Helen stood back waiting in line with Adele waiting for Adrienne, Marjorie, and Lucy to finish their pull-ups and move onto the next obstacle. As the PT instructor turned to shout at some of the women at the back, Adele rushed forward.

"Here we go PT Addies' style," Helen murmured to Lily under her breath watching the small woman rush down the small incline towards her bay mate.

Adrienne hung limply, trying to muster up the energy for one last assault on the bar. She could feel the lactic acid build up burning her muscles making her arms feel impossibly heavy, her fingers starting to lose grip on the metal bar. She was about to let go when she felt arms circling beneath her knees, gripping her tightly. Suddenly she was propelled upwards. "Oh my giddy aunt, seriously Adrienne it's been weeks Honey. We need to build those skinny arms of yours up."

Adrienne smiled as she recognized Adele's voice beneath her.

"I promise press-ups tonight," Adrienne grinned as her chin finally edged over the bar.

Adele released her legs and the red-haired woman dropped down to the ground.

"I promise," she huffed as she landed.

Adele narrowed her eyes, "Good now help me up onto the damn bar."

Adrienne boosted the smaller woman up, releasing her when she gripped the bar. Adele drew her legs together, immediately, and effortlessly she started to pull herself up. Adrienne looked on enviously before turning and continuing her way around the course. Lily and Helen skidded down the incline and launched themselves at their bars using their momentum to assist their first pull up. Completing the repetition, they dropped down and sprinted off to their next station.

It had been three weeks since those first confusing days of their arrival, and in those three weeks the women had done nothing but eat, sleep and talk about flying, Lucy had even woken the majority of the bay up one night by yelling out her pre-flight checklist. Their brains hurt from the navigation and Math classes they had during Ground School in the morning. They physically hurt from the afternoon drill, calisthenics, and exercise that they undertook to increase their strength and stamina. In some instances, their egos had taken a bashing as their flight instructors pounded on them. Flying the 'Army way' proved to be vastly different from their civilian flight procedures. They were learning to fly planes that were different and more complicated than the planes they were used to. They had engine dust under their fingernails from learning the basics of engine design in Ground School, the searing sun had browned their skin, makeup was a forgotten luxury, and they were lucky if they had the time or the inclination to pull a hairbrush through their hair in the morning. A week had passed before Adrienne realized that she had not even washed her hair, she was in such a tired fug. However, with all of the discomfort, tiredness, and regimen in their lives, not one of them would swap it for their life before Avenger Field.

They had settled into the rhythm of WASP life; as Helen had predicted privacy was not something that any of the girls had anymore. Their initial embarrassment about changing in front of each other had been replaced with easy camaraderie and it wasn't unusual to see one of them mopping the floor before breakfast while still in their bra and drawers. They had learned the hard way after the first Saturday morning inspection that civilian clean and Army clean were poles apart and were now used to washing the bedsprings under their beds, arranging their clothes in the correct order and ensuring that their ice buckets were emptied and polished.

Each morning as soon as the bugle played the women would rise, apart from Lily who still would sleep through the morning call.

However, the bay had developed a plan to ensure she was up; the first one to put their feet down onto the cool floor was responsible for using the 'Rosecroft Method' to wake Lily up. Lily had become accustomed to the morning ritual of being rudely woken up with a smack to the head; so much so that she could now tell who wielded the pillow just from the blow.

They had taken great pleasure in creating their radio call signs for each other and Lily was now 'Sleeping Beauty' on the airwaves, which made her smile anytime she radioed the tower during her limited airtime each day. Each woman was working towards the required hours, which would mean they would be allowed to go solo, no one from their class had yet achieved the honor, and everyone was desperate to be the first.

"You have gotta work on those arms. They're too weak," Adele shook her head as they huddled around, hunched over trying to get their breath back after their run.

"At least I can get up onto the bar," Adrienne scoffed. "You need to work on those legs, they're too short."

Helen turned her head towards Lily, both still breathing heavily, "Here we go. The Addies are about to start up again."

Lily snorted standing up straight and stretching out her lower back waiting for the show to begin. Helen averted her gaze from the sight of a sweaty Lily rolling her hips around to ease her back.

Her attraction for Lily had only grown during the weeks as she got to know her better. Her brain knew that they could never be more than friends; however, her heart and other parts of her anatomy didn't seem to be in on the message. The ease that the women felt around each other and their bodies only served to taunt Helen further. Despite her best efforts not to stare, Helen was fairly certain that she would be able to recite every aspect of Lily's body, even down to the small dark freckle on Lily's left breast. Helen was continually reminded of Peggy's frustrated words the night before she came to base, when oblivious to Helen's discomfort Lily would strip naked in front of her.

"Did you even meet the height restriction?" Adrienne asked teasingly knowing that Adele had sweet-talked the doctor that examined her into adding a half inch so she made the five two requirement.

"Shuddup!" Adele replied wide-eyed looking round to make sure that no officer overheard the conversation. She narrowed her eyes. "Did you make the weight requirement?" she parried back, knowing that Adrienne had been underweight for her height so she too had fudged the system firstly by hunching down to lose an inch in height to reduce the height weight ratio requirement, then by carrying fishing weights in her underwear so that she came in on the mark. "I hear when you went for your first medical there was a mighty strange clanging noise," Adele added, knocking her hip against the taller woman.

"You two, seriously you squabble more than me and Lucy and we're sisters," Marjorie remarked running a hand through her sweat soaked hair.

"We're only messin'," Adele smiled.

Foster put her fingers into her mouth and let out a loud whistle. "Ladies there's an extra flight line been called for your class today, so get your zoot suits on and get ready to march down," Foster yelled standing on the plinth used for the leader of the PT classes.

The six women looked at each other with raised eyebrows, another chance to fly was not something that they had expected today, however it was something they would not want to miss. They hurriedly picked up their overalls and sunglasses and fell in.

***

Lily pulled her parachute on over her overalls closing the fastening at her chest; from experience she left the leg buckles undone until she was ready to climb into the plane, otherwise the heavy equipment would hit against the back of her legs as she walked out of the hangar. She picked up her soft leather helmet and goggles and went to check what instructor she had.

"Rivera, you're with me."

Turning from the instructor list on the board Lily smiled as she realized whom she would be flying with that day.

"You got old man Rowe," Helen grumbled as she realized that she was going to be flying with Stark, who was notoriously difficult and known to bark instructions and insults through the radio.

"Luck of the draw I guess. Fly safe and happy landings," she smiled at Helen and squeezed her hand, before turning to greet her instructor.

It felt to Lily that since the night when they had been out after curfew they had grown closer despite them having little free time now that they were in the full swing of training and it seemed that if one person was in bay they all were. However, regardless that they had not managed to get any alone time, the bond between them had grown deeper; each seemed to have an in built awareness of the other woman's presence, it was as if they had a sixth sense for where the other was. A feeling of warmth would settle in Lily's chest when she turned to see familiar blue eyes watching her. They would give each other reassuring smiles and were happy in each other's physical space; it wasn't unknown to see one of them to be resting their head on the others lap when they were studying. Helen's touch would still cause Lily's skin to flush, however she had stopped trying to fathom the reason and simply enjoyed the feeling.

"Fly safe," Helen called.

"Ah Hollywood, I have the distinct pleasure of your skills this afternoon," Stark remarked snidely as he checked his clipboard. "Try not to kill me," he sneered and walked off towards the doors of the flight room.

Helen rolled her eyes and followed the instructor out; mimicking him under her breath as she walked, "Try not to kill me," she muttered. "It would be a pleasure!"

Lily climbed up onto the wing and fastened the remaining clasps to hold her parachute in place; before tossing her cushion onto the seat of the plane and pulling her soft leather helmet down onto her head and securing it under her chin. Rowe gave her an encouraging smile as he lowered himself into his instructor seat behind her. Nodding she climbed in and slipped into the seat gripping the stick nestled between her legs and settling her feet onto the pedals. Once settled in the cockpit she placed the headset onto her head and adjusted the microphone, she flicked the radio switch, lifted the control lock on the stick and completed her pre-flight control check.

"Control check complete," she said into the microphone as she checked the elevator trim ensuing that it was cranked to the correct position for two people. "Engine's ready, clear," she yelled, pulling the stick back into her lap and pumping the wobble pump handle to build up the fuel pressure to the necessary level. She pressed the starter button and the engine belched into life coughing blue smoke into the air around them, Lily smiled at the smell of the engine as she waited for it to heat up. A member of the ground crew pulled the chocks from the wheels giving Lily the thumbs up as they stepped back.

"Sleeping Beauty to control. Are we good to taxi? Over."

"Control to Sleeping Beauty. Proceed. Over."

Using the rudder pedals for direction Lily started to taxi the plane out of the lot towards the runway, she pulled up patiently waiting her turn as other classmates took off into the sky, eventually when it was her turn she steered the plane onto the runway, pointing into the wind. Lily pulled the microphone closer to her mouth, "Control. Sleeping Beauty. Ready for take-off."

The radio buzzed in her ears then eventually she heard a soft Texan accent replace the white noise, "Go ahead Sleeping Beauty. Happy flying!"

With her feet firmly on the brakes, she checked that her flaps were raised and started to run up the revs on the engine, she checked her counter and cylinder head pressure, pushing the engine up to full throttle, the plane danced about like a tiger fighting against a leash, desperate to be freed. She double-checked her flight controls and her seat harness, then took a deep breath and released her hold on the brakes. The plane surged forward building up speed. Checking her gauge, she felt wind start to break across the elevator and the tail lifted, with the tail up the plane started to speed faster. She watched closely until she reached the desired speed, as soon as the needle hit, she pulled back on the stick and the nose of the plane started to lift from the ground.

Helen watched Lily's take off from her position in the runway queue.

"Happy landings Liliana," she smiled, her smile turning to a frown as Stark's voice sounded in her ears.

"Hollywood, are you having a conversation up front there?"

"No sir," Helen responded her eyes following the flight path of Lily's plane as she rose up into the clear blue sky.

***

Forty-five minutes later, Lily was taxing back towards the hangar when she heard Rowe address her, "Rivera, I see you've logged eight hours flying time here at the field."

"I have Sir, yes," she replied.

"How 'bout you let me out and you log another half hour on your own?"

Lily could hear the smile in his voice as he gave her permission for her first solo flight as a W.A.S.P, she tensed her body in a quick celebration, "Sir, that would be a pleasure." After a quick turnaround Lily was back out on the runway and repeating the process that she had done only a short time before. However, this time, she was on her own.

Helen parked her plane up and unfastened her safety harness, she pulled herself out of the seat and automatically looked over to where Lily's plane should have been. She felt her stomach start to churn; Lily should have been back, her mind started to race, panicking that something had happened. She barely registered Stark's scathing assessment of her flying ability.

She jumped down and ran back to the hangar not bothering to relieve the discomfort of the parachute banging against her in her desperation to find out what had happened. She saw the Addies standing together in the shade of the hangar comparing notes of their flight, running up to them Helen yanked her helmet off her head and crushed it in her hand.

"Where's Lily?"

The two women looked up at her in surprise.

"Is she still out?" Adrienne asked, holding a hand above her eyes so she could see Helen better.

"She should be back," Helen said hitting her helmet against her thigh. "She went out in front of me, she should be back."

"Hey, don't be thinking the worse," Adele soothed. "Who'd she go out with?"

Helen took a couple of breaths, "Rowe, she was out with Rowe."

Marjorie and Lucy wandered up each pulling on a soda bottle, enjoying the cold cola after their flights. "Who was out with Rowe?" Lucy asked.

"Lily," Adrienne answered. "She's not back."

Lucy furrowed her eyebrows, "But Rowe's in the hangar, we just passed him." She looked towards Marjorie for confirmation, who nodded.

"So if Rowe's in there and Lily's plane isn't in the lot, then…" Helen stopped, all five women looked up into the sky. They walked out from the shade of the hangar and covering their eyes from the sun they started to scan the sky for their friend.

Marjorie started to smack Lucy's arm. "Over there!" she pointed; they turned and spotted the yellow wings of Lily's PT in the distance. None of them took their eyes off the plane as it neared the base, they watched as Lily leveled the plane and lowered it towards the runway. The wheels bounced on the tarmac and as she slowed the speed, the tail started to drop down until its wheel was also on the runway.

As Lily taxied back towards the hangar she could see her bay mates lined up cheering her as she passed; she gave them a thumbs up and a wave, her grin wide on her face. Maneuvering the plane back into its stall she let the engine idle for a couple of minutes relishing the relief at completing the first hurdle as a WASP. She pushed the mixture and the engine cut out, the propellers clicking to a stop. She had barely unbuckled her harness when Helen appeared on the wing beside her.

"You flew solo," she grinned.

Lily stood up onto the seat of the plane and leaned over to hug Helen.

"It was amazing," she laughed.

Helen pulled out of the hug and grabbed her hand dragging her down the walkway on the wing; they jumped down onto the ground where the rest of the girls were waiting.

"We got ourselves the first solo of the class," Adele yelled. "You know what that means."

"Wishing well!" the women shouted, hoisting Lily up between them. Ignoring her shouts of protest, they carried her towards the small pond of water that Helen and Adrienne had raced to on their first day.

As was tradition with each class, the first solo pilot had to be dunked, flight clothes and all, into the water. Within moments, Lily was lifted over the small wall surrounding the pond and unceremoniously dumped into its cool waters. As she lay at an impossible angle thanks to her parachute, which was still sitting just under her backside, with her soaked overalls clinging to her skin she looked up at the faces of her friends who were standing on the wall of the pool clapping and cheering from her. Her eyes locked with clear blue eyes, which were full of pride. At that moment Lily didn't think she'd ever been happier.

***

In the following week the rest of Bay Four completed their first solo flights; the joy of that however was overshadowed with the news that their first check flights would be happening soon. A civilian instructor who had not been out with them before would first take them out while they completed the necessary maneuvers. If they passed this then they would be taken out by an Army pilot for the second check, this would be the point when the class was expected to dwindle in numbers; nervousness pervaded every activity now.

The one piece of respite was that now that they had been on the base for one month they were eligible for an 'Open Post'. However, their excitement at their short leave was destroyed when they received news that there had been an infantile paralysis scare in the area, so all local swimming pools and cinemas had been closed and the recommendation was for all personnel to stay on base. The disappointment felt was palpable; as much as everyone loved being on Avenger Field, they were starting to get a little stir crazy and needed to blow off some steam. As a compromise the social committee at the field decided to organize a dance in one of the hangars, they hooked up the public address system to a gramophone in the office, and the sound of Glen Miller's orchestra bellowed out across the night's sky.

Still dressed in their uniforms the women entered the hangar full of excitement at the opportunity to let their hair down, all be it without the aid of any alcohol. The male Army instructor pilots that were in attendance were dramatically outnumbered by the WASP women and looked slightly intimidated by the ratio as the sound of saxophones playing the start of 'In the Mood' came over the speakers. The temporary dance floor started to fill with women who had been quick enough to grab one of the male attendees, joining them were women running out to dance together.

Helen grabbed Lily's hand and pulled her onto the dance floor while the trumpets responded with their section of the song. Helen registered the look of surprise on Lily's face.

"What Liliana? You've never danced with a fly girl before?"

Lily laughed. "I'll dance with you. But I'm leading!" she grinned, before twirling Helen under her arm and round to her back, releasing her hand and then reclaiming it with her other hand. They kicked and flicked their legs out in time with the music twirling, weaving, and spinning each other until they were dizzy. They held each other at arm's length moving round with one foot planted on the makeshift dance floor as the heel of their other foot rested on the ground twisting back and forth as they danced around in a circle. As the trumpet played its solo Lily pulled Helen close, their bodies pressed against each other as they stepped in rhythm, Lily's leg nestled in between Helen's as they danced in perfect step.

Helen's senses were filled with Lily; she allowed herself a moment to bask in the thought that she was in the arms of the woman that she was slowly falling in love with. She mentally shook herself; *this doesn't mean a thing, we're only dancing and there is no way that Lily had those sorts of feelings for me*. Feeling uneasy at the closeness, Helen pulled away putting Lily at arm's length again.

Lily felt a flash of confusion at the action worrying that perhaps she had been wrong to pull Helen in so close, but they had always been comfortable in each other's personal space and she had enjoyed holding Helen in her arms. It had felt as though the heat that she had become accustomed to when Helen touch her, had surrounded her entire being when their bodies pressed together closely. Her face flushed as she realized that the pleasure she felt went far beyond that of enjoying a dance with a friend.

They stopped as the music ended, their breathing increased; in part due to their energetic dancing and in part due to having been pressed against each other. An awkward tension descended between them, as they stood staring at each other still rooted to the spot where they had finished dancing, neither willing to move or say anything.

"Hey Lily," Adele ran up breathlessly, oblivious to any tension between her two friends. "Can you go git yer fiddle?"

Lily dragged her eyes from Helen to look at the small brunette. "Violin," she corrected. "Sure."

She didn't even think to ask why, she was just relieved that she had an excuse to leave. Adele grinned as Lily left them and walked out of the hangar doors.

"This is gonna be great," Adele smiled slapping Helen on the shoulders, then headed back into the throng of the dance floor.

Helen quickly looked around the hangar and spotted all of the Bay Four women on the dance floor laughing and having fun. As her eyes scanned the room she spotted Peggy watching her from, the tall blonde shook her head slowly, a worried look on her face. Helen gave her a half-hearted smile, then took a breath and decided to follow Lily.

The music from the hangar was playing through all of the speakers across the base so as Helen walked she continued to be treated to the music being enjoyed by the rest of the base down on the flight line. She softly opened the door to their bay; Lily was sitting on her bed, her back to the door with her violin case beside her. At the noise of the door opening, she turned and looked surprised at Helen hovering in the doorway.

"What are you doing?" she asked.

Helen opened her mouth to speak but nothing came out. Her mind was a maelstrom of emotions and she was not able to pick the words to describe coherently what she was feeling. She swallowed hard and took a step into the room, "I just wanted to see that you were okay, the dance, we..."

"I'm fine Helen," Lily interjected standing up; knowing she was anything but fine and that anytime she was close to Helen confusion grew in her.

Helen nodded slowly, unsure what to say next. "Okay," she turned and took a step out onto the wooden veranda that ran the length of the bays. As she did the music over the tannoy changed, the saxophones and clarinets that had everyone jumping earlier were now soft and gentle and playing the soothing melody of 'Moonlight Serenade'.

Lily's feet propelled her towards the door and before she knew what she was doing she was standing in the doorway with one hand holding onto the doorframe.

"Dance with me?" she whispered towards Helen's back.

Helen wasn't sure whether she'd heard correctly or whether her mind had simply created the words that she so desperately wanted to hear. She turned slowly, her eyes locked on Lily's. Gradually she let her eyes fall down towards Lily's left hand, she took a step forward and ran her hand down the back of Lily's hand, eventually lacing their fingers and lifting their hands up. Drawing her eyes from their hands, she looked deeply into Lily's eyes as she took a half step towards her and slipped her other arm around Lily's waist. Lily lifted her free hand and moving closer curling her arm around Helen's body, placing her hand on Helen's shoulder as they swayed to the music, their faces millimeters apart. They danced, never taking their eyes from each other, their feet shuffling on the dusty wooden floor of the veranda. The music sped up as the song came to a climax before hitting the final note. They stood unmoving in each other's arms, their breathing becoming shallower at their close proximity.

Helen watched as she could see the battle being fought in Lily's mind being played out across her face. Lily leaned in, her lips almost brushing Helen's. As she neared she felt the Helen stiffen in her arms. Suddenly her nerves hitting like a train at full speed, she pulled her head back quickly.

"I should get back. Adele will be wondering where I've got to," she reluctantly removed herself from Helen's embrace and re-entered the bay to collect her violin. When she came back out Helen had gone.

As soon as Lily had entered the bay, Helen was overcome with the need to get away and get some space between them. She had been sure that Lily was about to kiss her and her entire body had tensed at the anticipation of finally feeling those lips on hers. It felt as though her entire world collapsed on itself when Lily had pulled away, so she took to her heels and ran as fast as she could, sprinting round the corner of the bay where they'd watched Foster doing her nightly sweeps only weeks before.

She pressed her back against the wooden building and dropped her head allowing tears to fall freely down her face; slowly she lowered herself down towards the ground holding her knees against her chest tightly.

Time seemed to hold no consequence as she wept softly. She was so lost in her thoughts she didn't hear the approaching footsteps; it wasn't until a pair of shiny boots replaced the stones that her gaze was focused on that she realized she wasn't alone. Her eyes trailed slowly up the legs bearing the standard beige trousers until she reached sympathetic blue eyes.

"Hey Hell's Bells, how you holding up?" Peggy asked, moving to Helen's side and dropping down beside her.

"Please, Peggy, leave me," Helen pleaded.

Peggy pulled two cigarettes from her pocket, put them both in her mouth, and lit them. Removing one, she held it out to Helen who reluctantly accepted it. Taking a long drag on her cigarette Peggy stared off into the distance, "It'll never happen sweet cheeks. She's not like us." Before adding softly, "You're going to get your heart broken."

"Going to?" Helen laughed bitterly.

Peggy toyed with the loose tobacco sticking out of the end of her cigarette, "That bad?"

Helen blew out a long trail of smoke, "I can't stop thinking about her, the way she smiles, her entire face just lights up. I was dancing with her and our bodies just fitted perfectly, like we'd been made to fit together." She dropped her cigarette to the ground and let her head drop, clasping her hands at the nape of her neck.

"It's always the ones you can't have," Peggy said wistfully, she gave a small laugh. "I'm the last person to give you advice I'm in love with one of my bay mates."

Helen looked up and saw her pain mirrored on her friend's face. "We're a right pair," she smiled, wiping her tears. "So what do you do?"

Peggy shrugged, "What can you do, I want her in my life and the only way that I can have that is to continue to lock away the fact that I want toss her onto my cot and ravage her." She stood up slowly, groaning as her knees straightened, "Let's go back and pretend to be the best friends our girls will ever have." She tossed her cigarette and held out her hand for Helen to take.

Taking the outstretched hand Helen pulled herself up, "Lead on McDuff."

"You do realize that I hear that all the time," Peggy replied, rolling her eyes at the common phrase lobbied at her once people knew her surname.

Grinning Helen swatted Peggy's backside, "Margaret McDuff don't be such a moan."

Peggy shook her head. Looping her arm through Helen's, they started the walk back to the hangar.

***

Lily re-entered the hangar and swept her eyes around looking for Helen, unable to spot her blonde curls in the crowd.

"Why there you are...I was just about to come lookin' for ye," Adele grinned.

Lily held up her violin case. "You wanted this?" she said, distracted by the emotions coursing through her body. "Have you seen Helen?"

Adele accepted the violin. Gripping the handle she did a quick spin, a confused look dominating her face, "Nope, not since just after you went off. Sorry." She headed off towards where a stage, of sorts, had been erected. Standing on the stage were two other women one with a guitar and the other a fiddle, at the side was the piano from the recreation room that had been pushed across to the hangar. Adele jumped onto the stage and removed Lily's violin from the case. Lily looked up towards the stage startled by the familiar sound of her violin being tuned; it was only then that she realized that she had not asked any questions of Adele and had handed over her treasured instrument without a second thought.

Adrienne walked up to her and handed her a soda.

"You okay, you look like you've seen a ghost," the redhead remarked. "Or are you worried that short Stott there is going to wreck your violin?"

Lily's breath caught as she spotted Helen re-enter the hangar with Peggy, her eyes obviously red from crying.

"No, everything is okay. I've got to go."

She handed the soda back to a confused Adrienne and pushed past her to get to Helen. Adrienne took the bottle, shrugged, and watched as Lily approached Helen who was standing with her arms crossed pointedly trying to ignore the other woman.

Sensing that she was no longer required Peggy gave both Helen and Lily a quick glance, she gave Lily a wide smile and announced, "I'm off to get a drink."

She turned to Helen and gave her a cautious look, "Come get me later for a dance Hell's Bells."

Realizing that Helen was not going to speak first Lily took the initiative.

"Look, I have no idea what's going on," Lily said standing in front of Helen trying to get the other woman to look at her.

"Please. Helen look at me."

Helen half-heartedly looked up at Lily, her jaw tightened.

"You're my best friend here and I don't want there to be an atmosphere between us, I'm sorry I shouldn't have asked you to dance with me and…." Lily struggled to find the words. "We've probably just been stuck in Cochran's convent for too long," she joked trying to make light of the situation and the tension between them that she didn't understand and couldn't describe.

Helen gave her a weak smile.

"It's fine, you're right," Helen agreed. "Things get blown up out of all proportion, let's forget that anything happened. Friends?" She bit at her bottom lip to stop it quivering and revealing her true feelings.

Lily felt a mix of relief that their friendship would still be in place but at the same time a deep sense of loss, the reason for which she wasn't willing to address.

"Ladies and ladies, and you couple of gentlemen, wherever y'all are," Adele yelled. "Since we're here in the south we southern gals here thought that we'd bring a little bit of our music to you, this one's Soldiers Joy, go git a partner." Adele looked over towards the women that she shared the stage with and nodded, her foot tapping the quick beat. She lifted Lily's violin and rested it in the crook of her arm, her fingers started to move at lightning speed up and down the fingerboard.

Lily's eyes widened in surprise, she was impressed with the speed and nimbleness of Adele's fingers as she picked out the quick tune on the instrument. The dance floor started to arrange itself as Adele's voice rang out as she shouted out dance calls.

"How bout we dance and enjoy the rest of the night?" Helen said quietly taking Lily's hand and leading her out to where their fellow cadets were hooting and hollering and they tried to master the dance steps being called out.

Lily gave her a quick smile, "I'd love that."

Chapter Six

September 1943

Dearest Maria,

It's been six weeks now since I arrived at Avenger Field, you probably wouldn't recognize your dear old sister anymore; we do a couple hours of exercise a day. I'm fitter than I've ever been and more tired than I ever thought possible. We had good news yesterday our whole bay passed our first Army checks. There's only two bays that still have all their occupants in them and thankfully we're one of them.

We got paid...sort of! Two thirds of it went straight back to Uncle Sam for our accommodation and food. Good job I'm not doing this for the money! We also got our dog tags, feels like we're in the Army proper now. We've heard that they're still pondering over whether to accept us as a branch of the Army Air Corps, watch this space I guess.

Did I tell you that Adele (she of Tennessee) plays the fiddle like a dream? She never mentioned it and then we had an impromptu dance in one of the hangars as we were all base bound and she played my violin like it's never been played before. She's currently teaching me to play; it's as technically difficult as classical but really liberating at the same time.

The temperature is starting to cool here now which is a relief, especially in the afternoon when we're exercising or doing drill.

Lily paused; resting her head on her hand. She sat at one of the desks in the bay, her back to the beds, desperately trying to block out the rhythmic thumping that was pounding to her right and concentrate on finishing her letter. She thumped her pen down onto the desk and swiveled round in the chair.

"Helen, will you knock it off!" she yelled.

Helen plucked the small rubber ball from the air as it rebounded off the wall and brought it down to her chest, she tipped her head back on her pillow so she could see Lily albeit upside down.

"Sorry," she replied, dropping her chin back down and inspecting the small ball, rubbing her thumb across a small rough patch on the rubber.

Adrienne lay on her bed reading a letter from her husband, one hand absently toying with the gold ring that now hung beside her dog tags. She looked up at Adele, who was lying on her bed opposite studying, and raised a single eyebrow.

It had been over two weeks since the dance and in that time there had been a subtle shift in the dynamics in the bay. Lily and Helen seemed to be keeping their distance from each other, as much as they could with their living arrangements. There had been no blow out and nothing obvious but, as the women practically lived on top of each other almost twenty-four hours a day, subtle shifts were cataclysmic.

Turning back to her letter Lily looked at what she'd written so far, she closed her eyes and swallowed, she hadn't meant to snap at Helen but ever since their dance she struggled to be around the blonde. She refused to acknowledge that she had almost kissed Helen. However, despite her steadfast refusal to admit to it, in quiet moments she found herself replaying the incident, wondering whether she was more disappointed in what didn't happen than what did.

The ease of their friendship had given way to an awkwardness that neither was willing to address and instead had resulted in her finding fault with Helen for the smallest of things. Helen for her part was studiously avoiding making eye contact with Lily and would only speak to her when spoken to.

"You gonna come?" Adele asked closing her book and looking over towards Helen.

Helen turned her head still turning the small ball over in her hand, "Nope."

Adrienne folded her letter up and pulled herself up into a sitting position, "You've got to come, we've been paid, we've got a full day's pass, and we're allowed off the base."

Lily collected her things together and walked over to stow them back in her locker.

"Tell her Lily. She's got to come."

Lily glanced over her shoulder towards Adrienne who was prompting her with her head, sighing and rolling her eyes, she turned round to face Helen.

"You should come."

Helen raised her eyebrows slightly at the tone of Lily's voice, for the first time in two weeks there was the sound of genuine care there. Lily shrugged, "What else you going to do?"

Marjorie and Lucy burst through the door to the bay giggling carrying two buckets with ice in them.

"One of the girls says that Casablanca is playing in Abilene," Lucy gasped between giggles.

"Now you have to come," Adele said picking up her pillow and tossing it towards Helen.

"What do you mean?" Lucy asked confused before turning to Helen with a confused tone. "You weren't coming?" She stopped staring at Helen to check the clock, wishing that the minute hand had reached twelve so that their official leave could start and they could get off the base.

"Of course she's coming," Marjorie smiled, picking Adele's pillow from Helen's bed and throwing it back.

Helen huffed before sitting up and spinning her legs off the bed. She glanced up at the clock, "Well we have two minutes before our leave starts, we should get ready to go." She slapped her thighs and stood up, smiling towards her friends, evading Lily's stare as she did so.

***

"I remember when I shopped for girly things," Lucy mused, as she swung her brown package containing her newly purchased long johns.

The girls laughed as they paid their entry to the Paramount movie theatre and entered through the wooden doors, making their way towards the theatre where their matinee would be playing.

Helen hung back hoping that she wouldn't have to sit next to Lily. However, her ploy backfired as the other women edged their way into the row leaving them at the end. She gave Lily a small smile and held her hand out to indicate for her to go first, then slipped in behind her.

They watched the film in silence, each transported to Rick's Café and enchanted by the love story unfolding before them. Lily stiffened in her seat as she shifted slightly causing her bare arm to rest against the hot skin of Helen's arm. She closed her eyes tightly, listening to Ingrid Bergman tell Humphrey Bogart how much she loved him and still loved him.

Lily tried to control her heartbeat, which was racing at the most innocent of touches. The sensation of Helen's skin next to hers had restarted the fire inside her that had been ignited when she'd been held in Helen's arms. A fire that she could not comprehend and was trying desperately to quell, swallowing she opened her eyes as Rick and LIsa kissed.

Helen glanced down at their arms and returned her eyes to the screen, silently cursing herself that she so desperately craved the touch of Lily, that she was unwilling to move an inch in case Lily withdrew her arm. Despite her promise to be the best friend that she could be to Lily, the circumstances were too much for her to deal with. Being around Lily was just too hard, pretending not to feel what she felt was exhausting, and she had consciously withdrawn to protect her heart. However sitting next to Lily, feeling the warmth of her skin against her own, her resolve was all but gone.

Lily heard a gasp beside her as Rick told LIsa that she was to go with her husband and board the plane. A small sob escaped from Helen as Rick lied to protect LIsa's relationship with her husband. As the movie theatre filled with the all too familiar sound of airplane engines Lily moved her arm to open her purse. She plucked out a small white handkerchief, flapping it slightly before handing it across to Helen. She gave her a small smile then returned her attention back to the screen.

Helen took the handkerchief with a look of embarrassment; she daubed her eyes and gripped the material in her hand. As the film ended, the lights came on and the six women blinked at the brightness. Lily sat forward in her seat looking down the row at the line of red-eyed women, her eyes widened slightly in surprise.

"All of you? Really? You all cried?"

They stood up and shuffled out behind the other patrons. Marjorie was still dabbing at her eyes as she walked.

"You didn't find it sad?" she asked Lily's back incredulously.

Lily shrugged without turning round.

"You don't think it was romantic that they were in love but couldn't be together?" Lucy asked. Her brow furrowed as she projected her own sadness at being apart from her husband onto the images they had just watched.

Lucy's comment hit a nerve somewhere in Lily and her mind suddenly raced towards Helen who was inches in front of her as they waited for the crowd to ease their way through the exit doors.

"You can't always get what you want," Lily said quietly, her eyes still trained on the blonde curls in front of her.

***

They checked their leather A2 jackets, hats, and purses in and straightened their uniform blouses out. Grinning they entered the Abilene USO, the swing music from the live band filled the large room, the dance floor was filled with a mix of uniformed men from the nearby Camp Berkeley and girls in short summer dresses. The WASP women looked at each other slightly unsure of themselves in their uniform white shirts and beige skirts.

A young GI approached Adrienne, "Do you wanna dance?" She turned and raised her eyebrows at her friends.

"I would love to," she smiled, taking his hand and allowing herself to be led towards the dance floor, where they immediately started to dance energetically.

The others headed to grab a table, losing Adele and Lucy to the dance floor on the way. Helen opened her mouth to speak when a young GI came up behind her and whispered in her ear, she laughed and turned following him onto the dance floor.

"Looks like it's just me and you," Marjorie sighed, as Lily watched Helen dance with the young dark haired man, her brown eyes darkening as she watched him grip Helen by her waist and throw her into the air.

"Looks like it," Lily replied, tearing her gaze from Helen and her dance partner and slipping onto one of the seats.

"You girls from Avenger Field?" the waitress asked coming to take their drinks order.

Lily smiled proudly, "Yes we are."

"I think it's just wonderful what y'all are doin'," the waitress smiled. "What can I get'cha?"

Marjorie and Lily ordered on behalf of the rest of their friends and settled in to enjoy the music; laughing as Adele's dance partner tossed her high in the air bringing her legs down to his side. Grabbing them under his arm and holding them tight to his body, he released her upper body using her momentum to spin her round his back and flip her back into his arms. They clapped wildly at the dance move as their drinks were placed in front of them.

Moments later, an out of breath Adrienne collapsed into one of the chairs. "Did you see Adele being tossed like a doll? One of the benefits of being tall is that they don't do that to you," she grinned, taking a long drink from a glass.

The occupants of the table changed during the next hour as each woman was asked to dance; there was particular excitement when Marjorie brought back a GI who had whiskey in his possession, which was subtly added to their glasses. During all the coming, and goings, Helen still had not returned to the table, she was still dancing with the GI that had grabbed her on her arrival.

"He's cute," Adele remarked, puffing slightly from her last exertion on the dance floor.

"Hmm?" Lily responded absently her eyes still following Helen's every move.

"Helen's pick up, he's cute," Adele clarified, nodding towards the dance floor, she caught the slight flicker in Lily's eyes. "Did you want to hook up with him?" she asked.

"What?" Lily asked confused.

Adele shrugged, smiling at the soldier who was hovering to ask her to dance, "I just thought that you liked him. You look kinda' jealous. Gotta go be thrown around," she grinned, taking a quick swig of her drink before heading back out.

"I'm not…" Lily responded to the space vacated by Adele, she tossed her hand in the air looking round at the empty table. "I'm not jealous," she said to herself shaking her head as she continued to watch Helen dance. Her stomach clenched as the music slowed and the young GI changed his hold to bring Helen in closer.

"Would you like to dance?" a nervous blond soldier asked.

Lily shook her head, her eyes full of unbidden tears that she had no control over, "No, sorry, thank you for asking, I'm going to sit this one out."

She gave him a small smile, which he returned, he nodded sadly and left Lily sitting watching the dance floor before putting her head back to look up at the ceiling blinking back tears as Helen's dance partner placed a soft kiss on her cheek.

***

The six women fell through the door to their bay, four of them slightly drunk from the whiskey that the GI's had been slipping them.

"Sshhhh, you'll get us in trouble," Adele slurred falling onto her bed.

Adrienne flopped onto her bed lurching forward to remove her shoes, "You'll get us in trouble."

The two women started to a laugh loudly.

"What, what are, are you laughing at?" Lucy asked, pursing her lips and shaking her head as she leaned against the doorframe in an attempt to stay upright.

"Nothing. They're drunk," Marjorie answered taking her sister's arm and guiding her towards her bed.

"We's not drunk," Adele hiccupped. "We's jus' happy s'all."

Lily laughed, pulling Adele's shoes off and placing them on the floor. "And tomorrow you'll be paying for being happy," she grinned, leaning down and placing an affectionate kiss on Adele's forehead.

"Pfft tomorrow, tomorrow is another day," Adele laughed.

Adrienne stood up wavering slightly. "An' frankly my dear," she said, waving her arms as if conducting an orchestra, and on time she was joined by Adele, Lucy and Helen who was edging her way slowly and somewhat haphazardly towards the bathroom.

"I don't give a damn," they chorused.

Adrienne nodded emphatically, the effort making her lose what balance she had and tipping her back onto her bed,

Marjorie, who was attempting to undress her rather reluctant sister, looked up at Lily as snores were now coming from Adrienne and Adele's bed. "You should check on Helen," she nodded towards the bathroom.

Lily hesitated slightly; with a deep intake of breath, she walked towards the bathroom where Helen was standing attempting to brush her teeth.

"You okay?" Lily asked closing the bathroom door behind her.

Helen took her toothbrush out and pointed it to her chest. "I'm okay," she pointed the brush in Lily's direction. "Are you okay?"

Lily gave a mirthless laugh. "I'm just fine Helen," she replied sarcastically.

Helen frowned stumbling slightly, "Now why'd do you say that?" she asked sadly. "'Cause we both know that we're not okay."

Lily swallowed the lump in her throat that threatened to choke her, "We're fine Helen, just hurry up and get to bed."

"See, I think you're lying," Helen slurred. "I think, I think that you're angry with me," she lifted her shoulders up to her ears and held her hands out. "For what, I, I don't know, but you're mad," she creased her face up into an over exaggerated scowl.

Lily cocked her head to the side and took a step forward. "You want to know what's wrong with me?" she asked, biting her top lip.

"Yesh," Helen replied, blinking furiously trying to focus on Lily in her new closer position.

Shaking her head Lily asked carefully, "Did you have a good time tonight?"

Helen looked confused, "Yes…I had a lovely time thank you."

"You enjoyed being pawed by that soldier?" Lily's pent up frustration and jealousy finally finding a vent. "Enjoyed being in his arms? Enjoyed him kissing you?"

The confused look on Helen's face grew. "He's shipping out next week, hell he could be dead in a month," she added swaying as she spoke. "It didn't cost me anything to be nice to him. He only kissed my cheek Liliana."

Helen felt her own anger rise, "And he wasn't pawing me and what business is it of yours if he was?"

"You're right," Lily shook her head. "It has nothing to do with me. I'm glad you had a good time and stop calling me Liliana. It's Lily!" She turned on her heel and walked out of the bathroom, yanking the door closed behind her as she left.

Helen stood still wavering slightly from the effects of the alcohol she'd consumed, she put her toothbrush back in her mouth. "Wha' the hell jus' happened?" she muttered to herself, slowly brushing her teeth, her fugged brain unable to decipher the meaning behind the conversation.

***

Helen gingerly opened one eye instantly regretting it as the bright light in the bay made her blink rapidly, her face contorted at the action. Slowly, her other eye opened and the room blurred into focus. She turned her head carefully to the side, her brows furrowing in confusion at the empty made up bed beside her. If Lily was up before her then she knew she was in trouble.

She raised herself up onto her elbows and looked across the bay. There were groans and snores coming from the other occupants depending on where they'd gotten to in their waking up process. Adele's bed was empty. However, Helen recognized the woman's snores, which appeared to be coming from the floor between Adele and Lily's beds.

Giving herself a small headshake and groaning at the resultant pounding it caused, Helen slowly planted each foot onto the floor and sat up. Looking over towards Adrienne, the red-haired woman appeared to be in a similar predicament to Helen. She was sitting on her cot, her hands flattened against the mattress at her sides. She gave Helen a bleary-eyed half nod of acknowledgement. Helen turned her head gradually towards Marjorie and Lucy's cots. Like Lily's bed, Marjorie's was empty and made. However, there were two dirty soles of feet where Helen usually would see the top of Lucy's head. She opened her mouth to speak and closed it again releasing a breath, as her brain could not seem to find the correct combination of synapses to allow words to form.

She was contemplating attempting to stand, when the bathroom door opened. Lily and Marjorie emerged fully dressed, banging the tin ice buckets used by the bay and singing a WASP marching song loudly at the tops of their voices.

Lucy sat bolt upright instantly, her hands flying to grip her head as if holding her skull together. Adrienne lifted her pillow and weakly tossed it in the general direction of Lily and Marjorie who were now parading up and down the small walkway between their beds. Helen cast them an unimpressed look through her still half-closed eyes and stood up shakily.

Marjorie and Lily stood beside the door and finished their rousing chorus of one of the songs sung during drill. They surveyed what remained of their bay mates. Helen was standing albeit she hadn't moved since getting to her feet and was swaying slightly. Adrienne was sitting cursing them under her breath, Lucy was still gripping the sides of her head as if her life depended on it and there were loud snores coming from the floor from Adele.

"Well, that didn't work," Lily muttered to Marjorie, who grinned in response.

"Ladies, the bugle has been and you have two minutes to drag your sorry asses into the bathroom and try and disguise the fact that you smell like a distillery," Marjorie shouted loudly as she walked towards Adrienne and gave her a gentle shove from behind to encourage her to move.

Lily walked over to the slumped figure beside her bed; poking her toe against Adele's arm. "Stotty! Wake up," Lily shouted. Not getting any response she leaned over and pinching her nose shouted, "Mountain Momma this is Tower, you have permission for take-off."

Adele sprang awake, "Whaa?" She looked around; her eyes not focused on anything as she brought the palm of her hand up to her face and ran it down dragging the skin with it causing her face to distort. "I'm up," she muttered, looking at her position on the floor in confusion.

Lily straightened up laughing and noted that Lucy and Adrienne had now made their way to the bathroom. Helen, however, was still standing with a look of concentration on her face.

"Helen…you need to move," Lily said gently walking over towards her friend and gripping her by the shoulders and maneuvering her towards the bathroom.

Helen allowed Lily to guide her, she'd been watching Lily try to rouse Adele and there was something playing in the blonde's mind; something that was there but that she couldn't quite get access to. She knew it involved Lily but frustratingly it seemed to be out of her reach.

***

After a subdued breakfast, the girls were sitting in rows facing each other in a classroom, small wooden boards separating them. Glancing over the top of the board Lily couldn't help but smile at the red eyes looking back. They had plugged their four worse for wear friends full of coffee. However, no amount of caffeine was going to help them through two hours of Morse Code training.

They sat scribbling the translated messages transmitted by the instructor at the front of the class, their hangovers worsening at the incessant beeping and concentration required to make sense of the noise. Every now and again Lily's stomach would flip as she looked up and caught blue eyes looking thoughtfully at her.

When she had eventually gotten into bed the previous night, she had tried to process her emotions and had realized that she was being unfair to Helen. It wasn't Helen's fault that she was confused about her feelings towards the other woman. Lily had decided to stop projecting her anger and frustration and just accept that she was confused. She'd had had a friend in the orchestra who had gone to an all-girls school and she'd mentioned once that it wasn't unusual to grow attached to other females in that sort of environment. So it seemed to Lily that what she was experiencing wasn't unheard of, she just needed to get beyond it and not destroy the friendship she had with Helen in the process. She made up her mind to apologize to Helen for her recent behavior when she got the chance.

However, that chance was not coming any time soon. As if to compound their wretchedness, their schedule then had them in the Link trainers for an hour.

"I'd go back to Physics class and Math like a shot," Lucy whimpered as they walked towards the classroom that housed the mechanical beasts that simulated flights to allow them to practice instrument flying.

"I have no idea what I wrote during that class," Adrienne remarked from behind her sunglasses.

"Can y'all still hear the beeping?" Adele asked waggling her finger in her ear.

Marjorie and Lily shared a smug look. "Well you now know why they call it the demon drink," Marjorie sang as she skipped ahead of them. "And just think now you have a whole hour in the dark being spun around."

"Just breathing in the hot stale air inside the Link," Lily added. "Hot stale alcohol-fumed air."

The four hung-over women groaned as they entered the room lined with the wooden boxes painted in the blue and yellow colors of their trainer planes. They each walked to a Link, climbed inside the small compartment, and waited for their instructor to speak to them. After receiving their initial instructions, the instructor closed the small side door and lowered the lid on the Link plunging the occupants into darkness; the only light coming from the instrument panel in front, which seemed to lurch forwards in the gloom. The women put on their headsets and waited for the first radio waves to be sent to allow them to respond and fly the plane blind.

After an hour of the electrically operated simulators tossing and turning them, their Link time was up. The instructors opened the lids revealing in some instances some rather green looking faces and provided the cadets with their charts, showing the course that they had 'flown', and going over where errors had been made and what actions would have corrected them.

Helen felt surprisingly better following the Link training. Whether it was having to concentrate so her brain ignored the physical discomfort her hangover was putting her through or the fact that the heat that built up in her simulator meant that whatever alcohol was still buzzing around her system was immediately sweated out, she wasn't sure. However, some of the others hadn't faired so well; the moment they had cleared the classroom the Addies sloped off to find a quiet area to gracefully throw up.

After lunch the effects from the previous night were starting to lessen which was probably just as well as the women were now sitting on the flight line waiting for their turn to 'shute' up and go up in their new nemesis the BT 13B Vultee Valiant, or 'The

Vibrator' as it was more commonly known as by cadets. Having passed their army checks in the PT planes, they had now advanced to the more complicated and powerful BT. They'd had a week of flying it so far and the more complex instrument panel meant more pre-flight check; it felt as though they had about a million things to remember before they'd even left the ground.

Checking the instructor list Helen groaned inwardly she was with Stark again; the little man seemed to take great delight in finding fault with her flying. She had a range of bruises on the inside of her thighs from where the annoying little weed would rattle the stick back, and forth, hitting the sensitive area of her legs when annoyed with an action she'd taken.

"Hollywood, you and me again," Stark yelled from the door of the hangar.

Helen pulled on her parachute and started to run so that the instructor would be less pissed with her before she had even gotten near the plane. They walked over in silence towards the plane and just before Helen climbed up onto the wing walkway. Stark said the same as he did each time they went out, "Try not to kill me."

She rolled her eyes, climbed up and slid open the canopy, settling into the bucket seat she adjusted her position so her parachute was in place.

Once she heard Stark settle in his seat behind her she released the control yoke and secured it with the spring clips then fastened her shoulder and safety harness giving it a quick tug. Helen checked the carburetor heat, the oil cooler shutter and the mixture, before pumping the wobble pump handle, priming the engine. She cracked the throttle and turned the ignition switch, she used her foot to move the starter switch pedal then flipped the starter switch. The plane started to hum as the engine grumbled into life and she worked the wobble pump to smooth the engine. As she waited for the oil temperature to rise she radioed in to the tower to check that she had permission to taxi.

Once settled on the runway she completed her take off final checks. Stark's voice came into her ear, "You keeping your canopy open Hollywood?"

"Sir, yes, sir," she responded. "Like to feel the wind in my hair," she lied; the desire to leave the canopy open had more to do with her wanting to wash away any residual cobwebs from the night before. She cranked the flap handle and slowly advanced the throttle, the difference in the BT to the smaller lighter PT places was marked. The Vultee accelerated much faster along the runway giving her less time to prepare for the actual take-off.

She curled her hand around the pistol grip of the stick as they trundled along the runway. The tail started to lift and the plane started to feel lighter as it started to defy gravity, she applied a little backward pressure to the stick, and the nose of the plane lifted skywards.

As they cruised, gaining altitude, Helen looked out of the side of the plane down towards the cotton fields below and listened for Stark's instructions. As he yelled 'Stall' through the radio, she immediately took the necessary actions to place the plane into a controlled stall; pulling the stick back and climbing for what seemed an eternity into the clear blue sky. When the canopy started to shake indicating that the plane was about to stall, she released the backward pressure and allowed the nose to drop leveling off.

"Good Hollywood."

Helen raised her eyebrows, *that's a first*, she grinned to herself waiting on her next instruction.

They performed a series of loops, snap rolls and a half-roll reverse and were just completing a spin recovery when Helen felt her harness loosen during the spin, her eyes widened as the clasp released while she popped the stick to recover. The negative g-force propelled her out of the cockpit. Her headset ripped off, taking her helmet with it. The last thing she saw of the plane was

Stark's wide eyes and open mouth as she spun out into the Texan sky.

She felt the air pass by her at rapid speed as she freefell towards the ground. A calmness descended upon her as she was buffeted by the air before her training kicked in and she pulled her ripcord. Her parachute shot out and immediately her descent slowed. Floating towards the ground Helen gave out a loud whoop.

"I'm flying!" she yelled. Her laugher was cut short however as she looked down toward the rapidly approaching ground.

"And now I'm landing!" she groaned, as the cotton field beneath her got closer.

She landed ungraciously in a heap, her canopy floating down to cover her beneath a pile of silk. Lying on the mud and with no other outlet for her exhilaration, she pounded her arms and legs on the ploughed earth like a toddler having a tantrum.

"I'm alive!" she shouted laughing hysterically as she twisted onto her back.

She lay underneath her parachute for a moment savoring the emotions then reluctantly released the catches of her harness and started to crawl out from underneath the material. She stood up and placed her hands on her hips looking around trying to work out the direction she was from the base. Squinting at the sun she worked out that she was east from where she needed to be, she leaned down and started to pile up her parachute for the long walk home.

***

Lily stood on the flight line taking a long drink from her bottle of cola, laughing as Adele and Adrienne rejuvenated from their flight were now standing singing WASP songs replacing the words for rude versions. Lucy looked up shielding her eyes, watching the next plane line up for landing. "That's Marjorie coming in," she remarked bringing her hand back down. "Just Helen to come."

The women had a rule that no-one left the flight line until their bay were all back on safe ground. They watched as Marjorie had a bumpy landing, before their attention returned to the sky where Helen's plane was now lined up to come in.

"And there she is, all present and correct," Lucy smiled.

They waited for Marjorie to taxi and waved at her as she wandered over towards them walking awkwardly, grumbling that she had taken a stick hit from her instructor during the flight. Lily watched Helen's plane carefully as it parked up.

Her eyes narrowed as she couldn't see the blonde in the front cockpit, she dismissed the thought, opting to think that her eyesight was playing tricks. However, when only Stark got out of the plane and leaned into the front cockpit she felt panic start to rise.

"Guys, there's something wrong," she padded the back of Adrienne who turned to look toward where Lily was looking with wide eyes.

"What?" Adrienne asked.

"Stark's back and Helen's not in the plane," Lily yelled over her shoulder her feet already propelling her towards the instructor. "Where's Helen?" she grabbed the man's shoulders looking wildly between him and the plane in the vain hope that Helen was still in it.

"She..." the small man looked as though he was in shock, he shrugged. "Her harness, the clasp broke, she bailed out!" he said looking up wide-eyed at a distraught Lily. They had been joined by the others and shouts of disbelief surrounded the instructor. "She just fell out," he added numbly.

"Where?" Lily asked trying to get him to focus on her. "Where did she fall?"

Stark pointed up towards the sky and Lily rolled her eyes.

"I know she fell out up there, but where might she have landed!"

He shook himself out of his reverie, his thoughts filled with the surprised look on Helen's face as she dropped out beneath the plane, "About eight miles east."

Lily released him and grabbed Marjorie pulling her along behind her.

"Aaahhhh, my legs. Lily, What?.. Wait. Where are we going?" Marjorie yelled as Lily dragged her along by the collar of her overalls.

"To get Helen!"

***

Helen heaved the heavy parachute up, gathering the lose material that had slipped to her knees threatening to catapult her forwards again for the sixth time. She grumbled to herself as she made her way back towards the base along the deserted road.

She was on her second verse of the WASP song to keep her occupied when in the distance amongst the heat haze rising from the road she could make out something coming towards her.

"Oh thank God," she breathed, continuing to walk.

Lily sat forward on the seat, pointing in the distance.

"Is that her?" she asked Marjorie, as the car got closer and Lily could make out the figure of Helen clutching her parachute she started to bounce on the seat. "It is her...she's alive!" she thumped Marjorie's arm excitedly. "Slow down," she yelled as they got near. Lily pulled her feet up onto the car seat ignoring Marjorie's shouts of protests and before the car slowed to a stop, she jumped from it and ran the final distance to Helen, engulfing her in a tight hug.

"I thought I'd lost you," she said breathlessly, holding a grinning Helen tightly.

***

Lily sat on her bed, her mind working through the event of the day when the sounds of squabbling from Marjorie and Lucy invaded her thoughts. She looked over to where Marjorie had been pinned to her bed by her younger sister who was desperately trying to grab a photograph that Marjorie was holding at arm's length.

"Lily help," Marjorie squawked. "Lucy has taken a photograph of herself in her long johns that she's going to send to Peter."

Lucy's eyes widened. "Are you just going to tell everyone?" she gasped.

"Nope I'm going to show everyone," Marjorie giggled, twisting so that her hand and its contents were still out of Lucy's reach. "Lily, you wanna see?"

Lily laughed and stood up and plucked the photo from Marjorie's grasp she looked appraisingly at the photo.

"Nice, Lucy," she grinned.

Lucy looked from her sister to Lily. Her eyes narrowing, she tensed her muscles and Lily's face registered that she had realized that the younger woman was about to pounce. Before she could grab Lily, the taller woman had taken to her heels and was standing on one of the cots. Lucy gave chase as they bounded across the cots, Lily finally landing on the floor and throwing the bathroom door open.

Helen lay in the bath trying to block out the fact that Adrienne was sitting on the john, her trousers puddled around her ankles and her nose deep in one of their text books, while in the shower Adele was singing 'I'm a Ding Dong Daddy from Dumas', still wearing her overalls.

The warm water was soothing her sore muscles from her day's exertions and she had just closed her eyes when the bathroom door flew open. Opening her eyes she sighed as Lily entered the room with Lucy and Marjorie on her tail. Lily held one hand aloft dodging back and forth as Lucy tried to jump and grab whatever Lily had in her hand. The smaller woman was determined and backed Lily towards the bath; the sides of the tub hit the back of Lily's legs causing her to stumble. Lucy's eyes glowed as she realized that she had an advantage. She lunged at Lily tumbling her into the bath on top of Helen. Lucy snatched the photograph, sniffed haughtily at Lily, and turned to exit pushing at her sister on her way past.

"Hello," Helen said dryly to Lily, who was now lying on top of her facing the ceiling.

They heard a toilet flush as Lily turned her head slightly.

"Hi," she replied sheepishly. "What is Adele doing?" she asked confused as she watched the tiny woman in the shower in her overalls.

"Laundry," Adrienne replied, washing her hands and leaving the bathroom.

Lily nodded as if that was the most obvious thing in the world, "Ah, makes sense."

Helen bit her lip, "Liliana?"

Lily turned again, "Hmm?"

Pulling a wet hand out from the water Helen swiveled her hand back and forth between them, "You're on top of me, in my bath."

"Oh God yes, sorry," Lily apologized. She put her hands on the side of the tub, but was unable to get the momentum to push herself out. "Sorry," she repeated, shifting and putting one hand into the water to get more downward force.

Helen squeaked as Lily's hand landed in the gap between her thighs, she placed her hands onto the other woman's soaked back and gave her a shove to help her get back out.

"Really sorry," Lily blushed as she stood up and looked back down at Helen, a very naked and wet Helen. "I should let you," she nodded her eyes focused on Helen's breasts.

A small smirk played on Helen's lips as she leaned forward to put her face in the line of where Lily's eyes had been staring. "Yup, you should," she grinned.

Snapped out of her staring Lily flustered another apology and bundled herself out of the room. The sound of shower water shut off and Adele stepped out her soaked overalls clinging to her tiny frame, "Quite a day, Hollywood. Quite a day!"

***

Lily woke up suddenly as the sound of yelling pervaded her dreams, she sat up blinking looking around the bay in confusion. Adrienne and Marjorie were awake and rubbing their eyes trying to locate where the shouts were coming from. Lucy and Adele were still sound asleep.

Another burst of noise came and Lily turned toward the source; in the bed next her Helen was flailing her arms and legs wildly against her blankets mumbling and shouting incoherently.

Lily waved towards her bay mates, "I've got this, go back to sleep." With that she pulled the blankets on her bed back and put her feet onto the floor. Her toes twitching at the coldness, she stepped across and sat on Helen's bunk.

"Don't wake her, you're not meant to wake them," Marjorie mumbled, snuggling back into her bed.

"That's sleepwalkers," Adrienne whispered, thumping her pillow before flopping back down.

Lily tore her gaze from the chatter and back to the twisting woman beside her she ran a soothing hand across Helen's brow, "Sshhh, you're okay, you're safe."

"Mmmm, sky, ground," Helen mumbled.

"Shh, you made it, you're safe," Lily repeated. Remembering what she used to do for her younger sister, Maria, when she had nightmares, she shifted Helen gently over in the cot and stood up to change her position. Lifting the blankets that were caught around Helen's body she climbed underneath, slipped an arm between the space under Helen's neck and snuggled herself against Helen's back pulling the smaller woman into her arms, "I've got you, you're okay."

The movement and noise from Helen abated and soon her breathing had returned to normal. Lily smiled and gently tried to extricate herself. However, as soon as she moved her arm Helen clamped a hand down on it, holding her in place. Frowning slightly Lily sighed. "Guess I'm staying," she muttered and settled down to sleep. The peacefulness of sleep found her quickly as she held Helen tightly against her body; their bodies fitting together perfectly like pieces of a jigsaw.

***

Chapter Seven

October 1943 – Avenger Field, Sweetwater Texas

Helen woke up slowly. Disappointed that she was alone in her bed, she turned her head and smiled at Lily sleeping in her usual, arms and legs out of the bed, position. It had been six weeks since her inadvertent parachute jump; the day when she joined the small but illustrious 'Caterpillar' group, the name given to servicemen and women who had bailed and deployed their parachutes. Her medal of honor from the jump; her ripcord, sat proudly in her locker.

During the six weeks, their relationship had settled back into an easy equilibrium. Helen had experienced a few nightmares during the period and had gotten used to waking up in the morning snuggled safely in Lily's arms, there was always a sense of let down when she woke up and found Lily in her own bed. The only positive was that it meant that her sleep had been uninterrupted by the recurring dreams of falling through the air minus her parachute. Lily had apologized for being 'snippy' with Helen but neither seemed willing to tip the balance of the relationship to discuss the reasons behind it. They settled for just enjoying being around each other again.

The bugle sounded and Helen slipped from her bed lifting her pillow as she rose, thumping Lily gently on the shoulder with it to rouse her.

"Mmmm…morning Helen," Lily muttered her eyes still closed.

Helen smiled it had become Lily's habit to say the name of the person that she thought had hit her, before opening her eyes to confirm it was correct and so far, she'd a hundred percent record.

"Morning Sleeping Beauty," Helen responded, tossing her pillow back onto her bed and collecting her wash things from her locker.

The Bay Four morning two-step started, the women seemed now to anticipate each other's movements. The Addies would stand sleepily at the sink Adrienne squeezing toothpaste onto both their brushes. Marjorie would make hers and Lucy's bed, while her sister showered and as if by telepathy would know when to go into the bathroom to switch places with her younger sister. They tidied the bay finishing with the habitual mop of the floor to rid the bay of the incessant Texan dust that appeared to get everywhere, especially as winter was approaching and the winds had picked up.

They marched with the rest of the cadets to the mess hall and lined up with their mess trays to collect breakfast. Mealtimes were an invaluable source of information as it was one of the times that all classes were together and Adele was the local Bay Four gazette, amassing an amazing amount of the latest gossip before she hit the drinks section of the line. The tiny woman sat bouncing on her seat waiting for her bay mates to join her before telling them all that she'd found out. When, finally, their entire bay was sitting Adele started to dish the dirt with wide shining eyes.

"Someone two classes below had a man in their bay!" she leaned forward to whisper. "Hid 'em in their locker!"

"How the hell did they manage that? I can barely get my stuff in mine," Lily laughed, prompting laughs and murmurs of agreement from her friends.

"I know!" Adele replied, nodding her head, her short brunette curls bobbing. "Aaaand Helen broke Stark's collar bone," saving the best piece of information as her pièce de résistance.

Helen's head shot up.

"Whaaaat? I did not. The stupid little man broke his own damn collar bone."

"Oh whatev'r you say Hollywood," Adele laughed. "Indirectly, or not, you broke the little man." Adele held her tin mug aloft, "An' I for one, along with my thighs am grateful to ya!"

"I fly like a dream Stotty," Helen motioned with her hand the smoothness of her flying.

During the six weeks Helen had again been placed with Stark, his 'Don't kill me' pep talk before each flight had been replaced with 'Try to stay in the plane'. During their last outing on the longest cross-country flight that Helen had completed to that point. She had become aware that at some point during the return flight, the small man had fallen asleep. He remained asleep during Helen's landing and the short taxi to the hangar. Helen opened the canopy and taking his unconsciousness as an indication of her flying expertise had simply left the man sleeping in the plane as she closed the canopy and completed her post flight papers. Around ten minutes after they landed Stark opened his eyes. His still half-asleep brain registered that there was no pilot up front and the engines weren't humming beneath him, thinking that something had gone wrong he flipped the canopy open and bailed from the cockpit deploying his parachute, which unfortunately wasn't sufficient to break his ten foot fall from the plane onto the concrete floor of the hangar.

"Like a dream," she reiterated.

***

The usual routine of Ground School in the morning included navigation, Morse Code and more time in the dreaded Link trainer. After lunch, they changed into their dark blue PT kit and lined up outside watching the muscular Lt Latham's actions as he had them performing star jumps, pushups and other exercises designed to increase their strength. Their PT class ended with a quick circuit of the assault course.

Helen and Lily stood with Adele waiting on their friends completing their pull-ups on the bar. They grinned watching as

Adrienne pulled herself effortlessly up to complete her required number.

"You okay?" Lily asked an unusually quiet Helen.

"Hmm...Yeah I'm fine," Helen replied, giving Lily an absent-minded smile over her shoulder as she replaced Marjorie on the bar.

Lily narrowed her eyes watching her friend pull herself up and tuck her chin over the bar. Regardless of what Helen said, Lily was worried about her. She was happy that their relationship was back to where it had been before she had started to project other feelings onto it, but in the past week Lily had noticed a change in Helen. She was distant and dark circles were starting to appear under her eyes, which couldn't all be down to the nightmares that plagued the blonde woman regularly.

"Rivera, snap out of it!" Lt Latham shouted, halting Lily's musing as she ran to the now vacated bar and started her chin ups.

***

On the flight line the women had been plunged into ever more varied experiences during the six weeks, night flying was added to their curriculum and they had been 'flying under the hood' where they sat in the instructor's seat in the Vultee and used only the instruments to fly.

Blind-flying was disconcerting enough when in the Link. However, if they got that wrong all that was likely to happen would be a ticking off from their instructor, but flying blind in an actual aircraft was a whole new ball of wax. Their airtime had been building steadily as they were now in the midst of the cross-country flying that could potentially form part of their duties post-graduation, delivering new, or fixed aircraft, to bases across the country.

As darkness fell across the base the women returned to their bays, chatting happily about their day's experiences, the close calls, and the gentle ribbing about kangaroo landings.

Throwing herself down onto her cot Adele sighed deeply, "God-damned stomach pains. Be gone curse, leave my body!"

Adrienne pulled the top of her zoot suit down tying the arms around her waist, "Isn't that the problem Adele, the curse is leaving your body, which is why you're all moody!"

Adele sat up on her bed, "I am not moody Adrienne Jane Rosecroft. I am a woman!"

Adrienne laughed at Adele's haughty response as she pulled her wash bag and towel from her locker.

"We all know you're a woman Adele, you've spent the past three days complaining about it," Marjorie added.

Adele scowled at her, "I would give my first born for some chocolate around now."

"There's some in my locker," Adrienne yelled over her shoulder as she went to the bathroom to wash the aircraft dirt from her body.

Adele scrambled off her bed and lunged towards Adrienne's locker, as she rummaged around she knocked a pile of letters onto the floor. She cursed bending down to pick them up and, as she did so, a photograph fell out. On the reverse of the photo the words, 'My darling wife, Adrienne I'm so proud of you, yours for eternity. Ben' were written in neat handwriting. Adele looked at the message and then up towards the bathroom where Adrienne was, a look of confusion clouding her features. She turned the photo over and the confusion grew into astonishment at the picture of a handsome black man in an Army Air Corp uniform. She still had the photo in her hand when Adrienne stepped back into the room.

"What are you doing?" Adrienne yelled, rushing forward and snatching the photo from Adele. The other Bay Four occupants stopped their activities to watch the interaction between their friends.

"It fell out, I'm sorry," Adele apologized as Adrienne replaced the photo in her locker brushing her aside in the process.

"Here's your damn chocolate," Adrienne hissed thumping the small bar against Adele's chest.

"Addie, please, I'm your friend," Adele soothed. "Why didn't you say?" she asked softly.

Adrienne sat down heavily onto her cot. "I thought that would be obvious," she laughed, turning to face the others in the bay who were studiously now trying to ignore the flare up between the two women. "You all might as well know now, I'm married."

The women started to mutter sounds of astonishment and encouragement. They stilled as Adrienne held her hand up. "My husband is Negro. So technically, in Texas, I'm an outlaw!" she added sarcastically, tears falling from her face as her fingers gripped her wedding band on her chain. "He's flying with the 332nd Fighter Group in Europe."

Without another word being spoken, the women of Bay Four moved to comfort their friend. As the six of them sat squashed on Adrienne's bed she reached up the brought the photograph of Ben down handing it to Helen.

"He's good looking," Helen smiled. "What the hell does he see in you?" she joked earning a half sob half laugh from Adrienne. Ben's photo was passed around, each of the women commenting on the man.

"How'd you two meet?" Lily asked when it was her turn.

Adrienne smiled, happy to finally be able to share her whole life with her friends. " He's a lawyer and worked for my father. I taught him to fly," she said proudly. "We get such a hard time even in Boston where our marriage is legal," she sniffed loudly. "I love him, so much." Her lip started to tremble as she thought of Ben, miles away fighting.

"Ahh honey, love ain't got a compass," Adele laughed pulling a handkerchief from her overalls. "If'n it did, I wouldn't be with Mathew. That boy's dummer than dirt," she laughed shaking her head. "If he survives this war without blowing his own darn head off I'll be shocked," she patted Adrienne's thigh.

Adrienne smiled gratefully at Adele.

"Thank you," she mouthed.

"Oh don't thank me," Adele shook her head and handed Adrienne the bar of chocolate back. "You're gonna need that for energy cause we're gonna be spearing your ass for details all night!" she grinned getting comfortable on Adrienne's bed.

***

Lily lay on her cot, the sound of her sleeping friends providing a comforting soundtrack to the night. She cursed herself for the amount of cola she'd drank over the course of the evening, the volume which was now providing her with the dilemma of getting out of her warm bed to go to the john or staying where she was and trying to ignore the painful pressure on her bladder. She opted to stay and try and find a more comfortable position. She turned over to face Helen, frowning at the empty and stripped bed beside her. She sat up looking around the room in confusion for the blonde woman. Spotting a soft light coming from underneath the bathroom door she got up and padded towards it. Opening the door gently she sighed at the sight that greeted her. Illuminated by candle light was Helen sitting in the bathtub swaddled in her bedding, her nose buried in her Ground School notebook.

"What are you doing?" she whispered closing the door behind her.

Helen, who had been so engrossed in her studying that she didn't hear Lily approach, jerked in surprise. She gave Lily a defeated smile, "I'm studying."

Lily gave a soft laugh as she sat on the toilet. "At this time? It's the middle of the night Helen," she whispered from the john.

"I'm going to fail Liliana," Helen whispered in response, her eyes filling with tears of frustration. "I'm going to get washed out cause of navigation, I'm just not getting it," she thumped the book down onto her lap.

Lily flushed the toilet and washed her hands, as she turned back towards her friend she noticed the tears flowing down her cheeks.

"Wait there, don't move."

She left the room, retuning moments later carrying her blankets and pillow. "Scootch forward," she indicated to Helen with her pillow. Doing as instructed, she watched as Lily threw her pillow into the tub, swung her blankets around her shoulders, and climbed into the tub. Nestling in behind Helen, she plumped her pillow behind her back then pulled the smaller woman back so that she could see over her shoulder, "Now tell me what you're struggling with."

Helen sat back snuggling against the warmth of Lily's body and the two of them worked through the night picking apart the aspects of navigation that Helen wasn't getting until the candle's flame extinguished.

As dawn broke Adele padded towards the bathroom, hopping as her feet met with the cold floor, she entered the bathroom only pausing slightly at the scene in front of her. Lying asleep in the tub were Lily and Helen nestled against each other.

"Ain't that a sight for the minds camera," she murmured smiling before remembering the urgent nature of her visit.

***

The following four weeks were spent continuing to build up their airtime and skills; they had progressed to the point where they had been allowed to fly buddy flights with a fellow WASP to practice instrument flying, which both Lily and Helen savored. Following their first time flying together, they were giddy for days at the shared experience. Helen had received one hundred percent in her navigation test following continued tub study periods with Lily during the night when the rest of the bays were asleep. The whole bay had celebrated with some whiskey that Adrienne 'acquired' when they passed their BT army checks and had been promoted onto the Advanced Trainers AT-6 Texan, which had been a peach of a plane to fly. They had now moved onto their final trainer plane, the AT17.

When they had arrived, every woman had looked at the aircraft and wondered whether they would ever see the day when they got to fly the twin-engine planes that could carry passengers. Theirs was now the only bay in their class that still had a full complement of filled beds. Two of the classes in front of them had graduated and they, along with all other cadets, had proudly taken part in the ceremonies, marching and saluting to the assembled dignitaries at the passing out parade.

Texas was now in the grip of winter and the women were now donning the heavy flight suits and boots for their flights. When Adele had first put hers on, it appeared to drown the small woman and she practically had to lift her legs with her arms to be able to walk.

They had rapidly been building up their air time on the AT completing cross country flights, desperately cramming in as much time as they could in the air to hit the air time requirement in addition to studying for the remaining Ground School tests that would allow them to graduate. Something that for them, was now only a matter of six weeks away.

They sauntered into the ready room with the carefree ease of old timers; smiling at the eager faces of the newer cadets who were still finding their feet at the base. Adrienne nonchalantly gazed over their orders posted on the notice board along with what plane they were to take. Her eyes widened in excitement as she spotted the letter RON on the order sheet. She jumped in the air and spun around towards her arriving bay mates.

"We're going to Atlanta in the AT-6's," she grinned, her brows furrowing as she didn't get the reaction from her friends that she expected. "We've got RON orders. We're going to Atlanta." When still they didn't match her excitement she threw an exasperated hand in the air, "Overnight. We're to remain overnight."

The women smiled in response their chatter becoming more animated as they discussed the possibilities.

"Ladies," Foster smiled coming up behind them to pin something onto the notice board. "You've seen your orders, go get packed," she laughed shaking her head as the six women ran off playfully pushing at each other as they went.

***

Adrienne strained her neck, looking down from the cockpit and spotting the easily identifiable control tower at the Atlanta base.

"Tower, this is Red Devil, permission to land?" she said into her radio.

The radio crackled and a voice responded, "Permission denied Red Devil, we only take orders from the pilot, can you put him on, over."

Adrienne hooted loudly, "Tower, I am the pilot, now give me God-dammed permission to land. Over!"

A sheepish voice came back on the radio, "Permission granted Red Devil. You have permission. Can you roger that."

"Roger tower. Red Devil, coming in. Over." Adrienne lined up for landing still chuckling to herself. "Put the pilot on," she scoffed.

Forty minutes later and their whole class had landed and were shrugging off their heavy leathers as they waited for the army pilot who was accompanying them. Captain Ward landed shortly after and joined them. "Ladies, the base has no bays for women so we're staying in a hotel in Atlanta and, if you're asked, you're a baseball team."

The women looked at him in surprise, "I know, don't yell at me, but it's just a damn sight easier if you just tell 'em that."

The women gave him a filthy look before stowing their leathers and parachutes in the ready room allocated to them on the base before changing into their civilian clothes and being transported to their hotel in downtown Atlanta.

They pulled up outside a hotel and Captain Ward ushered them out of the bus and into the hotel, where they waited to be checked in. The Captain was handed a sheet from the hotel receptionist.

"You're sharing rooms so come forward and get your keys when your name is called," the blonde haired man shouted.

The women stood patiently listening for their names, "Richards and Richmond, Rivera and Rosecroft, Simpson and Stott."

They moved forward to collect their keys and headed towards the allocated rooms.

As Helen unlocked the door to their room and entered Marjorie hung back and turned to Lily. "If Hollywood starts with one of her nightmares, I don't know what to do," Marjorie whispered her tone full of worry.

Lily smiled, "It's okay you go share with Adrienne, I'll share with Nighthawk there."

Marjorie grinned. "Thanks, see you in a bit," she called over her shoulder, running after the taller woman. "Hey Adrienne wait up, my legs are shorter than yours."

Shaking her head Lily entered the room.

"Marjorie there's a bathroom! One bathroom for just of two of us," Helen shouted coming back out of the bathroom and looking puzzled at Lily standing in the room instead of her expected roommate.

"Marjorie said you snore, so we swapped," Lily smiled, tossing her suitcase down onto the bed. "There's only one bed?"

Helen laughed, "Yes, but look at it!" She took a run and leapt at the bed. "It's a proper bed," she giggled, bouncing up and down on it. "I can't feel the springs."

Lily chuckled and pushed her case onto the floor before jumping onto the bed. "It doesn't creak or squeak either," she remarked lying down beside Helen. They lay side by side looking at the ceiling for several moments before Helen turned onto her side and propped her head with her hand.

"So was it 'cause of my nightmares that you swapped?" she asked quietly.

"What? No!" Lily responded unconvincingly, she looked at Helen who had raised an eyebrow. "Okay. Yes, it was the nightmares."

Helen chewed on the inside of her mouth and nodded, "Thank you, for stopping them."

Lily turned to face her, "You want to talk about them?"

Hesitating, Helen shook her head. "No, not really, they're fine," she dismissed the topic with a wave of her hand. "I just never said a proper thank you before. I am surprised that I manage to wake you up with them since you manage to sleep through most everything else."

Lily shrugged, she had wondered the same thing herself and in the end concluded that it was just another indication of how attuned she was to Helen. Her hand toyed with the edge of the pillow, "You know the night we found out about Adrienne's husband?"

Helen nodded flopping back down onto her back, "Hmmm?"

She paused unsure whether to continue the conversation she'd started, they'd been living side by side for four months now and there was only a few weeks left before their final tests and graduation and Lily didn't want those final weeks to be filled with an atmosphere, but she couldn't hold it in any longer. She was sure that somewhere along the line that it was more than a girlish crush and that she had fallen in love with Helen. When they shared a bed or during their study sessions, the heat that suffused her body had become almost unbearable. Her body thrummed with a need that she had never felt before. She had to find out whether those feeling were in any way reciprocated before they finished at Avenger Field and were posted.

"Adele said something about love not having a compass."

"Yeah, I liked that," Helen took her bottom lip into her mouth, she knew without a doubt that she was in love with Lily and that she was fooling herself that Lily felt anything other than friendship for her. Following the period after their dance when things had become strained between them, Helen had followed Peggy's advice that having Lily in her life as a friend was better than not having Lily in her life at all. However, the physical closeness between them was driving her insane. She was constantly in turmoil, trying not to read too much into the sleeping in the same bed or the bathtub study session where they would sit cuddled up under their blankets. She felt as though she was constantly battling not to accidentally blurt out her feelings for Lily.

"Me too," Lily took a quick intake of breath. "Helen I..." Whatever she was about to say was cut off as their room door flew open and the rest of the Bay Four girls entered giggling.

"You got a huge bed!" Marjorie groaned. "I should have stayed with Nighthawk." She passed Helen an open bottle of whiskey and flopped down onto the bed, "And it's comfy."

They were soon joined by Adele, Adrienne and Lucy.

"How is it even when we're not in the bay, all six of us end up in the same room?" Lily grumbled shifting to create space for the other women.

"It's love is what it is," Adele grinned, taking a swig from the whiskey bottle. "That'n it's time to go eat downstairs." She jumped back off the bed and took a swipe at Lily's stocking clad legs bringing them with her, "So gerrup' cause I could eat a horse with scabies right around now."

"Let's hope that's not on the menu," Lucy moaned pulling her sister off the bed by her arms.

"Or grits!" Adrienne remarked, placing the whiskey bottle down on the nightstand and following the others out of the room. "I've had enough of grits to last me a lifetime."

***

An hour later, after dinner, they traipsed back up the stairs to their rooms.

"Grits, what is it with the South and grits!" Adrienne grumbled. "Always with the grits."

Adele pushed her up the hall towards their room. "Stop yer whining, you love 'em, see y'all in the mornin'," she called over her shoulder.

Marjorie and Lucy grinned after the Addies.

"Goodnight," they called.

Lucy turned the key in their door. "Night," she called to Lily and Helen who continued on to their room.

"Night," the two women replied as they reached their door which Lily unlocked. They entered and Lily locked the door behind them throwing the key down onto the nightstand where it clinked against the bottle of whiskey left by Adrienne.

"Ooo, we have the whiskey," Helen smirked, a gleam in her eye as she picked up the bottle and headed off to locate glasses from the bathroom. She returned holding the glasses above her head victoriously. "We have glasses, you want a nightcap?" she asked pouring herself a glass.

Lily pulled her shoes off and walked over to Helen enjoying the feeling of carpet under her feet for once.

"That would be lovely."

She took the glass from Helen, "What should we drink to?"

"To your amazing tutoring skills," Helen laughed. "For getting me through navigation."

They clinked glasses and took a long nervous drink; one working up the courage to put words to her feelings, the other trying desperately to tamp down those feelings in case her mouth betrayed her. When they heard yelling from the street below they moved across to the window, they placed their glasses down on the small table to get closer to the glass for a better view of the street below, some GIs were drunkenly singing as they walked along.

"Someone's had a good night," Lily remarked turning to look at Helen who was still looking out of the window entertained by the antics of the men below. Lily took a moment to observe Helen, her features illuminated by the neon lights of the hotel sign, her dimple twitching in her cheek as she smiled.

"Someone definitely has," she replied, turning she blinked in slight confusion at the look of what she could only describe as longing that Lily was giving her. "What?" she asked, tilting her head slightly.

Lily's eyes flitted from Helen's eyes to her mouth and back to the blue eyes regarding her.

"Nothing," she shook her head then took a deep breath. "Just…" she exhaled slowly and, leaning forward, pressed her lips against Helen's. The blue eyes widened in shock then slowly closed as she melted into the kiss. She reached a hand up threading her fingers through Lily's locks to hold her in place as she deepened the kiss, her tongue slipping into the warmth of Lily's mouth.

Lily felt her heart rate increase as Helen's actions ignited the fire that had been burning within her for weeks, the blaze threatened to consume her as her cheeks flushed. Her hands rose to Helen's body propelled by no thought other than her desire.

Helen moaned against Lily's mouth, as hands clutched desperately seeking some form of purchase that would increase the contact between their bodies. Stumbling backwards slightly, Helen's hip brushed the small table with their glasses. She thrust her hand out behind her to steady the table only succeeding in knocking a lamp to the ground. The room was plunged into darkness as the lamp's cable tore from the socket. Ignoring the destruction that they were causing, the two women shuffled towards the bed. Their progress slowed as determined hands clawed at clothing, desperate to rid the barriers stopping them feeling their skin pressed against each other.

Quickly unbuttoning Lily's shirt, Helen peeled her mouth away and started to trail wet kisses down Lily's neck. Her lips settling on Lily's now throbbing pulse point, the blood flow so rapid that Helen stilled her lips to relish the feeling of Lily's neck pounding against her mouth. She pushed Lily's blouse over her shoulders, tossing it aside once she had freed the material from Lily's' body.

Lily threw her head back granting Helen more access to her sensitive neck as her fingers fumbled with the buttons on the blonde's shirt, which were stubbornly halting her progress. Pulling the shirt from where it had been neatly tucked in, Lily focused her attention on operating fingers that, under normal circumstances, had no problem nimbly playing the most complex of music on her violin.

However, with Helen lavishing kisses on her neck, those usually compliant digits were struggling with the easiest of functions. She gave a small yell of satisfaction when finally the last of the buttons popped open, allowing her to rid Helen of the piece of clothing. She snaked her arms around the small frame of Helen's torso, which was pressed tightly against her own. She dropped her head and started to kiss along Helen's shoulder, shivering as she felt fingertips dance up her spine.

The dance stopped at the clasp of her bra, which was deftly released. Helen roughly pulled the underwear off, dropping down to capture a swollen nipple in her mouth. Lily's knees threatened to give as every fiber of her body felt alive and craving the touch of Helen. She reached around the smaller woman to work the catch on Helen's bra, pausing as her addled mind couldn't process the direction required to open the catch from this new angle. She felt Helen's lips spread into a smile against her breast, as the blonde woman removed her hands from Lily and reached around to her back to undo her own bra, allowing it to drop to the floor between them.

Grasping Helen's face Lily pulled her back up, so that she could kiss the lips that had been teasing her breast so expertly. Exploring Helen's mouth with her tongue she tentatively cupped Helen's breast, her touch gaining in confidence with each soft moan that echoed it. She felt the back of Helen's hand brush against her stomach, followed by the waistband of her skirt loosen as Helen unbuttoned it and pushed it over her hips until it fell to her ankles.

Never removing her lips, or hands, from exploring, Lily toed off her shoes and stepped backwards out of her clothing, the heel of her foot caught the edge of her earlier discarded suitcase causing her to fall backwards onto the bed. They landed with a soft bounce on the mattress.

Using her position to her advantage Helen removed the remnants of Lily's clothing before hurriedly casting the last of her own garments aside. She stood at the bottom of the bed, her head tilting slightly as she regarded Lily lying naked on the bed, her dark locks strewn like a halo around her head.

Lily watched as the look of lust that had been in Helen's eyes disappeared. She had a moment of panic that the blonde was having second thoughts, before she placed the look that was now on Helen's face, it was a look that she recognized from the myriad of expressions she'd seen animate Helen's face over the time they'd known each other.

This one resembled the look that would appear when she spoke about flying.

This look was one of awe.

Helen smiled softly. She'd seen Lily naked before. Living in each other's pockets the way that they did in the bay Helen was sure that by now every woman knew every freckle and blemish, on each other's bodies. However, this was different. This time, Lily was naked for her.

She caught brown eyes looking at her in wonder and struggled to find power in her voice to ask the question, but she needed to. Despite the fact that a response of no would break her heart irreparably.

"Are you sure?" she asked tentatively.

"Never more sure of anything," Lily replied confidently.

With a smile Helen leaned down and started to kiss her way slowly up Lily's thigh. Their eyes locked as she continued her progress, Lily bit her bottom lip trying to control her breathing. When eventually Helen's lips concluded their torturous trail towards Lily's mouth, she lowered her body down on top of Lily relishing the sensation.

Lily's breathing quickened as she held Helen's face in place plunging her tongue into the blonde's mouth in a searing kiss. Hips moved involuntarily, moaning as they found the friction that they desperately longed for. Helen groaned into Lily's mouth, she trailed her fingers down hot skin, drawn toward the heat of Lily's center. Lily bucked her hips as finally, Helen's fingertips caressed her where she needed, arching her back she moaned and sensing her need, Helen wasted no time with teasing as she built up a steady rhythm.

Lily's stomach and thigh muscles contracted in time with the rhythm created by Helen, until finally the tension built up by Helen's ministrations released in an explosion and Lily's lungs emptied in a massive rush.

***

Lily didn't think she could be happier; she was lying with Helen in her arms, not because she was comforting the woman after a nightmare or because they were crammed into a bathtub studying the wonders of navigation. She had Helen dozing in her arms after they had spent the night making love. She trailed the back of her thumb lazily up Helen's arm, which was thrown protectively across her stomach. Helen moaned softly and snuggled closer, shifting her head until she found another comfortable spot on Lily's chest.

"What time is it?" Helen mumbled, her breath tickling Lily's breast.

"Five thirty," Lily replied, checking her wristwatch.

A blue eye popped open in surprise. "And you're awake? Are you...are you okay?" she asked nervously, wondering whether Lily had been lying regretting their time together.

"I'm fine," Lily smiled and seeing the anxious look still on Helen's face she added. "Honestly I'm okay. Are you?" she chewed on her lip. "Are you okay? I mean I sort of took you by surprise last night. "

"You certainly did that," Helen laughed. She traced patterns on Lily's stomach as she spoke. Her fingertips reaching to circle the small freckle on Lily's breast that she had admired so often, "I imagine you surprised yourself too," she said lightly, her tone not fully disguising a hint of seriousness.

Lily chortled, "Damn near shocked myself."

She teased fingers through Helen's curls, "I never thought..." she paused as her mind shuttled between thoughts. "I mean, I've never..."

Helen placed her hand on Lily's chest, "I know. It's confusing at first."

Shuffling down so she could lay on her side and face Helen, Lily asked quietly, "Was this your first time?"

Smiling Helen reached out a hand to touch Lily's face; the brunette moved her cheek further into the caress.

"No and yes. No, as I have been with other women, and yes because I've never before experienced what we had last night."

She groaned softly as Lily leaned forward to place a light kiss on her lips. When they separated she saw a thoughtful look on Lily's face. "I'm assuming that you've never…"

Helen let the question hang.

Lily shook her head, "No I didn't date much in school or college, mainly because I was so focused on either flying or my violin. Then after I graduated college I wanted to stay in New York so started to play in a women's orchestra and found out that I could make more money if I also played in nightclubs. So my time was filled with music. Then I met Henry, he played in one of the nightclubs and our relationship kinda grew." She frowned as she compared her feelings for Henry with those she had for Helen, "I thought that I loved him, but I think now I loved the idea of him more than anything. He was what I was supposed to want." Her eyes hardened as she considered her marriage, "But in reality I didn't have what I wanted, he was sweet to begin with, but he changed after we got married. I ended up with a man who as well as being an adulterer undermined my confidence and dictated what I could and couldn't do." She felt the familiar anger rise as she thought about her late husband, "He made me quit playing in nightclubs he wasn't playing in, and when we flew together, he would always take control despite the fact I was a better pilot." Her eyes softened and the anger disappeared faster than it had appeared and as she returned to the present, she looked deeply into blue eyes full of more concern than her husband had shown in their years of marriage. She smiled softly, "You make me feel confident; that I can accomplish anything I set my mind to."

"You can," Helen responded with conviction, before pulling Lily's hands to her lips and kissing her knuckles. She spoke quietly, "I grew up thinking I was Huckleberry Finn." She narrowed her eyes playfully at Lily's soft chuckle. "Hey no mocking, Huck was great," she grinned. "Seriously though, my brother was only a year older and what he did, I did. It never occurred to me that we were supposed to be different. It was only as I got older that I realized what those differences were meant to be and yet still I didn't feel them." She gave a small shrug, "I just figured that I wouldn't marry since it didn't feel right and I was going to be one of those old spinster aunts, with cats." She gave a laugh at her younger self. "And then," she sighed, "I landed in Hollywood and I realized that there were others that were different. I wanted to tell you, but I have lost people that I cared about in the past when I was honest." She looked deeply into Lily's eyes, "And selfishly, I didn't want to lose you."

Lily pulled Helen into her arms and held her tightly as a loud sigh escaped her lips.

"Still okay?" Helen asked, her anxiety less but still not completely abated.

"I'm just savoring this time," Lily replied.

Helen frowned as shifted her position so she could see Lily's face, "You sound sad."

Pressing her lips onto Helen's, Lily sighed then pulled back, "We go back today."

Their night together had been wonderful, amazing, life changing, and now that she was changed irreversibly Lily did not want them to return to base as if nothing had altered in their relationship.

Helen sat up, kneeling in front of Lily. "No, we fly to Avenger Field today. We," she pointed between them. "We don't go back," Helen took a deep breath. "Do you remember the night we were out after Taps?" Lily nodded smiling. "I said that I'd never met the right person."

"That someone that made it feel like you were flying," Lily laughed softly at the memory.

"Exactly, well I have. Liliana, when I'm around you. I'm flying!" she smiled broadly her dimples highlighting her joy. "I get the same kick out of a smile from you from across a room as I do from doing an inside loop." She leaned forward and took Lily's hands into her own, "So we aren't going back to the way it was before."

Lily pulled Helen close to her, and in one easy action had spun their bodies until she was lying on top.

"Impressive one eighty," Helen laughed as her back thumped against the mattress, her hands trailing up Lily's hips and sides.

"I'm a terrific flyer," Lily replied in a cocksure tone. "In fact I'm going to give you a lesson now." She smiled as Helen cocked an eyebrow.

"You are?"

"I am, Lesson one, pre-flight check, you should give the body of the plane a once over checking for damage from previous flights." She lifted herself up, looking down the length of Helen's body beneath her. "Check!" she grinned.

"Then when in the cockpit, adjust your seat." She eased her legs between Helen's, using them to part the blonde's thighs. She sat up knelt and pulled Helen's knees up, before leaning back down. "Then check the instrument panel." She looked lustily at Helen's breasts. Helen started to laugh, squirming slightly at the attention she was receiving.

"Check!" Lily smiled, lasciviously licking her lips.

"You then need to prime the engine," she dipped her head and took a nipple into her mouth, toying with it for a second before pulling her head up slowly, lightly dragging her teeth over the sensitive bud. She smiled at the gasp she received in response. "Once you've primed the engine, if you've got the mix right, then you should be able to crank the throttle a little." She thrust her hips, feeling the moisture from Helen's arousal wet her skin. "I think the mix is right. Check!" she lowered her head back down to Helen's breast. "Work the wobble pump," she smirked taking Helen's other breast into her mouth, ignoring the laughter that burst from Helen.

"Wobble pump, really!" Helen giggled before her laughter stalled in her throat; replaced by a moan as Lily thrust her hips once more while using her tongue to circle the nipple held firmly in her mouth.

Lily released Helen's nipple with a soft pop. "Check! Then it's a simple matter of flicking the ignition switch." She lowered her hand between their bodies, groaning at the swollen arousal her fingers found, she slowly started to rub small circles, biting her lip as Helen started to moan noisily and move her hips in time with Lily's fingers. "You should hear the engine start to hum and the plane start to dance with the power," she murmured seductively as she increased the pressure on Helen, eliciting a louder moan and a slight bucking of Helen's hips. "Check! The last thing is to check the flaps and radio the tower, so Hollywood, this is Sleeping Beauty. Permission for take-off?" she smiled dipping her fingers through Helen silky arousal. Helen nodded quickly.

"Permission granted. Roger," she groaned and gripped the bedding in tight fists as Lily's slender fingers entered her.

Lily chuckled bringing her lips down onto Helen, "Just one thing. It's Liliana, not Roger."

Chapter Eight

Lily and Helen sat with the rest of their bay during a lively breakfast, each stealing glances as their minds escaped the chatter that surrounded them and took them back to moments during the night. Helen sat smirking as she recalled the 'flying' lesson that Lily had given her earlier.

"Don't you look like the cat that ate the cream?" Adrienne remarked with a raised eyebrow at Helen's expression.

"She's right. For once!" Adele added, getting a playful slap from Adrienne. "What you thinking about?" she nudged the blonde woman.

Helen's eyes locked with Lily who was sitting feigning innocence while sipping her coffee.

"Just going over my pre-flight checks in my head," she smiled.

Lily choked on her coffee, spluttering and coughing loudly as Lucy pounded on her back.

"Ladies, finish up, we should be getting back to the airfield," Ward said coming up to their table.

***

The bus trip back was filled with Adele and Adrienne relaying their bawdy versions of the WASP songs. The two women stood in the gangway announcing that they were like the Andrew Sisters only cheaper. Helen and Lily sat laughing at their friends antics, their hands planted on the space on the seat between them, their pinkies curled around each other.

Pulling their heavy leathers on, the good-natured banter continued between the Bay Four women.

"Hey, Stotty, you think that at tomorrow's game, you might try and hit a pitch?" Adrienne yelled, referring to the regular baseball game that replaced their PT sessions.

"You wanna stop throwing no balls," Adele countered shrugging her heavy jacket into place. "Then maybe I will!"

"They're not no balls," Adrienne snorted. "I can't help it if your head height is everyone else's waist height!"

The women laughed as Adele waddled over in her heavy leathers to swat Adrienne with her flight helmet.

"I bet you two weeks mopping, I hit a homerun Red."

Adrienne held her hand out. "Deal. Good job you're good with a mop!" she yelled climbing up the wing of her plane.

"I ought to be, I spend enough time cleaning up your mess," Adele shouted in return. "Happy landings ladies," she nodded to Lily and Helen. before climbing up into her ride home.

"Happy landings," they chorused in return.

***

Several hours of flying later Lily was parked in the stand completing her post flight checks, when the canopy of her plane opened.

"Did you see them?" Helen said breathlessly, still dressed in her flight leathers.

"See who?" Lily asked confused.

"The Addies, you and me were the last to go, and they're not back," Helen replied, running a frustrated hand thought her curls. "I thought maybe you'd seen them."

"How late are they?"

Helen stepped down the wing walkway to allow Lily to climb out of the plane, "A half hour."

Lily frowned as she jumped down onto the ground beside Helen, "I'm sure there's a simple explanation."

They joined Marjorie and Lucy who were sitting on the wooden benches that ran the length of the exterior of the hangar. Helen shook her head as they approached, the two sister's expressions fell as the hope that Lily may have seen them disappeared.

Nodding over towards a small group of women huddled together, Lily removed her leather helmet and ran a hand through her sweat damp hair. "What's going on over there?" she asked.

They shrugged as Lucy slapped her thighs and stood up, "Might as well go be nosey while we're waiting,"

Helen sat down in her place to wait. Lucy returned to them moments later a sad look on her face, "A newbie is late back from her first PT solo."

"How long's she been out?" Marjorie asked, pulling her leather jacket onto her lap to make space for her sister.

"Forty minutes or so," Lucy replied sitting down.

They waited in a nervous silence for twenty minutes until the still of the afternoon was broken by the sound of engines approaching. Marjorie squinted into the sky.

"That's a BT," she said sadly.

They dropped their hopeful eyes and sat quietly again as the plane came into land. Lily reached for Helen's hand, feeling the need for her comforting touch.

Ten minutes later another engine hummed in the distance. "That's an AT engine," Lily said standing up.

The others joined her quickly as they waited for the plane to come into view. As soon as the plane bounced along the runway, the four women started to run. The plane had barely stopped in the stand when they climbed up the wing and flung the canopy back. A startled Adrienne looked up in surprise.

"Well that's what I call a welcome!"

"Where the hell have you been? We've been worried sick," Helen yelled.

Adrienne gave a sheepish look, "I'm not that late."

"Almost an hour," Lucy yelled from her spot on the ground behind the wing. Adrienne raised herself up and peered out of the cockpit to glare at Lucy.

"*Thank you,*" she said sarcastically, standing up onto the bucket seat of the plane.

"So where have you been?" Lily asked her face scrunching as she caught a whiff of something from the cockpit. "What's that smell?"

Adrienne frowned waving them away so she could climb out. "I got caught short," she admitted. "I had to use the pilot relief tube."

"How the hell did that make you late?" Marjorie asked her jumping down to stand beside Lucy.

"Firstly no judging, I got knocked off course," Adrienne held a finger up to stop them responding as she climbed out and walked down the walkway on the wing before jumping down to the ground. "Secondly, I had to strip," her eyes widened for emphasis. "And I mean strip. I was flying the damn thing wearing only my bra. Apparently undressing, and dressing, while flying will cause you to veer drastically off course!" she exclaimed. "Once I got the leather off, then the zoot suit as well as my uniform pants, I remembered the damn long johns, so the shirt had to go, then the long johns and finally my underwear," Adrienne ticked each item off on her fingers as she listed them, "Aaaand the damn relief tube is tiny so…" she paused.

Lily's eyes widened, "The smell, it was pee!"

"You peed in the cockpit," Marjorie asked incredulously.

"No," Adrienne clarified with a shake of her head. "I peed in the tube, only it's not built for women," she finished quietly looking at the faces of her friends. Finally realizing they were missing someone she looked puzzled, "Where's Adele?"

***

Darkness had fallen and the five women sat huddled together on the bench, their hands plunged into the pockets of their flight leathers trying to ward off the drop in temperature that night had brought.

Foster watched the five of them from a distance, their body language a mix of hope and despair. Heads rested against the hangar behind them, eyes stared into the distance no doubt not seeing anything, heels of their heavy boots kicked against the ground disconsolately. She took a breath then approached them.

"You should try and get some sleep," she said kindly.

Lucy was the only one who turned to look at the officer, the others still lost to their thoughts.

"Thank you Ma'am we're good," Lucy replied before returning her head to rest against the hangar with a quiet thud.

"You'll freeze," Foster tried again. "You should come in."

Adrienne still starting straight ahead set her jaw determinedly.

"We always wait," she swallowed hard and turned to look at Foster with eyes red from the tears she refused to shed. "We go out as one, we come in as one," she nodded to emphasis her point. Helen took her hand gripping it tightly. "We're not going anywhere until Adele is home," she added in a tone that left Foster in no doubt that the discussion was over.

An hour later Foster returned with another officer, bringing a tray of hot coffees and blankets, which the women gratefully received.

The sound of the first notes of reveille roused them, hands rubbed tired eyes, necks twisted back and forth to alleviate the pain from the awkward position that sleep had forced upon them. They looked up at the sound of footsteps as an ashen-faced Foster approached. Adrienne leapt up as she watched Foster's progress towards them. Helen stood slowly, standing next to Adrienne and looping her arm through the taller woman's.

"We just got a call from a farmer twenty miles east of Abilene, he went out to his fields this morning, and…"

"No," Adrienne yelled. "Adele is a damn good flyer, the conditions were perfect. You've made a mistake!"

Foster blinked back tears as she shook her head. "He gave us the plane and her dog tag numbers, I'm sorry," she gulped down the lump in her throat. "It looks like she and the newbie who was soloing yesterday collided," she swallowed hard before adding another useless apology.

Adrienne crumpled to the ground. "No," she cried into her hands as Marjorie and Lucy held each other and sobbed, each trying to comprehend the blow they'd been dealt.

Helen looked down at Adrienne, balled tightly against herself and lost in her grief. Feeling hot tears flowing down her cheeks, she turned her head towards Lily who was standing frozen to the spot, stricken by the fate of their friend. Helen pulled her by her leathers into a hug as sobs broke free and wracked both their bodies.

***

"Permission denied," Captain Hardy said, looking up sadly at the women standing opposite his desk, their faces carrying the scars of their nighttime vigil and the grief that followed in the day.

"She was our friend Sir," Lily pleaded.

"I know and I'm sorry for your loss, but you graduate in a few weeks and we can't allow you time you don't have."

"I don't care about the God-dammed graduation," Adrienne spat. "Sir," she added as an afterthought.

Hardy stood up, "Given the circumstances, I'm going to ignore that outburst cadet. Permission not granted. Dismissed."

The women saluted and marched out of the office.

"I'm sick of this," Adrienne raged. "Why won't they let us take her home!" she smacked her palm against the wall in frustration.

Marjorie rubbed Adrienne's back, "I know, we'll see what the funeral home say, when we go."

"She was our friend," Lucy said quietly. "We should get to escort her."

They walked out into the parade ground ignoring the pitying looks from the class doing drill there as they returned to their bay. Entering, they immediately noticed the difference in the room they had left. Adele's bed had been stripped and her locker emptied of her belongings.

"What the hell!" Adrienne yelled, spinning and leaving the room, stomping off in search of Foster.

Lily gave her friends a quick glance. They seemed rooted to the spot, still looking at the living space that Adele had occupied.

"I'll go," Lily said simply and set off in pursuit of Adrienne. She found the red-haired woman pointing her finger and yelling in Foster's face.

"How dare you!"

Lily grabbed Adrienne's arm and tried to pull her away.

"You had no right, she's not even gone twenty-four hours, and you clean out her stuff."

"I was trying to help," Foster said helplessly, "to spare you." Her eyes pleaded with Lily who nodded her acknowledgement.

Adrienne put her face close to Foster's and snarled, "Well you had no damn right," before storming off back to the bay.

"She's hurting," Lily offered an explanation. "We all are," she bit her trembling lip and left Foster, who was looking hopelessly at the ground.

***

The five women stepped into the Sweetwater funeral home, a somber older woman greeted them and asked which of the WASP they were here to see. They looked momentarily confused until they remembered the newbie, whose name they hadn't heard until just now. They were led into a room where a simple pine box with no adornment lay.

"We're waiting on her family contacting us to tell us what they want to do," the women said.

"What's that?" Helen asked. "That's not Adele?" she looked at the faces around her in confusion. "When it's a military death there's a proper coffin, and a flag," her voice broke. "She should have a flag."

The funeral director looked sadly towards Helen, "I'm sorry dear, but your friend wasn't military. We don't get paid for a casket or for the transportation, so…" she left the rest of the sentence hanging.

"Get her a proper casket," Adrienne said, her eyes fixed on the wooden box. "I'll pay for it. Just put her in a proper casket."

"We'll pay," Marjorie corrected. "We'll all pay."

The Bay Four women each added their contribution and selected a casket for their friend, as they stood to leave Lily whispered, "Can we?" She cleared her throat, "Can we go see her again?"

The woman nodded and led them back to the room. They walked over to the coffin, each laying a hand on the smoothed wood.

"We live in the wind and the sand, and our eyes are on the stars," Lily said softly, reciting the WASP motto. "Happy landings Adele," she added, tears falling down her face splashing onto her hand.

"Happy landings," the others repeated their voices thick with emotion.

***

Foster watched the five remaining Bay Four women leave the memorial service in the Sweetwater church.

"How are they?"

She turned to the source of the enquiry, flashing a quick smile at Captain Hardy.

"It's only been a couple of days, they're holding up Sir," she replied, watching as the women huddled together, their blank faces masking their emotions.

"Do you think they'll walk?" Hardy asked, returning the salutes from women walking past.

Foster tipped her head to the side and frowned, "What? Leave the program?"

Hardy rested his gaze on the slight woman, "They're civilians, they're free to go anytime. What I'm asking you is do you think that their friend's death is enough to make them walk from the program?"

Frowning Foster looked over towards the five women and regarded each one of them. Playing through her head what she knew of each, slowly she shook her head, "No. No, I don't think they'll walk."

Taking a deep breath Hardy nodded, "Good, their training cost twenty thousand dollars and that bay has some of the most talented flyers we've had through the program. I've already lost one brilliant pilot in this accident, I don't want to lose more because of it," he looked over towards the women. "Do whatever you need to do to make sure that they come back from this," he gave a solemn nod of the head then turned and walked to his waiting car.

Foster watched his departure. "You're all heart Captain Hardy, all heart," she said to herself, before moving to round up the women to return to the base.

***

The bay was quiet as they lay on their beds staring at the ceiling, lost in their own thoughts. In the days that had passed no one had much energy to speak, their focus had been solely on putting one foot in front of the other and supporting each other during the period. Lily rose from her cot and walked wordlessly to the bathroom, waiting a few moments Helen rose and followed her.

"You okay?" she asked as she closed the door behind her.

Lily looked up from the edge of the tub where she had perched herself and nodded slowly.

Helen walked over and positioned herself between Lily's legs, looping her arms loosely around her lover's neck. Lily gave a sad smile at the action and wound her arms around Helen's waist pulling the other woman close to her. She snuggled against Helen's chest, listening to her steady heartbeat.

"I just keep thinking that could have been any of us and it just seems so random so…" she brought her shoulders up taking a breath as she struggled to find the words.

"Such a waste?" Helen said, expressing her own thoughts on Adele's death.

Lily moved her head, resting her chin on Helen so she could see her face.

"Such a horrible waste," she agreed. Helen nodded and lowered her head pressing her lips against Lily's for a slow comforting kiss.

Despite her grief Lily felt her body start to respond to the kiss, worried that someone might come in and find them kissing, she reluctantly pulled away. "I feel a bit better now," she smiled, a hint of life sparkling in her eyes.

Taking a deep breath Helen looked down at Lily's lap. "I love you," she said quietly. "I don't need you to say it back. I just needed to tell you so you knew in case…"

"Nothing is going to happen to you," Lily interrupted. She smiled and ducked her head so that she could see into Helen's eyes, "I love you too."

Lily felt a weight lift at the admission, she had known for a while that the depth of her feelings went beyond friendship but finally saying it out loud, suddenly she felt like throwing open the window and yelling it across the base.

Helen grinned briefly before her features returned to a somber expression, "I feel bad that I'm so happy right now."

Reaching up to brush blonde locks from her forehead Lily soothed, "Sssh, me too. But Adele wouldn't want us to mope around forever. She had too much life in that small body of hers to want us to waste ours. Come on, let's go back in."

Helen pulled away from Lily, dropping her hand down and taking Lily's, leading her gently back into the main section of the bay. They dropped their hands as they walked in, surprised to see Foster standing in the doorway of the bay, their friends looking at her suspiciously.

"Hi, I…" she made a small growl like noise. "I wanted to come make sure that you're okay, actually I wanted more than that." She stepped in and closed the door behind her, "I'm part Irish and when we have a death, after the funeral there's usually a hoolie that goes on, where we stop mourning the death and celebrate the life." She hesitated as she realized that her speech had sounded more rousing in her head when she had practiced it walking over and it was not having that effect now, "Anyway, I thought that maybe you should have a small wake in the bay and celebrate Adele's life." She dug her hand into her leather jacket and pulled out a whiskey bottle, "Now I know that Nolan County is dry and we're not allowed alcohol on the base." Adrienne avoided eye contact at that comment. "But given the circumstances I thought that you could use it. Although if you get caught with it at bay check, I'll deny knowledge," she grinned.

"Who's doing bay check tonight?" Lucy asked.

Foster smiled broadly, "Me, but I'll still deny it." She held the bottle out, there was a brief hesitancy before Adrienne rose from her bed and walked over.

Taking the bottle, she saluted Foster. "Thank you," she smiled. "And I'm sorry about what I said."

"I have no idea what you're taking about Rosecroft," Foster smiled and gave the rest of the bay a quick nod before turning and leaving.

Adrienne stood facing the door and let out an audible sigh. "Best go get some glasses girls," she said turning round, a small smile on her face.

An hour later and the mood in the bay had lifted, there were tears rolling down their faces. However, this time, it was tears of laughter as they each recounted their favorite moment with Adele during their training.

"Oh God, remember the time when she fell in, in the morning and she still was wearing slippers!" Adrienne laughed wiping a tear from her face. "I thought Foster's face on the first day with my high heels was a picture but when she caught sight of Adele's furry feet, I thought the vein in her head was going to pop," she exploded with laughter at the memory. As the laughter died down Helen started to chuckle to herself.

"What is it Hollywood?" Adrienne demanded.

"I'm just thinking about the times that she would lift you up over the 'chin up' bar, I'm surprised Lt Latham didn't spot you suddenly shooting up in the air."

Adrienne picked up her towel and tossed it at Helen, who shot a hand up and plucked it from the air.

Marjorie stood up and walked over to Lily's bed, the other woman looked up in surprise as Marjorie brought out Lily's violin.

"Play something for us Lily. Something that Stotty taught you."

Lily placed her glass on the floor and took the violin from Marjorie's outstretched hands. She put the case down on her bed and opened the catches, picking the instrument out of its padding. She plucked the strings and twisted the pegs to tune the instrument before slipping it under her neck and picking her bow to check the tuning properly. She drew her bow across the A string checking the pitch before playing the other strings.

"Y'all ready for this?" Lily said in her best approximation of Adele's Tennessee drawl. "Well get up and get ready to dance like she taught you." She used her bow to poke Helen's leg, spurring her to get up.

They quickly pushed their beds back out of the way to create more space then Adrienne, Marjorie, Lucy and Helen stood facing each other holding hands. Lily nestled her chin against the violin then started to pick out the fast notes of a song that Adele had taught her to play. The other women bowed and curtseyed to each other before setting off at lightning pace. Skipping sideways down the extended pathway between their beds, before returning up the length of the room. They performed a series of steps that Adele had tried to teach them; each correcting the other when they went wrong, laughing as they remembered Adele's frustration as she had tried to co-ordinate them before eventually giving up exasperated, shouting that it was a miracle that they could fly, since none of them seemed to know their right from their left. As the song drew to a close they dropped laughing, and out of breath, onto the cots.

Lily put her violin down and collected their glasses passing them to the breathless women; she raised her glass up.

"To Stotty!"

The others sat up and clinked their glasses together.

"To Stotty!" they repeated.

***

Life returned to normal the next day, they rose early went to breakfast, completed their Ground School classes and headed out to the flight line. It was getting close to sun down and their class was still out using every ounce of sunlight they could to fly to build up their airtime before graduation. Foster watched the class coming in to land, ticking off the planes and pilots in her head as she counted her girls back in like a mother hen. She stamped her frozen feet on the hard ground, lightly dusted with snow that had appeared overnight, her breath frosting in front of her face.

"They all in?" Captain Hardy asked coming up behind her.

"We don't usually see you down on the flight line sir," Foster remarked as the red-haired man rubbed his gloved hands together. "All in bar the Bay Four girls," she watched the sky nervously for any sight of their planes.

"I wanted to check that they went up okay, it's their first day back in the air," Hardy said softly. "And despite what you might think Foster, there is a heart beating in this chest."

Foster smirked looking at the captain out of the corner of her eye, "Yes Sir, it just that sometimes I think the medals on your chest make it hard to hear it beating."

Hardy guffawed at her comment.

"I will take that on board. Thank you," he smiled shaking his head slightly.

The hum of engines in the distance stopped further conversation. Squinting into the sky Foster sighed as she spotted five dots in the distance.

"They're flying formation," Hardy remarked noting the positioning of the planes.

Nodding Foster smiled at him, "I think they're about to say a final goodbye."

They looked up at the low flying planes overhead, the plane at the lead of the formation pulled up and out of the arrangement peeling off west. Foster and Hardy saluted watching the plane fly into the fading sunset.

Chapter Nine

<u>December 1943 – Avenger Field, Sweetwater, Texas</u>

Their last weeks on base were a frenzy of activity as they crammed for exams and flew every spare second they had. They had received with much excitement their newly approved Santiago blue uniforms that they would wear during their graduation.

Taps had just been played and the lights of their bay snapped off, plunging them into darkness.

"I wonder where we'll be based?" Lucy mused aloud studying the shadows on the ceiling.

"We'll find out in a few days, they usually post the orders a couple of days before graduation," Marjorie replied.

Adrienne snuggled deeper under her blankets for warmth, "Well, wherever we get put, we have to stay in touch."

Lily felt her chest tighten, she felt foolish. In all of the activity and focus on graduation, the thought that they would split up after graduation had not occurred to her. She spoke quietly her eyes seeking Helen, "We only have a few more days together."

"Which is why we have to stay in touch," Adrienne repeated.

The bay quieted as the women drifted off to sleep one by one, the sound of steady breathing and soft snores soon filled the room that had been their home for five months.

Still thinking about the separation that could soon be forced upon them, Lily lay unable to sleep. She pulled her blankets from her bed and as she had done countless times before she rose and slipped into the cot beside Helen. The blonde stirred and sleepily whispered, "Was I having a nightmare?"

"Shh, no. I just wanted to hold you," Lily whispered in her ear.

Helen smiled and sighed happily. Her eyes sprang open as she felt a warm hand start to wander beneath her pajama top.

"What are you doing?" she hissed quietly as she felt fingers graze her breast.

Lily gave a soft chuckle against her ear, "Checking your wobble pump."

Any protest that Helen was about to mutter was stilled as she felt Lily's hand trail down her stomach and underneath the waistband of her bottoms.

"You need to be really quiet," Lily whispered. "I need you and we might not have a lot of time left," she started to dot kisses beneath Helen's ear as she felt the blonde woman push her body further into hers, writhing against her touch.

Helen closed her eyes and concentrated on Lily's caresses, as Lily's rhythm increased she felt the pressure build within her and, conscious of making any noise, she turned her face into her pillow burying into it to muffle the sound that she was unable to stop from leaving her lips as her body shuddered into a climax.

***

Two days before their graduation, they were sitting around the wishing well discussing how their Morse Code examination had gone, when Foster came up carrying envelopes.

"Ladies, I have your orders," she smiled, waving the wad of papers she had in her hand.

They stood up nervously waiting to see what duty they had been assigned to. She handed them their envelopes, which they tore open quickly like children at Christmas. Adrienne gave a quick fist pump as she read the contents of her envelope.

"Fleet Command," she said. "In Romulus, Michigan."

Marjorie grinned, "They always put the tall ones in Fleet Command. I got Engineering Command, Bainbridge, Georgia."

Lucy sighed disappointed, "I'm going to Bryan, Texas. Engineering too."

Lily opened her papers, "Fleet, Las Vegas."

She looked hopefully at Helen, her hope falling as she saw the look in Helen's eyes.

"Dodge, Kansas. Training Command," she said quietly, her tone full of sadness.

Foster smiled, sensing Helen's reticence. "Dodge is a good one; you'll probably get to fly all sorts of planes there."

Helen gave her a half-hearted smile as she thrust her order papers into the pocket of her jacket.

As they walked towards their bay Lily and Helen hung back.

"We don't have to report until January, and we're done here in two days," Lily said trying to make both of them feel better. "We have almost two weeks leave, we could go somewhere together, New York maybe?"

Helen smiled looping her arm through Lily's, "Christmas in New York sounds perfect."

***

The day of their graduation dawned, the women rose and instead of their usual beige slacks they donned their blue skirts, each of them stood a little taller in their official uniform. For almost the first time since their first morning, they queued in front of the mirror conscious of their appearance. Lily reached up to fix Adrienne's tie.

"You got anyone coming today?"

Adrienne gave a small laugh, "You know what with everything I forgot to invite anyone, you?"

Lily shook her head, "Nope, I forgot too." She looked at the others, "Has anyone got family coming today?"

Helen gave a quick headshake, Marjorie nudged Lucy with her hip, "I have my sister, but I didn't invite her, she just showed up."

Lucy laughed and nudged back harder. "Well I guess it's just us then!" she laughed as Marjorie stumbled.

There was a knock at the door and Foster opened it poking her head round the door.

"Morning Ladies, I hope you don't mind but you have a visitor," she pulled back and guided a small woman into the bay.

The women gave quick glances at each other, wondering who the woman was here for. Adrienne finally made a small noise as she recognized the woman, the features on her face so familiar but strange to see on another's face.

"Mrs. Stott?" Adrienne said moving forward.

"You'll be Adrienne?" she replied, her accent thicker than her daughter's but her voice holding the same mischievous undercurrent.

"Yes Ma'am," Adrienne smiled taking the small woman's hand in her own.

"She said you was tall and she wasn't kiddin'," Mrs Stott said with a sad smile, garnering a laugh from the women. "You're Lily?" she asked looking at Lily.

Lily nodded, "I am."

"She said you was tall too but not like a beanpole, no offence," she said to Adrienne.

"None taken," Adrienne shrugged smiling.

"She also said your skin was the color of our Maisie." Seeing the look of confusion on the Lily's face she moved to clarify her comment, "Maisie's our prize milker."

Laughing, Lily replied, "In that case, I'm honored."

"I can see a family resemblance so you'll be Marjorie and Lucy?" she asked, nodding her head towards the two women.

"We are," they replied in unison then indicated who was who.

"Which leaves Hollywood," she smiled towards Helen. "You're as pretty as she said."

"Thank you."

"She wrote about you all, an' she loved being with y'all. I just had to come say thank you for what'n you did for her."

Adrienne gulped back the lump in her throat and gave a small cough.

Adele's mother patted Adrienne's forearm, "I hope you don't mind, but I wanted to tell you 'bout somethin', cause I don't want your parents to go through what we have." She opened her purse pulling out a dog-eared telegram and opened it, "I received this from the War Department." She held out the paper toward Adrienne.

The red-haired woman read the contents, a look of disgust and anger flashed on her face.

"I'm sorry that you found out that way."

She passed the paper to Lily who gasped in astonishment as she read the telegram, typed in capitals were the words

'YOUR DAUGHTER WAS KILLED THIS MORNING.

WHERE DO YOU WANT US TO SHIP THE BODY TO?'

Adrienne shook her head in disbelief, "She deserved more than that. She was a good friend and one of a kind."

Mrs Stott gave a small nod, "An' by all accounts a lousy baseball player."

The bay laughed at the woman's comment.

Lily moved forward to shake the woman's hand, "Yes she was."

They led Adele's mother in and gave her a small tour of the bay punctuating it with stories of her daughter. Mrs Stott filled with pride as she listened to the descriptions the woman gave her.

"We would be honored if you'd stay as our guest, we graduate today," Helen asked hesitantly.

Smiling a smile that was hauntingly similar to her daughter's Mrs. Stott accepted their invitation.

***

They paraded with pride and stood to attention as the General inspected their lines. They never wavered during each speech and their excitement grew as they got closer to the part of the ceremony when they would be given their wings.

Finally the visiting General stood with Jackie Cochran with the list of names to be called. They watched as the other members of their class marched up to collect their wings as their names were called.

As Marjorie's name was announced the rest of her bay mates felt the satisfaction of having completed their training wash over them. They watched as Marjorie marched back towards the line with a broad grin on her face.

When Helen's name was called, she stepped out of line, marched towards the podium and climbed the stairs. She shook hands with the General who spoke fondly about her father. She moved on to shake the hand of their founder and the very woman who had interviewed her all those months ago.

"Congratulations," Jackie smiled, pinning the silver wings onto Helen's uniform. Stepping down from the podium Helen caught Lily's gaze, she marched back to her place, a large grin plastered on her face.

Lily smiled as Helen stepped back in line. Her stomach churning as it got closer to her time. She swallowed back a lump in her throat as her name was said and she stepped up to receive her coveted wings. The sound of clapping around her disappeared and Lily was only aware of her heartbeat as she marched quickly towards the stage. She accepted her wings with a deep breath, almost unwilling to believe that it had finally happened. She had done it.

She was a fully trained WASP with the silver wings to prove it.

Chapter Ten

<u>December 1943 – New York</u>

So are you two with TWA?" the female cabbie asked in a thick Jersey accent as she pulled out of LaGuardia Airport, checking the uniforms of the two women in the back seat.

Helen and Lily exchanged a quick smile before the blonde responded on their behalf, "No…we're WASP"

"We're not hostesses. We're pilots. We fly military planes," Lily added.

The cab driver's eyes widened in surprise, "You're pilots? Well I'll be! It's a real pleasure then ladies." She grinned into the rear view mirror as she drove them towards the address in Greenwich Village that Lily had given her.

It had been almost two days since their graduation and despite being allowed to forgo their uniform due to their length of leave, neither had been willing to travel in civilian wear on their flight to New York. It had been hard saying goodbye to their classmates in particular the other Bay Four women. Many tears were shed and hugs were plentiful in the hours after graduation.

Marjorie and Lucy had been first to go, the prospect of their long drive back to Oregon urged them to leave almost as soon as the graduation supper had finished and they were released officially. The other three women had stood under the archway that had greeted them on their first day and waved until the white car was a dot on the horizon. Turning back, they had looked towards the base, each of their minds returning them to the first time they had driven underneath the airfields welcome sign adorned with Fifinella. Small smiles grew larger as they looked across the planes standing in rows; the planes that they could now fly as well as they could sign their own names. They weren't sure who started it but the smiles developed into giggles which then transformed into gales of laughter, they held onto each other as the stress and strains of the previous weeks drained from them finally as they walked haphazardly, wiping tears of laughter from their faces, back up the long drive towards the base.

The next morning had seen yet another tearful farewell to Adrienne, as Helen and Lily set off on Helen's motorcycle up to Amarillo to catch a plane to New York.

The journey turned out to be rather an uncomfortable one. Lily's previous experience of the bike had been limited to excursions into Sweetwater, which had not really been sufficient to prepare her for the long journey from Avenger Field with their luggage perched on the bike with them. However, they'd had a pleasant flight east, enjoying the novelty of not wearing leathers and parachutes while up in the air.

Helen had never been to New York before and she felt as though she was in sensory overload. After months of wide-open expanse, the sky now looked very small, squashed between the tops of the tall buildings. The streets were filled with a variety of uniforms; people wrapped up against the bitter cold weather, going about their business, oblivious to the awed face staring out of the cab window absorbing everything as they drove through the city.

Lily smiled watching Helen's head swivel back and forth, every now and again she would lunge across the expanse of the seat to see something out of Lily's window, her face was flushed with excitement at the sights of the city. They pulled into the tree-lined street where Lily's apartment building was. Lily paid the cab driver and walked, grinning, up to Helen who was staring straight up, one hand keeping her uniform beret on her head.

"You live here?" she asked, looking up at the tall red building, laundry hung from wrought iron balconies and the fire escape which zigzagged up the height of the building.

Lily followed her gaze upwards. "Yup, I live here. I should warn you my roommate can be gnarly," she smiled, walking up the steps towards the door of the building. Her fingers circled keys that she had not held in her hand for months; their familiarity linking her with her life pre WASP.

She pushed the door open and waited for Helen to join her before they climbed the stairs toward her apartment. The staircase was filled with the familiar sound of a screaming child. "That'll be three B. Her children scream all the time," Lily smiled, feeling comforted that although she may be different and forever changed by what she experienced in Texas, her home had not altered.

There was a clatter of footsteps above them. Lily paused recognizing the scampering sound of children. She had been barreled out of the way too many times not to heed the oncoming approach. She looked around and pulled Helen to the side of the stair, placing her arm protectively in front of her as three children of various ages, dressed in warm coats, scarves, hats and gloves piled down the steps at a rapid pace, their momentum carrying them quickly past the two women. The youngest and slowest child came running down picking up his small legs as he attempted two steps at a time in the same manner as his older siblings. His slower pace meant that he was able to take in the women waiting their passing.

"Sorry Mrs M," he said, pushing his flat cap out of his eyes with the heel of this hand so that her could look at Lily, before dropping his head down to concentrate on his descent.

"Robbie, be careful," Lily called after the small child.

"I will, don't worry," his voice drifted up the staircase.

Turning, Lily shrugged, "Five A, they run riot, come on." She indicated with her head towards the stairs. Helen followed Lily up the steps; they walked along the short hallway pausing at a green door. Putting the key into the deadlock Lily took a deep breath, wondering what would greet her on the other side. She swung the door open and walked through the small hall, putting her case and violin down on the floor and indicated for Helen to do the same.

She pushed open a door revealing a small living space; the room had a dark red carpet with a soft blue sofa. A bookcase filled with an assortment of books and a music stand stood in front of window dressed with lime green curtains that matched the flower patterned wallpaper on the wall. Beside the window and complementing the soft yellow paint on the other walls, a yellow lamp sat on top of the dark radio-phonograph.

"It's lovely," Helen said taking in the neat room.

Lily smiled proudly. "Let me show you the kitchen," she said pulling at Helen excitedly. She opened a door off the living room and entered a square room lined with patterned linoleum. A small red table sat at the side with two seats pushed in, the large white refrigerator dominated the space along with the pristine white cooker.

Lily shrugged, "So this is home." She pulled her beret off, threw it on the table, and started to undo the belt on her blue blazer. Following her lead Helen put her hat onto the table.

"Lily Rivera, as I live and breathe. Girl I thought we were getting robbed. What you doing sneaking in at this time of the day?"

Lily looked up, a wide smile on her face as she regarded the small woman standing in the kitchen doorway wielding an umbrella as she rubbed her eyes sleepily. She gave the tiny woman a quick once over.

"Eva Wilson, is that my robe you're wearing?" she asked pointedly, taking in the red silk robe pulled tightly around Eva.

Eva narrowed her eyes and smirked. "Was you here? 'cause the whole war effort is about not wastin' stuff, an' a beautiful thing like this laying in your drawer, well that's a God-dammed travesty," she grinned, holding her arms out for a hug, which Lily quickly provided.

"Helen Richmond, this is my roommate Eva Wilson."

The small black woman regarded Helen and sucked air in through her teeth. "Well I doubt you could have brought a whiter woman home for Christmas Rivera," she laughed, holding out her hand for Helen to shake.

Immediately liking the woman and her humor Helen shook her hand energetically, "It's lovely to meet you."

"So back to my other question. What you doing sneakin' around at this time of the day?" Eva said pulling one of the kitchen chairs out and plonking down onto it. She picked up Lily's beret and put it onto her head at a jaunty angle. Lily busied herself around filling the kettle with water before placing it on the stove.

"Grab a seat Helen," she pointed to the spare seat beside Eva. "And woman, it's three in the afternoon, normal people have been up for hours."

Eva tsked. "Normal people weren't singing in a club until the wee small hours," she scoffed, taking the hat off and putting it back onto the table. "You gonna come hear me sing?" She asked looking between the two women.

Helen leaned forward over the table. "I'd love that, can we?" she asked Lily expectantly.

Lily nodded as the kettle started to whistle, "Sure. We can go tonight."

Helen gave her a satisfied nod and smile then settled back into her seat as Eva started to pepper her with questions.

***

An hour passed where they shared histories. Helen learnt that Eva had come from Houston to New York to pursue her musical career and in turn she'd shared her stories of Hollywood and air racing before Eva announced that she should go try and get a bit more sleep, otherwise she'd be nodding off during her spot later. As she left the room, leaving them alone Helen rose and circled her arms around Lily's neck.

"I thought you said she was gnarly?" she asked nuzzling into Lily's neck.

"She was on her best behavior there, no one wants to get on the wrong side of Eva, believe me," Lily laughed, enjoying the sensation of Helen's lips nibbling her neck.

"So a classical violinist and a jazz singer, under one roof?" Helen remarked pulling away to look into Lily's eyes. "How does that work?"

Lily gave a small laugh. "I have an eclectic taste in music and wasn't asking too much rent," she replied, skirting the reasons why Eva had moved into her apartment.

Helen smiled and leaned in to whisper into Lily's ear. "There is one room that I haven't seen yet," she purred seductively.

Lily felt her stomach flip as she pulled her bottom lip between her teeth.

"That was remiss of me, let me rectify that right now," she said grabbing Helen's hand and pulling her towards her bedroom.

They stripped their uniforms off with less precision than they had dressed, quickly discarding the symbols of their hard work at Avenger Field for the desire to feel each other. Their lips roamed freely, exploring each newly exposed piece of skin as they made their way towards the plump bed that dominated the room.

Kissing her way down Lily's neck, Helen allowed her tongue to play lazily with Lily's nipple. It had been far too long since she had been able to revel in Lily's body and she had craved the taste and feel of it, living still in close quarters in the bay she'd had to resign herself to looking surreptitiously at her lover's body as she dressed in the morning or got ready for bed in the evening. The curves that she longed to caress tantalizingly out of reach. Apart from the night when Lily had quietly slipped into her bed, the two women had not been together since Atlanta and both were taut with desire.

Lily groaned as her breast was teased, she brought her hands to Helen's head raking her fingers through soft blonde curls, watching intently as Helen savored taunting her. Lily closed her eyes as Helen trailed kisses down her firm stomach her muscles twitching in response. Lily bucked her hips involuntarily as she felt Helen's lips ghost across her arousal, hot breath teasing as she waited hovering on the edge of ecstasy before moaning loudly as Helen finally took her into her mouth. Helen lost herself in every twitch, gasp, and moan that she elicited from Lily, each one increasing her own need for release. Lily gripped Helen's shoulders holding her in place as she felt her body tense, every muscle in her body screamed in response to Helen, finally with a loud moan the tension disappeared leaving her feeling a warm haze, her deep brown eyes watched from under hooded lids as Helen crawled back up her body.

"I like this room," Helen said smiling.

***

They had fallen asleep wrapped in each other's bodies, a sheet carelessly thrown across their nakedness. Eva opened the door to Lily's bedroom her eyebrows raised slightly at the sight of Lily asleep with Helen wound tightly against her back.

"You two planning on getting up and coming with me to the club or are you gonna lay there naked all night?" she asked loudly.

Helen sprang awake clutching at the sheet in a panic.

"Now, now," Eva waved her hand. "Ain't no business of mine what you two get up to, besides you live long enough in Greenwich you see it all, men with men, women with women. Just be careful if you go into them queer clubs, the police have been harassing them a lot lately. Damn shame if you ask me, people just trying to find love and gettin' beat up for it." She shook her head slightly stopping her rambling, "Anyways, you comin'?"

Lily lifted her head from the pillow and looked sleepily at her friend, "We're coming."

Eva gave her a brisk nod and left them closing the door as she left.

Helen let out a long breath that she had been holding since Eva came in, Lily laughed, "Relax, like she said, in Greenwich you see it all." Lily got out of the bed and pulled a robe from her wardrobe, "I'll go get the cases from the hall."

Forty minutes later Lily was looking into the mirror as she swept her dark red lipstick across her lips, she touched the red flower pinned into her dark locks and stood back to appraise her outfit, she gave herself a small nod of encouragement at her black polka dot dress. It felt positively decadent to have all of her wardrobe at her disposal after the previous months of frugal living. She picked up her red purse to match her shoes and beaded necklace and stepped out into the hallway and into her living room.

A few moments later Helen came out of the bathroom and entered the room, she hovered nervously in the doorway, her fingers worrying the seam of her dark blue halter swing dress.

Lily's breath hitched and she smiled broadly, "You look amazing." As she appraised Helen she whispered absently, "I've never seen you in that dress before."

"You like?" Helen asked giving a small twirl the material swishing around her thighs.

"I like you whether you're in your zoot suit, leathers or a bed sheet," Lily said appreciatively, moving across to take Helen into her arms. "I really like it when you're not wearing anything though."

"I'm goin', whether you two are comin' or not!" Eva shouted from the front door.

Lily rolled her eyes and slipped her hand into Helen's. "Wait. We're coming," she yelled in response grabbing coats for them both as she pulled Helen along behind her.

***

They followed Eva through the backdoor and into the nightclub.

"I thought we were going to a jazz club?" Helen asked weaving her way past the assortment of musicians gathered in the hallway, trying to keep up with Eva and Lily's fast pace.

"We are, but most of us play a set at one of the supper clubs first before doing the fun stuff," Lily replied over her shoulder.

At the thought of when the night might end, Helen almost rued not sleeping more when she'd had the chance… almost.

Eva grabbed a young bus boy in passing, "I need a table up front for my guests." She pointed at Lily and Helen. "Go tell Jacob," she barked.

The boy nodded quickly, a fearful look on his face as he scurried off to do Eva's bidding. The small woman gave Lily a quick wave as she slipped through a door to get ready.

Lily chuckled to herself; she had forgotten quite how intimidating Eva could be when you didn't know her properly. She turned to speak to Helen as they waited on the bus boy returning, as she turned her eye caught sight of a tall man walking towards her wearing a tuxedo and carrying a shining brass trumpet in his hand, a large grin on his face, she yelled in excitement, "Eli!"

Helen watched in confusion initially thinking that the smile on Lily's face was directed at her. Then realizing the brown eyes were looking over her shoulder, she turned her head slightly just as a man brushed past her and enveloped Lily into a bear hug spinning her around. He plonked her back down and held her at arm's length to inspect her.

"Mmmmm," he murmured appreciatively.

His voice was so deep that Lily could feel the vibration in her chest when he spoke.

"Altitude does wonders for you," he grinned.

Helen felt a surge of jealousy rise in her as the dark skinned man continued to make noises of approval while he twirled Lily around. Lily laughed at Eli as he spun her once more, her gaze catching the darkened look on Helen's face; she felt a flood of warmth diffuse through her at the possessive look that Helen was failing to disguise as she took in the scene in front of her.

"Eli," Lily sang. "This is Helen Richmond."

She held her hand out indicating the women standing observing Eli cautiously.

Eli turned, seeing the blonde for the first time. "This is Helen?" he remarked looking back at Lily, small dimples appeared as he smiled, turning back to Helen his smile broadened. "Well hello Hollywood! She didn't do you justice in her letters," he remarked. "She said you were pretty, but shit girl, she's beautiful," he laughed playfully pushing Lily. He held out his hand to Helen, "It is my sincere pleasure to finally make your acquaintance and thank you for looking after our girl here while she was down in the Deep South."

Helen smiled as she shook his hand, unsure what exactly Lily had written about her in her letters home.

"Did you read my letters to Eva?" Lily exclaimed in mock horror.

"Only way I find things out," Eli said smoothly. He held his hands out from his body with a look of wide-eyed innocence on his face, the light from the hallway catching the trumpet in his hand.

"Helen, this is Eli. He's Eva's beau," Lily laughed slightly at the introduction.

"Fiancé," Eli corrected.

"What? She said yes finally? she never mentioned it," Lily said surprised.

Eli shook his head, "Not exactly, but I'm working on it. You coming to the club later?" he asked as other tuxedoed musicians started to bundle him towards a door. "I'll see you there," he called over their heads before turning and moving with the wave of black jackets.

"See you there," Lily yelled in response as Eli disappeared.

Helen gave Lily a quizzical look. Lily sighed wondering how to describe the complicated nature of her friend's relationship, "He and Eva have been together for years, he wants to get married, she doesn't and every six months or so he forgets this and asks her." She shook her head as she thought about the couple, "She says no, and then breaks it off with him for a few weeks, kinda' like smacking a puppy's nose." Lily directed Helen towards the busboy, who had returned and was waiting on them, "Then they get back together, it's a dance they do, I've known them three years and have seen it happen enough times."

Pursing her lips thoughtfully Helen frowned. "Why doesn't she want to marry him?" she asked.

Giving a shrug Lily laughed, opening her eyes wide, "'Cause she's Eva!" They followed the boy through a door leading to the club. "I know she loves him because she was devastated when he went to sign up, and relieved when they found something wrong with his heart or something, I can't quite remember now," Lily shrugged. "Plus she says that a mouth that plays the trumpet in the way his does, has to have spoken to the devil himself," she grinned as they were led to a table with a prime view of the stage as the band struck up a lively swing number. The boy offered to check their coats. As Lily shrugged off her fur, Helen licked her lips as Lily's curves reappeared from the depths of her coat.

Lily smiled as she recognized the lusty look that Helen had just given her. The blonde smiled guiltily as she slipped her own borrowed coat off, realizing that Lily has caught her ogling. Sitting down they ordered their drinks and looked towards the stage. Finding the brass section Helen spotted Eli playing, his trumpet swaying with the music. He was a handsome man, however, the danger that Helen could see, was that he knew it. She leaned across towards Lily as their drinks were placed in front of them.

"So what did you tell Eva about?" she asked, lifting the wine glass to her lips and taking a delicate sip.

Lily dragged her eyes from the stage, still bobbing her head in time with the music. "Nothing exciting, I left out the details on how I thought I was going mad with desire for you," she smiled affectionately,

"Mad with desire? Really! We should explore that in more detail I think later," Helen purred as she let her hand drop from the table onto Lily's lap. Lily could feel the heat from Helen's hand through the thin silky rayon dress she was wearing, her touch almost burning into Lily's leg.

"If you don't move your hand, the whole club will get to see just how mad," Lily said ominously out of the side of her mouth. Helen was about to reply when the bandleader introduced Eva onto the floor.

They ate a light supper as they listened as Eva belt out song after song; Helen thought it almost impossible that such a large voice could come from such a small frame. The tempo dropped, Eva stood at the microphone, her eyes closed as she nodded in time with the intro to the song. Slowly opening her eyes she lifted her head up and leaned into the microphone, her fingers clicking at her side and her voice filled the room.

Eli's trumpet balanced out against her voice, playing a response to the tune crooned by the small woman. Her rich voice sounded like it was coating the lyrics with honey as she sang.

Eli sat back down and the saxophonist stood up taking up the mantle of supporting Eva's voice.

They clapped as Eva took a step back from the microphone and accepted the applause before stepping out of the spotlight, grinning towards Lily and Helen as she left. They took Eva's cue and rose from their seats, as they left the table they had to squeeze past the cigarette girl with her tray, selling a packet of cigarettes to the table next to them.

Collecting their coats, they stepped out into the night, the chill almost ripping their breaths from them. Five minutes later Eva joined them and putting her fingers in her mouth whistled a passing cab to take them to the center of the jazz scene in New York; 52nd Street.

The neon lights shone brightly, stark against the dark of the night, as they parked outside the club. Following Eva, they entered the club, which had a distinctly more relaxed atmosphere than the supper club they had come from. After checking their coats in they walked into the dark club and found a table, Eva joined them clicking her fingers in the air for the drinks waiter.

"You're in for a treat," Eva said as their drinks appeared at the table. "We've got a fantastic singer tonight."

"Modest as ever Eva!" Lily remarked.

"Not me, fool! Her," Eva nodded as the man at the microphone announced. "Miss Billie Holiday."

Lily's eyes widened, she had heard her sing a year previous and had been moved by the most distinctive and soulful voice she had ever heard. She could not wait for Helen to experience the joy of hearing 'The Lady' sing for the first time.

Helen felt a tingle in her spine as the first notes came from the woman on stage.

The hairs on Helen's arms rose and a shiver played on her neck as her body reacted to the voice filling the room. She sat awestruck listening to the most remarkable voice she had ever heard. She looked across in excitement at Lily, receiving a knowing smile in return. Feeling like a child at Christmas, experiencing the magic of seeing presents laid out before her for the first time, Helen sat enthralled letting the music wash over her.

At some point during the set, Eli slipped into the booth beside Eva. Had her life depended on it Helen would not have been able to tell you when he arrived; she was so absorbed in the music. Several drinks and songs later the set was over, Helen wanted to leap from her seat cheering,. However, she resisted and settled on clapping wildly from her seat in the booth.

The band started to play an instrumental piece and Lily became aware of Helen's pinkie tapping on the back of her hand, Lily frowned, as the beat that Helen was keeping didn't relate to the rhythm of the music being played. It seemed unusual, as she thought from her experience of dancing with her, that the blonde had a decent sense of rhythm. Lily's puzzlement disappeared as her training kicked in and her brain started to pick up patterns, slowly her mind automatically started to translate the patterns into letters.

Helen paused for a moment before starting to tap again. This time Lily was fully focused and a few minutes later was grinning as she had deciphered the message Helen had been relaying onto her hand. Leaning close so Eva and Eli couldn't hear her, Lily whispered nonchalantly, "You got your W mixed up with your L." She turned to cock an eyebrow at Helen.

"I did?" Helen replied quietly as she repeated the message, her head nodding as she converted the letters trying to spot her mistake.

Lily snorted quietly. "I'm pretty sure you don't want to drag me out of here, get me naked so you can make wove to me," she whispered in response.

Smiling Helen leaned forward, her lips almost brushing Lily's ear. "I weally weally want to make wove to you," she breathed.

Lily held up one finger motioning for the waiter, "Check please. Eva I'm really sorry, it's been a long day and I'm so tired, I need to get to bed." She plunged her hand into her purse and smacked a handful of bills onto the table, before grabbing Helen's hand and dragging her from the booth.

Eva smirked knowingly against the rim of her glass, "Sure you do Honey!"

Chapter Eleven

Lily and Helen spent the next forty-eight hours in a bubble in Lily's apartment, neither wishing to go out in public where they would have to be guarded with their touches or glances.

Eva disappeared after the first night to give them some privacy, but not before she'd cornered Helen and given her a graphic speech about what would happen to her were she to hurt Lily in any way. Helen for her part had been somewhere between amused and terrified at the description of the pain that would be inflicted upon her person should that event ever occur.

They passed the time listening to Lily's eclectic collection of seventy eights, and cooking together in Lily's small kitchen. For the first time they deliberately shared a bathtub when it had water in it, laughing as they compared the experience to their late night study sessions. They knew that they were trying desperately to form shared memories to bolster them during their enforced separation. Each experience was tinged with an aura of sadness that their reality was going to be far removed from these few days in New York 'playing home'.

Lily finished giving Helen an impromptu, if rather naked, virtuoso performance of 'Flight of the Bumblebee' while standing on the end of the bed. She finished with a flourish; holding her violin and bow out wide from her side, she gave a flamboyant bow then jumped off the bed and placed them down onto the dresser before returning and crawling up the length of her lover's body.

"I'd have loved to have seen you perform with the orchestra," Helen mused lifting Lily's fingertips to her mouth, kissing the pads of Lily's fingers enjoying the roughness, caused from hours of violin playing, against her lips.

"Well maybe, when everything's back to normal, you will," Lily smiled. "We should get out of the apartment today." She started to kiss along Helen's collarbone.

"Nope," Helen said stubbornly, closing her eyes and shaking her head.

"We took a big step yesterday getting out of bed," Lily smirked continuing to kiss Helen's skin. "We should make sure we don't lose momentum."

"Nope," Helen repeated. "Not happening."

Lily moved her hands down quickly to Helen's sensitive sides. "We need to go out for your present," she murmured as she pressed her fingers into the soft flesh or Helen's side.

Helen wriggled frantically to get away from Lily's tickle assault, succeeding only in propelling them both off the bed and onto the floor. As they lay laughing in a heap still wrapped in their bed sheet Lily propped herself on her elbow

"Well it looks like we're up now," Helen moaned as Lily smiled leaning down to kiss her.

***

Lily's violin case brushed her leg as they walked along, Helen's arm looped tightly through hers, both were thankful that the cold weather gave them an excuse to huddle close as they walked. Helen was still walking around taking in the sights of New York; her head practically rotating three hundred and sixty degrees as they walked along the streets.

"Where we going?" she asked for fifth time since they had left the apartment. "Are we there yet?"

"You'll see and almost," Lily replied smiling as Helen turned walking sideways so she could still see the large billboard with a cartoon man advertising Camel cigarettes, smoke billowing from the sign through a hole where his mouth was. Stopping outside a door Helen, still slightly distracted by the advertisement, bumped into Lily as she shuddered to a halt.

"We're here," Lily announced, rapping her knuckles against the door. There was a long pause before the door opened, the door replaced by a tall black man stood in the doorway. "Chief," Lily smiled in greeting.

"Lily McAllister," the tall man said, his voice deep and rich, his lips parted into a broad smile. "I thought you'd taken to the sky," he said chuckling. "Come in," he said, stepping to the side and motioning for them to enter.

"I have, I'm on leave, I wondered if I might, you know. For old time's sake," she asked hopefully.

Helen looked between them confused, as she hadn't been in the city long enough to have any directional sense she'd not really been paying attention to where they'd walked in relation to Lily's apartment.

"Sure, no problem," the man replied. "You want the works?" he asked.

Glancing at an ever more confused Helen, Lily nodded, "Please."

"Miss, if you'd like to come with me," he said gently, taking Helen by the elbow. "Everyone calls me Chief, 'cause I'm in charge and I know how." He held up his large palm in a mock Indian greeting, chuckling at his own joke.

"Helen," she replied, trying to keep up with his long strides. She turned back to look at Lily, her brow furrowing even more as the corridor behind them was empty. "Where are we exactly?"

The Chief looked surprised at her question as he threw open a door. "Why, Carnegie Hall of course," he replied, sweeping his arm into the auditorium.

Blinking in surprise Helen entered the hall, her eyes sweeping around the rows of red seats and balcony tiers above her. She walked with the Chief into the hall and sat down where she was told. The tall man gave a signal to the back of the hall and the sound of a switch being flipped echoed around as the auditorium plunged into darkness. Helen looked around, her hand gripping the arm rests, still unsure what was happening. She blinked trying to acclimatize her eyes to the dark, when a spotlight snapped on. She turned back into her seat and looked towards the stage. Illuminated by the spot light was Lily, her violin poised beneath her chin. She drew her bow across the strings and started to play the piece that Helen had heard her play on their second night at Avenger Field.

Helen felt as though someone had placed a hand on her chest and pushed her back into her seat, her back flush against the cushioned fabric. Her heart thumped as Lily swayed with each movement of her bow, she listened as the music that had captured her attention those months ago in an aircraft hangar, was now being played on the stage at Carnegie Hall by the woman who had also captivated her heart and soul.

She felt wetness on her cheek as the depth of emotion that she felt for Lily overawed her, tears of joy left her eyes and trickled down her face. Lily paused with her eyes closed as she played the final note, standing with her bow in place as if she was going to continue. Helen leapt to her feet and applauded.

"Merry Christmas," Lily shouted from the stage, bringing her hand up to shield her eyes so she could see down into the stalls and see the eyes of the woman she loved.

***

On Christmas morning they rose and entered the kitchen, sitting on the table were two framed photographs of them, taken while they had been in the supper club a few evening before, underneath the frames was a hand written note.

An evening to remember, something to help with the days and nights, nights and days!

Fly safe always.

Eva and Eli.

They smiled at the gifts, lifting the photographs up, it was a thoughtful gift, however, it served only to remind them that their days together were running short. They made breakfast with a heavy silence hovering over them. After breakfast, Helen snuggled closer to Lily on the sofa as they listened to the radio.

"Thank you for the best Christmas present ever."

"I'm glad you liked it," Lily replied. "I had no idea what to get you and I wanted to get you a forever gift."

"It was. I will never forget how amazing you looked and sounded Liliana, although I also enjoyed the naked end of the bed performance. Just so you know," she smirked. "I have your gift." She extricated herself from Lily's embrace and skipped off into the bedroom, returning a moment later with a small simple rectangular box. Lily took the box studying Helen's face as her fingers tightened around it. She slowly slipped the lid off and examined the contents, a small gasp leaving her lips as comprehension dawned on her

"Helen, I can't," she thrust her hands out urging the blonde woman to take the box back.

Pushing the box back towards Lily, Helen smiled, "You can. I want you to."

"I can't take your father's wings," she said looking at the US Army Air Force wings presented in the box.

"You can and you will," Helen said emphatically. "This is a forever gift as well Liliana. You're the caretaker of those wings until we can be together again and when that happens, I don't intend on leaving you again."

Lily looked at the wings then back to Helen. "I will take really good care of them," she said simply.

"I know you will," Helen said leaning forward to press her lips against Lily's.

***

At New Year's, the city seemed determined to ensure that all service personnel had the best New Year that New York could deliver. There were fairs, shows and parties put on all over the city; however, Lily and Helen were oblivious to the celebrations as they continued to cram as much time together in as possible. Their impending departure played on their minds, but by silent agreement, neither mentioned it. They celebrated the first moments of 1944 from the cocoon of their bed, maximizing what time they had left to indulge in each other's bodies.

All too soon, they were standing in the entrance hall of Amarillo's train station. Their flight back west had been punctuated with small talk, both too overwhelmed with emotion to discuss what they were facing into. The rain beat a tattoo on the roof of the building as they watched the clock inching towards the time when Lily's train would depart.

"You ride carefully," Lily warned. "The roads will be greasy with all this rain."

Helen nodded sadly, "I will, I promise." Sucking in a sharp intake of breath that caused the pain in her chest to intensify, "I could…"

Lily put her finger on Helen's lips, "I know what you're about to say and no, we agreed, if we try and extend this anymore it's just going to get harder." She moved her hand to cup Helen's face, the blonde woman squeezed her eyes closed and leaned into the touch. A call came for the train that started Lily's journey to Las Vegas. She dropped her hand from Helen's face and clutched at the blonde woman's hand. "I love you. Write to me every day," she said quickly swallowing the lump that was rising in her throat.

Helen nodded dumbly, "I will."

Lily pulled her into a quick hug then broke away, their fingers finally separating. As Lily moved swiftly away, Helen felt a breath rush from her body. "Liliana," she gasped, her voice breaking.

Lily turned, her face glistening with tears as she studied Helen's face. Knowing exactly what was being said without the words being uttered, she gave a small smile and nodded, then turned to enter the platform.

Helen puffed up her cheeks and let out a long breath before turning and heading out into the rain, she pulled her slicker close to her body as she dropped down onto her motorcycle. Rocking the bike off its stand she switched the ignition on and kick started the engine. As she heard a whistle blow behind her and the sound of a train start to chug its way out of the station, she tugged the throttle and smiled at the pleasure of hearing the engine purr in response. Sitting back on her seat, Helen pushed wet tendrils of hair out of her face and looked skywards allowing the rain to mingle with the tears on her face as her motorcycle throbbed beneath her, waiting on her to set it to life. Brushing her palm across her face to remove the water from her skin, she shrugged and gripped the handlebars of her bike. She set off, the engine roaring as the back wheel skidded back and forth before getting solid purchase and propelling her towards her new home.

Chapter Twelve

February 1944, Dodge City Army Air Base, Dodge City, Kansas

Helen thumped a pile of papers down on the desk, in the four weeks since her arrival at Dodge, the nearest she'd got to flying was when she jumped down the remaining stairs from the observation tower. She had realized that this might not be the prime posting that Foster had tried to sell it as, almost as soon as she'd arrived at the gate and had a half hour long conversation with the guard about her reasons for being there.

"Are you a nurse?" the guard asked for the fourth time.

Helen frowned pointing at her uniform, "No, I'm a WASP."

"No idea what that is, Ma'am," he shook his head and turned to walk away from her.

"Wait, I've been posted here, I have orders," Helen pulled her papers from her purse and flapped them around. "I have orders to report to Major Chiswell."

The guard had taken the orders and reviewed them with a suspicious look on his face, he moved back into the guardhouse taking her papers with him. Helen waited kicking her toe idly against the rubber of her motorcycle's front wheel. Ten minutes later he reappeared shaking his head. She walked back towards him.

"Says here you're a pilot. That right?" he asked, handing the papers back.

Helen practically snatched the papers from his hand annoyed at his condescending tone, "That's right, I'm a pilot."

He gave a chuckle, "That's about the most insane thing I think I've heard. I wouldn't get in a car with my wife driving it never mind up in a plane with a woman flying it."

Helen glowered at him. "Do I have clearance?" she asked not bothering to disguise her anger in her tone.

"What? Oh yes," he waved a dismissive hand. "Third building on the right."

Helen stuffed her papers back into her bag, stomped over to her cycle, and remounted, her frustration swelling as the cycle refused to start on her first kick. She gave it another attempt, catching the smirk on the guard's face as she struggled with the starter. Finally, the engine submitted to her demands and spluttered into life. She rode the bike the short distance to the guard and stopped the bike in front of him.

"I'm sorry was it the second building?" she asked innocently, planting her feet firmly at either side of the cycle.

The guard rolled his eyes and sighed. "Third. The third building," he corrected.

Helen nodded and thanked him; keeping her feet on the ground, she pressed on the brakes and pulled the throttle back hard causing the back wheel to spin and skid back and forth, dirt kicked up and hit the guard, smoke surrounded them. After a second, Helen released the throttle and the smoke subsided. She turned and looked at the guard, now covered in a fine layer of dirt and dust.

"Oops sorry," she sang. "Stupid machines, being a woman I'm not really sure what I'm doing." She gave him a dimpled smile as she sat down on the motorcycle and rode into the base, laughing to herself.

Her conversation with the major had not given her much more confidence, she was the first WASP to be placed at Dodge and they weren't set up to have her on the base. She spent her first night in a local hotel, until hastily arranged accommodation in the nurse's quarters was available. She moved in her seat picking up another manila folder, the rustle of paper in her pocket made her forget her frustration at her current situation and think of Lily. She pulled the letter that she had received that morning from her pocket and read it for the third time.

Dearest Helen

It was lovely to get your letter. I'm practically hounding the office when it's mail time to see whether I have a letter from you.

I've still not adjusted to the temperature change here; the weather in Las Vegas couldn't be more different to our time in New York. Although there were some hot moments in NYC I guess!

I am loving the planes here, I did a delivery last week. It was a lovely flight...looong though. I got there around dusk and I was really tired and I guess the guy on the ground was too, 'cause when I passed him my papers he handed me a box. I didn't really think much about it and headed to my hotel. When I opened the box it was a prophylactic! Guess we know what the guys get up to when they go there. (It's in my locker...unused!) I was back there a couple days ago with another plane and the same guy was working, he could barely look me in the eye. He apologized for giving me the kit though.

Did you get a letter from the other girls? I got one yesterday, sounds like they've settled in well to their bases.

There's so much that I want to say...

IWU

Yours

Liliana

Helen sighed reading the letter. She was happy for Lily that she was enjoying her posting, but couldn't help but feel a tad jealous that her own experience wasn't as positive. She trailed her fingers across Lily's cursive handwriting, her fingertips following the flowing IWU, smiling at the hidden message within the three letters. Knowing that their correspondence would not be private, they had agreed to use the letters as their own personal 'I love you', referring to Helen's Morse Code mix up. Feeling her anger rise again at the waste of her skills Helen folded the letter and placed it back in the pocket of her blue uniform slacks.

She selected a cigarette out of her silver carry case and placed it between her lips before striking a match. While inhaling deeply she shook her right hand to extinguish the small flame, tossing the spent stick into the ashtray sitting beside the typewriter on her desk. She needed this, because she knew that what she was about to do could get her in a whole heap of trouble. She let her head fall back and exhaled slowly watching the smoke swirl around her head. Her thumb flicked against the tip of the cigarette as she contemplated her approach. Having completed her mental pep talk, she ground the cigarette out in the ashtray and stood up, tugging the hem of her short Eisenhower jacket.

Helen lifted her beret and positioned it on her head, then turned and strode across the office and rapped her knuckles brightly against the door.

"Come in."

She reached for the door handle, tugged down on it sharply and strode into the room.

"Sir."

Marching swiftly into the center of the room, her footsteps echoed loudly off the tiled floor. She saluted the Major and waited for his acknowledgement.

Major Chiswell looked up, quickly saluting back. "At ease WASP," he barked. He was uncomfortable with a woman saluting him and even more so when he knew that the woman was the daughter of a three star Army Airforce General. "Richmond?" he asked picking his pen back up and holding it poised above his paper.

"Sir, I'm seeking permission to utilize my skills fully, Sir. I have been here for four weeks and I'm yet to fly, Sir." Helen felt the rage in her start to flow, overriding her usual respect for authority figures, particularly authority figures in uniform with bars on their shoulders. "I trained for six months to serve my country, doing the same training as the men here, Sir, and I would like to put that training to use," Helen let out her breath in a rush.

The Major put his pen down and stood up; Helen puffed her chest up and lifted her chin up defiantly. "What do you see here?" he asked pointing towards the gold oak leaf on his shoulder.

"Your rank insignia, Sir," Helen answered, facing forward unflinching.

"And that is?"

"Major, Sir."

Chiswell walked around the desk to loom over Helen standing in her personal space. "That's right, WASP. Major. So I make the decisions. I give the orders and if I decide that you're going to fly, you'll fly or if I think that you'll serve your country better by getting my coffee then that's what you'll do," his voice was a steady snarl. "Have I made myself clear?"

Helen's eyes flashed upwards catching sight of the flushed face above her, "Sir. Yes. Sir."

"Dismissed Richmond," he stated.

Helen saluted, spun on her heel, and marched quickly out of the room. As she carefully closed the door behind her, she slumped against it.

"Well, that went well," she muttered under her breath. She lifted her cigarette case and matches and left the office walking out into the cool air.

She stood at the side of the hangar smoking, her hands shaking with adrenaline following her encounter with the Major. The office door opened and the major strode out towards a waiting jeep. He saluted the driver and climbed into the passenger seat. Recalling what he had said to her, an image of Adele flashed into her mind. Her friend had died training to do this job and how could she hold her head up and honor that sacrifice if he wouldn't let her, something within Helen snapped. She threw her cigarette on the ground and crushed it under her heel, pushing herself off the wall she jogged towards the stand.

"Stewie, is this fuelled?" she shouted pointing as she ran towards the Mustang plane sitting on the stand.

The tall engineer's thick eyebrows raised as Helen ran towards him. He wiped his hands on a rag and nodded, "Just filled her up."

Helen grinned, "Great." She climbed up the wing walkway, opened the canopy, and jumped into the cockpit, pulling the canopy closed in one swift action. Quickly, she went through her preflight checks, and primed the engine. Stewie realizing what she was about to do, dove under the plane and removed the wheel chalks just before the propeller started to spin. The plane started to move slowly from the stand towards the runway. Adjusting the microphone Helen called into the tower.

"Control, this is Hollywood. Permission for take-off. Over."

"Helen, what are you doing?" a female voice in her ear asked.

"Betty, just give me clearance," Helen barked into the radio, hoping the civilian air traffic controller wouldn't ask too many questions.

Betty stood up and looked out of the window that circled the tower; she spotted the Mustang taxiing along and smirked to herself. She'd seen the mounting impatience in the blonde since her arrival and wasn't surprised at the feisty response to her grounding, "Proceed Hollywood. Fly safe. Over."

Helen smiled turning her head to look up towards the tower she spotted Betty watching her, she held up a thumb, grinned and sped up towards the runway.

***

Chiswell was sitting in the open Jeep when the buzz of an engine distracted him from the conversation he was having with his driver, he looked over his shoulder and into the air. The source of the noise was apparent, above him was a Mustang, performing a series of rolls, the spins finished and the plane pulled upwards, completing a flawless inverted loop. The plane pulled around until it was flying directly behind the Jeep following the line of the road below. Chiswell watched as it spun one eighty and stayed there, flying upside down. As it flew overhead Chiswell's eyes never wavered from the canopy, spotting blonde hair flowing as Helen flew over him.

"I will kill her," he muttered as the plane flipped back over and peeled off back towards the base. "Turn the Jeep around," he shouted smacking the dashboard.

Helen whooped as she pulled the plane back towards the base.

"Make your own damn coffee!" she shouted, bouncing up and down in the seat.

***

Chiswell threw the office door open, Helen shot to her feet behind her desk, standing automatically to attention.

"Office now," he barked not looking at her and marched into his office, he yanked his hat from his head and threw it angrily onto his desk, rubbing his hand over the close-cropped hair at the back of this head. "Give me one reason not to have you arrested or thrown off the base?" he yelled spinning round to look at Helen. "That has to be the worst demonstration of insubordination I have seen in all my years in this man's army, do you have anything, anything to say Richmond?"

Helen pleaded with her body not to betray her as she faced the major's wrath; she remained silent hoping that she could keep her face neutral against the assault.

"Well, do you?" the major repeated, his face incandescent with rage his nose practically pressed against Helen's. "I'm not surprised you have nothing to say. You not only disregarded orders, you flagrantly disobeyed them. That little stunt of yours has got you confined to barracks for the next six weeks; any leave you hoped to get has been cancelled as of now." He stepped back and put his desk between them. Helen stood and swallowed, praying that he would dismiss her so that she could get out of there.

"Now go make yourself useful, report to Lewis and tell him to get your name on the flight schedule for tomorrow. Dismissed," he sat down heavily on his seat, the rage having left him. Realization dawned on Helen that the major was letting her fly, she bit at her lip to stop smiling as she fell out and walked towards the door, her hand reached for the door handle when she heard the major say her name, she turned to face him, nervous that he would change his mind.

"Richmond, if I ever see you flying without a parachute again, I'll have you put in the stockade."

She nodded quickly and shot out the room. The major sat back on his chair and shook his head chuckling to himself, "That woman has balls."

***

March 1944 – Las Vegas Army Air Field, Las Vegas, Nevada

Lily let out a long breath, pulling the soft leather helmet from her head and running a hand through her hair. She had only been away from the base for three days but she could feel the change in temperature already, spring was coming. She finished her paperwork then unfastened her harness and pulled herself out of the seat.

Walking over the flight line towards the office Lily waved at Rita, a fellow WASP. Rita jogged up and took Lily's overnight case from her.

"Good trip?" she asked, stepping in time with Lily.

"Three days, three bases, three beds and three planes," Lily replied wearily summing up her journey.

"Almost as many beds as Sadie managed in the same time," Rita grinned, nodding wide-eyed as Lily looked at her for confirmation.

Rolling her eyes at the news Lily shook her head, "When will she learn, she gives the rest of us a bad name." Lily started to unbuckle her parachute as they walked. "Does she realize that her hopping in, and out, of officer's beds means we get hassle? They think we've all been tarred with the same harlot brush."

Rita put Lily's case down and held out her hands to help her friend shrug off the heavy parachute. "I'm not sure she's thinking about much," Rita surmised hanging the chute up.

Lily handed her paperwork in, pulled coins out of a zipped pocket of her leather jacket and slotted them into the soda dispenser, she tugged the knob then reached in pulling out a cool bottle of Coca Cola.

"So what did I miss while I was gone?" Lily asked placing the bottle against the metal opener and thrusting the bottle down, the cap released from the bottle with a small audible hiss. She gave Rita an expectant look as she took a long sip from the bottle.

"There's rumors of some of us being selected for bomber training," Rita replied excitedly, her blonde curls bobbed around as she spoke, creating a pang of longing in Lily for Helen.

It was late March and it seemed almost impossible to Lily that the time could have gone so quickly and yet it feel like a lifetime since she'd held Helen.

"Are you listening to me?" Rita smiled waving her hand in front of Lily's face.

"Sorry, million miles away there," Lily shook her head and focused on Rita.

"You know I scored pretty high in navigation in training and I'm pretty sure that Kansas isn't that far away."

Lily smiled, Rita had figured out that Lily had a sweetheart based elsewhere from the excitement that would flush her face when she received mail; however, Lily never discussed Helen with Rita or corrected the assumption that her sweetheart was a man.

"May as well be," Lily replied sadly. Rita looked in surprise at the unusually candid response from the dark haired woman. "So, bomber training?" she asked.

Rita opened her mouth to reply but halted at a shout of Lily's name. Lily looked in the direction of the shout and grinned as she realized that Doris was coming towards her, waving papers in her hand. Rita shook her head knowing that their conversation was effectively at an end.

"Come find me when you're done," Rita said rubbing Lily's arm.

Lily murmured an acknowledgment her eyes monitoring Doris' approach.

"'You got mail," Doris smiled handing Lily a small pile of letters. Lily took the papers and flashed Doris a smile full of thanks.

Lily entered her room, tossed the mail onto her cot, and placed her soda bottle on her nightstand. She shrugged off her leather jacket, opening her locker she hung it up then automatically opened her drawer and pushed her clothing to the side, to reveal the framed photo of her and Helen. She traced a finger affectionately across Helen's face.

"Hey Hollywood," she said softly, before replacing the clothing on top of the photo and unzipping her zoot suit. She pulled her arms out of the overall letting the top half drop to her sides and loosened her black tie, slipping the knot over her head. Opening the top button of her blue flight shirt, she picked up her half-full soda bottle and flopped onto her bed. Drinking from the bottle her free hand sorted through her mail, she recognized her sister's spiky handwriting style, Adrienne's looping letters, Lucy's neat print, finally finding the handwriting that looked like a spider had fallen into an ink well and crawled over the paper while doing a small jig. She was about to open it when the next envelope sparked curiosity. She picked up the brown envelope with her name typed neatly in the center. She balanced the soda bottle between her thighs and slipping her finger under the seal she opened the envelope and pulled out the papers. Lily took in a deep breath, puffing out her cheeks as she read that she had been selected to attend Bomber School and was to report to the training base in Florida in two weeks' time. She was flattered to be chosen but also nervous. She knew that Bomber School meant flying B26 Marauder's which had the worst reputation with pilots who had nicknamed it with a range of names from 'Flying Coffin' to 'Widowmaker' she let her breath out slowly putting the letter to one side and picked up Helen's letter deciding to distract herself with her favorite blonde.

She opened the letter and unfolded it carefully ready to read what Helen had been up to. Like most serving personnel, they were always careful in their letters not to give specific details of what they were doing in terms of the planes they flew but they also had to fight with the balance of missing each other and wanting to express that while not exposing the nature of their relationship. Lily found it a difficult line to walk when she wrote meaning her letters were usually short and filled with hints towards what she couldn't say. Helen's letters on the other hand were full of stories from the base.

Dearest Liliana

Greetings from your favorite machine-gun fodder! Things have been hectic here recently now that I'm flying. I'm not just doing training flights, they have me doing test flights for the mechanics as well... my feet barely touch the ground. Remind me to tell you some of the hair-raising stories of that when I see you!

I've finally been allowed off base, seems the major isn't one to hold a grudge. He maintains that I'm less of a danger in the air than in the office, apparently my coffee making abilities could be the Allies' secret weapon. He reckoned that if we served up my coffee to Hitler the war would be over in no time... not sure how to take that!

Matty has settled in, have to say it's nice to have another fly girl on the base. Now that I'm off the hook with Chissy (As I like to call him) we went to the movies on Saturday and saw 'Four Jills in a Jeep' movie wasn't much to write home about, but Alice Faye sang. I thought that you'd enjoy the song. Now I might get some of the words wrong but I think it went something like...

"You'll never know just how much I miss you

You'll never know just how much I care

And if I tried, I still couldn't hide my love for you

You ought to know, 'cause haven't I told you so

A million or more times?

Have been thinking (a lot!) about your pre-flight instruction technique, your handling of the wobble pump in particular along with your take off is something that impressed me -and something that I long to put into practice. I look forward to being your co-pilot again soon.

IWU

Helen

Lily let out a frustrated growl and smacked her hands down on the hard mattress, her head thumped against her thin pillow. She raised her hand and re-read the final paragraph again before kicking her legs rapidly against her bed.

"Someone having a temper tantrum?" Rita remarked from the doorway.

Lily looked up, surprised at the voice. "Something like that," she replied sitting up and stuffing Helen's letter back into its envelope. She stood up and straightened her shirt. "I have to report to Florida in two weeks," Lily announced, masking her concern at being chosen. Rita jumped slightly in celebration, hopping forward to hug Lily.

"Congratulations!"

Lily returned the hug, then pulled away and picked up Helen's letter to stow it with the ever-increasing collection of correspondence from the blonde.

"What am I going to do without you for six weeks?" Rita mused.

"Try and keep Sadie's knees together," Lily joked about her roommate and her nocturnal habits.

"How 'bout you give me something easier! Like World peace," Rita replied dryly, sparking a guffaw from Lily. "I came to see if you wanted to eat, mess will stop serving soon."

Lily's stomach growled in response.

"I guess that's a yes," Lily smiled, quickly grabbing her tie and Eisenhower short jacket and dressing as they walked.

***

Lily was woken to a thud on the head.

"Morning, sunshine," Sadie sang.

Grumbling a response Lily sat up and checked her watch, not believing that the night had passed already. Wearily she got out of bed and padded behind her roommate.

Sadie stood in front of the mirror, pulling at the skin her eyelids. "All the squinting because of the sun is giving me wrinkles," she complained, pouting her full lips. As quickly as the pout appeared it left her face again replaced with a large smile, "We're flying short haul together again today."

For the past two days the three WASPs had been delivering utility planes to a nearby base. Lily tried to match Sadie's smile and enthusiasm for the trip but two days of doing the same hour-long flight before boarding another plane home to repeat the process several times a day, was starting to bore her.

Rita entered the small shared bathroom, wash bag in one hand the other rubbing sleep from her eyes.

"How exciting," she yawned.

"It is 'cause today we're going to spice it up," Sadie trilled hopping onto her toes.

Lily and Rita exchanged slightly worried glances at what the blonde's plans to 'spice' up their day would bring.

***

"Sleeping Beauty. It's Hot Lips. Do you read me?"

Lily looked over to her left, through the small cockpit window towards Sadie's plane.

"I read you Jones," Lily point blank refused to call Sadie 'Hot Lips'. Therefore, when she could she would ignore her call name when on the radio, "What's up?"

Sadie pulled back her lips in a smile, "You see those suspension lines ahead? You think you can fly under them?"

Lily focused her attention to the front, spotting the poles holding the high wires that Sadie referred to. Doing a quick mental calculation Lily broke from their formation and swooped down, easily clearing the lines that crisscrossed their way across the landscape. Whooping as she pulled the plane back up to the formation Lily chuckled into her mouthpiece, "What you mean? Like that?"

"Show off," Rita interjected laughing looking across to Lily's plane.

On their fourth trip of the day it was Lily's turn again to navigate the impromptu course they had created for themselves to relieve the boredom of the flight. She dropped the plane down, However, this time, she misjudged the sag in one of the lines. The cable snagged on her wing, causing the plane to list momentarily. Lily fought with the controls to keep the plane level, her heart started to race as for a split second she thought she was going down. Fortunately, the wire snapped from the poles, wrapping itself tightly around the wing. Taking a deep breath Lily put the plane back into a climb to join her friends.

"Good luck explaining that when we land," Sadie laughed inspecting the wing of Lily's plane from her vantage point, remarkably there seemed little damage to the wing itself. However, it was bearing a rather telling length of thick cable wound around it.

Lily laughed, the relief evident in her tone, "Let's go for boring next time we do the trip. That was a bit more spice than I have an appetite for."

***

Sitting out on the flight line, Lily tapped her lips with her pen, she loved coming out here to relax. She felt an overwhelming sense of comfort from the noise and activity around the hangars. It reminded her of her childhood and despite the racket from the engines, she felt at peace, there were only two other places in the world that provided that feeling, sitting in the orchestra, lost in the music that was playing and the other...Helen's arms.

Helen,

Machine gun fodder? Explain!

I'm glad that Matty is making Dodge a more enjoyable experience for you.

Lily paused, she was happy that there was another WASP on the base, as she'd detected in Helen's letters an unhappiness, despite obvious attempts to keep her correspondence upbeat. The first weeks particularly seemed to have been tough, Lily was grateful that in her first few weeks she had been kept busy flying, which gave some distraction to her misery at being parted from Helen. Up until her little flying display – which, when Lily had read about it, had caused her to laugh for a good ten minutes at Helen's description of the major's face as she flew over him - it seemed that Helen had been office bound. Having seen Helen when rain kept them grounded during training, Lily could not imagine Helen not flying regularly, the thought of the blonde sitting behind a desk conjured up the image of a tiger that Lily had seen when she and Henry had visited the zoo in Central Park on one of their first dates. She had watched as the tiger prowled back and forth in its small enclosure and had felt sorry that those strong muscles would never get the chance to run the speed and distance they were designed for, instead destined to only pace back and forth. Helen was destined to fly.

It's good that you're getting the chance to fly, I hope however that you're not doing any more dangerous aerobatics.

Lily smiled to herself thinking of her own recent moment of insanity and more so, the ground crew's faces when she had parked in the stand with a long length of wire attached to her wing. At their quizzical looks, Lily had merely shrugged and announced that it must have been there when she picked it up, before hopping into the truck beside her laughing friends to be driven to their ride home.

I've been selected for Bomber Training and so will be leaving Las Vegas soon. I'm slightly apprehensive! Although I will be returning homeward for it, so hope to get a day or so to see family on the way there.

I miss our preflight check training session; flying solo is nowhere near as rewarding or fun. If you think that my pre-flight checks are something wait 'til I take you through my landing procedures, I am particularly good at reverse thrust.

IWU

Liliana

She released a small groan as her mind drifted to what she wanted to be doing with Helen. Deciding it would be better not to work herself up on the flight line, she folded her letter and headed back towards her bunk for a cold shower.

Chapter Thirteen

<u>March 1944 - Dodge City Army Air Base, Dodge City, Kansas</u>

Helen shouted to Matty to release the target. Pulling the lever the tall brunette woman watched as the long white sock flew out of the back of the plane, fluttering behind them. She walked back up the length of the aircraft her hands pressed against the walls to steady herself. She sat back down in the co-pilot seat and raised her thumbs. Helen nodded, pulling the plane round in a steep bank and flying over the anti-aircraft mounds below. The sound of gunfire punctuated the air they flew, the noise eventually trailing off as they flew beyond the range of the guns. Turning the plane around again, they took another fly over the stations. Despite this being a regular training activity for them Helen still felt her heart rate increase. Her thoughts would often drift to her father and what it had been like for him in those final moments before gunfire took his plane down. These flights were always tense and doing them had reignited her nightmares, she was only grateful that she had a single room on the base, so her yells did not disturb anyone. She had become accustomed to waking up in a cold sweat, panting at the images her brain tormented her with.

They repeated their fly over a further two times before she brought the plane down to a low level and Matty released the target. The material fluttered down to the ground to be collected and analyzed; each gunner's bullets left a different colored mark on the fabric allowing their accuracy to be assessed.

Matty and Helen were walking back to the flight line, when they saw the officer in charge of gunnery practice frog marching a young GI, who looked no more than nineteen, towards them. They gave each other a quick look before watching the approach with a mix of amusement and confusion.

"Captain Vallance," Helen greeted the tall dark haired man. He gave a curt nod in response, his lips terse.

"Richmond, Gordon," he replied, shoving the soldier in front of them. "Say hello Private Dickson," he barked. The GI looked at them sheepishly and murmured a greeting. "Now say sorry," Vallance ordered.

Helen and Matty exchanged bewildered glances.

"What exactly is he apologizing for?" Matty asked eyed the GI suspiciously.

Vallance turned to the soldier. "Well?" he prompted. "Tell them soldier. That's an order!" he yelled as the GI looked reluctant.

"I'm sorry. I'm sorry that I misunderstood my orders, Ma'am."

Helen gave the captain another puzzled look, the tall man clipped his hand against the back of the GI's head. "Genius here, after you passed over for the fourth time, asked what the sock flying out of the back of the plane was for. We're all damned lucky that he couldn't hit a cow's ass with a banjo, 'cause the whole time you were up there he was firing at the damn plane and not the target." He gave the sheepish man another smack for good measure.

Helen's puzzled look grew into surprise before settling on a mild fury. "You idiot!" she yelled. "You're using live ammunition. You could have killed us!" she stepped forward ready to pummel the idiotic youngster. Her progress halted by Matty snatching an arm out to hold her back.

"I'm sorry," the private said repeatedly, backing away in terror, attempting to put the captain between him and the small woman glaring at him.

Helen breathed heavily through her nose, her nostrils flaring.

"Hey pocket rocket," Matty stood in front of her and made their eyes connect. "Why don't we go for a long walk, in that direction?" she nodded in the opposite direction, pushing on Helen's shoulders turning her away from the two men. She spun her head round and looked directly at the young GI, "You got lucky today, not just that you didn't kill us, but that she didn't kill you. Do better."

Vallance watched the women walk off.

"Idiot," he muttered, cuffing the GI once more.

***

April 1944 – Tyndall Army Air Base, Panama City, Florida

"Oh my giddy aunt."

Lily froze at the voice that had shouted a phrase that Adele had used to express disbelief or excitement. Her mouth spread into a broad grin as she chuckled to herself and turned around, standing behind her arms outstretched ready for a hug was Adrienne.

"Looks like the tall girls get all the good jobs again," Adrienne laughed as Lily practically skipped over into her arms.

"You're looking good," Lily smiled inspecting her friend.

"I could say the same of you," Adrienne smiled. "So you ready for this?" she asked nodding towards the screen where they were about to be shown their instruction film on how the fly the B-26. Lily gave her a halfhearted smile. "Yeah I know what you mean," Adrienne said out of the side of her mouth as they sat down. "Back at my base they call the plane the prostitute, 'cause it has no visible means of support," she whispered as she shot Lily a wide-eyed look.

"I hear that male pilots hate flying them," Lily whispered as the lights dimmed.

Adrienne reached over giving her hand a quick squeeze, "We're gonna love it then."

***

May 1944 - Dodge City Army Air Base, Dodge City, Kansas

It had been four weeks since Lily entered the training program, and in those four weeks Helen had only received one letter, she knew that the training program was intense and from the letter she did receive, it appeared to be taking its toll on Lily.

The sheer size of the plane twinned with it being multi-engined was taking everything out of her. Helen was only glad that Adrienne was there to provide support and encouragement. She didn't envy the altitude training that they'd gone through. Sitting in a pressure chamber being asked to write your name on a chalkboard as they increased the pressure didn't sound like a barrel of laughs to Helen. Lily had said that when she looked back at what she'd written it looked like a toddler's attempt at writing or close to Helen's own scrawl. Helen also did not envy the pre-flight checks that the plane apparently required. From Lily's description, the checks lasted longer than their first flights at Avenger. She curled up on her cot to concentrate on her letter.

Dearest Liliana... and Adrienne,

I hope that you're both well and coping with the training. Things here at Dodge are good. I haven't been shot at this week, so that's always good... one gunner clipped our tail last week. Matty had to sit on me to stop me kicking his ass.

We had a 'brass' visit this week, Chissy had me ferry the visitor back. He refused to get in a plane with me 'cause I'm a woman! Chissy told him he either flew with me or he walked... he flew with me! - I kept the plane the right way up the entire way too.

I'm getting some leave soon...three whole days...do you know when you will be finished? Would be good to see you.

There's not much gossip going on in the base, Matty has her eye on Lewis, the surly one I told you about. They went to a dance together last Saturday.

Fly safe

IWU

Helen

***

Lily and Adrienne stood waiting to be called into the major's office, both unsure why they'd been selected from their class, the training had completed and both would admit that it had been the toughest six weeks that they'd experienced, physically and mentally.

They were just plain worn out.

Adrienne had been putting extra time in on her upper body strength as the plane was a fickle one, particularly on take-off and landing, you had to fly it every inch of the way and she needed every ounce of strength that she had to control the wheel. The door opened and they were motioned inside.

"Well, that was a turn up," Adrienne remarked as they walked back towards their rooms.

Lily was still slightly shocked by the turn of events. "I'm not sure whether to be flattered or terrified," she laughed.

"I'd go with flattered."

Thanks to acing their training, they had been selected as part of a scheme to show male pilots that the B-26 could be flown safely, they were to tour bases flying the B-26's. They wouldn't be returning to their own base for a number of weeks until they'd visited their share of the bomber bases.

"Flattered and petrified," Lily said, throwing her arm around her friend's shoulders.

***

July 1944 - Dodge City Army Air Base, Dodge City, Kansas

Helen had received a telegram from Lily as letter writing appeared to be proving difficult while she did her new assignment. She had been touring the country for eight weeks and in eight weeks Helen had received one lousy telegram and had not been able to write back as she didn't know the schedule; to say she was pissy would be an understatement of her current mood. She had taken her three days leave and visited home; enjoying being looked after in the way only a mother could do with lots of home baking and cuddles.

Since her return back to base Helen was trying hard to be upbeat and peppy, but the effort was starting to take its toll, particularly when the engineers at the base seemed out to kill her more that the gunners. They'd had a few run-ins over her time there; where things that were meant to have been fixed, weren't, as they were so busy with the fixes that they would lose track of what had been done and what hadn't. The bulk of the planes she and Matty had flown that week had resulted in their having to perform emergency landings and she was getting sick of it. She fastened her seat harness on the Bobcat and turned to Matty to complete their pre-flight checks.

They trundled along the runway building up speed, Helen pulled back on the stick taking the plane into a steep climb. When she heard Matty's voice in her ears.

"What the hell?"

She turned to look at her friend and immediately saw what Matty was referring to; out of the window black smoke was billowing around them.

"Hollywood, you're on fire!" Betty's panicked voice came onto the radio from the observation tower.

"Is that what the smoke is?" Helen said tersely into her microphone. "I'm gonna turn round and come back in."

She turned the plane back towards the strip and took the pressure off the throttle, immediately the smoke stopped.

"There's no oil," Matty said, looking out of the window. "The smoke stopped when you eased up, there must be a problem with the oil line."

Helen shook her head, "I may kill someone today."

Matty looked around at the small blonde, sitting with a determined look on her face, "Just make sure it's not me."

Laughing Helen lined up for landing. They limped back to the stand and were greeted with the crew chief looking white faced, "What happened?"

Helen leapt down from the plane yelling, "I'll tell you what happened. You didn't fix the damn oil line, that's what happened."

"I did," he yelled back.

"Really!" Helen shouted ignoring Matty tugging on the back of her zoot suit. She reached a hand up towards the wing and wiped her hand across, bringing down her hand slick with oil, she wiped it on the crew chief's face. "Then what's that? Next time we go up in a plane, your ass is going to be sitting right next to mine. So you better make damned sure that it's fixed."

Matty pulled harder on the back of Helen's zoot suit.

"What?" Helen yelled, turning away from the blackened face of the crew chief to look at her friend.

"That," Matty pointed up towards the sky.

A large aircraft bearing down on the strip dominated the landing line, its two large propellers spinning as it approached. Around twenty male pilots joined them on the flight line, watching the plane as it came down at speed; its wheels touched the tarmac and screeched before slowing as it taxied along the runway.

There were murmured approvals from the pilots at the landing as they watched as the bomber taxi onto the far end of the stand. Helen felt as though her heart had stopped as she waited watching for who would get out of the plane. Finally, three figures came into sight, however Helen's focus was on the one whose swagger she would recognize anywhere. She pulled her helmet off her head and threw it to the ground, taking to her heels at full speed, running as fast as her legs would carry her towards Lily.

Lily looked over at the pilots lined up, they were accustomed to this type of welcome, and usually the noise of the engines from the bomber would ensure that they had an audience for their arrival. Then would come the shock from the male pilots that two women had completed the landing they had just witnessed. Then the posturing would happen, where they would try to either hit on her and Adrienne or show off their own flying skills.

However, as they walked towards the offices, the welcome she was about to receive in Dodge was going to be completely different to the other bases they had visited. She had spotted Helen as soon as she had rounded the plane, and it would appear from the sprinting woman that she had recognized Lily. Lily grinned as Helen's blonde hair, which had grown since they had seen each other more than six months previous, bounced around as she ran towards them. She had no time to say anything before arms were wound tightly around her neck and she was held in a tight embrace.

"You're here," Helen whispered. "You're really here." She finally released her grip and placed her hand against Lily's cheek, immediately seeing her error as she'd managed to cover her in the oil from her earlier altercation with the crew chief. "Oh God I'm sorry," Helen laughed stepping back, and spotting a smiling Adrienne out of the corner of her eye. She turned and held out her arms towards the tall red head.

"Not with that hand you won't," Adrienne held her hands out in front of her and took a step back. "But it's good to see you too Hollywood."

"Welcome to Dodge," Helen grinned, looping her arm through Lily's and walking her at speed towards the base.

***

Sitting at dinner the three friends quickly became reacquainted, catching up on all the things that they hadn't been able to say in their correspondence. Shortly after finishing their meal, however, Matty walked up and tossed a letter down on the table beside Helen.

"Hollywood, I picked up your mail," she smiled, slipping into the space at the table next to her.

"That's Lucy's writing," Adrienne noted pointing her fork towards the envelope. "Let's hear what she's got to say for herself. It's been ages since I got a letter from her."

"Me too," Lily added, nodding towards the red-haired woman sitting next to her.

Helen put her cutlery down and picked up the mail, "Maybe if you two spent more than two nights in a base, your mail would catch up with you." She slipped her finger under the seal and pulled out the letter. Scanning it before she read it aloud, her face fell.

Noticing Helen expression Lily reached her hand across the table and placed it on top of Helen's.

"What is it? What's wrong?" she asked gently.

"Marjorie and Lucy's husbands have been captured," she looked up from the letter. "They're in a prisoner of war camp." She placed the letter down on the table and pushed it across to Adrienne.

Sitting in silence each woman sat contemplating the news, each silently counting her blessings.

***

Helen lay in her bed staring at the ceiling; unable to believe that somewhere else in the quarters was Lily. After today's news, she was thankful that for once in almost seven months she knew exactly where she was. A quiet tap at her door roused her from her thoughts; pulling back the covers, she slipped her feet into her slippers and padded across to the door. She opened it slightly and poked her head around the corner. Standing in the hall in her zoot suit was Lily. Her hair was down and cascaded softly around her shoulders, looking blacker than usual in the dim corridor. Helen smiled, pulling the door open wider to allow her lover to enter.

Lily checked the hallway to make sure she was unobserved; she pulled the zip down on the front of her zoot suit and shrugged the overall from her shoulders letting it fall to her feet, revealing her nakedness underneath. Helen's eyes widened and she shot her head out of the doorway scanning the hall she grabbed Lily's arm and yanked her inside, Lily stumbled slightly on her zoot suit, puddled around her ankles. Helen simultaneously closed the door and pulled Lily to her, her hands tangled in Lily's dark locks as she kissed her furiously with a kiss full of seven month's worth of longing. They lost themselves in the kiss as finally the dreams of being together that each had had were given a corporeal outlet.

Lily shook her legs to liberate her feet from the confines of her flight overall, giving a quiet yelp of victory against Helen's mouth when she was free. They pulled apart breathlessly.

"I thought I'd come say hi," Lily whispered her hands slipped down to toy with the waistband of Helen's shorts.

"I'm glad you did, I believe you had a reverse thrust landing procedure that you wanted to share with me?" Helen asked, grinning pulling her t-shirt over her head. Lily gave her a broad smile.

"I do," she replied, quirking her eyebrows and pushing Helen's bed shorts over her hips. Stepping out of the clothing, Helen took Lily's hand and led her towards her bed, pushing Lily gently onto the cot; Helen lowered her body slowly against her lover. Their breaths caught as they felt their skin connect. Helen swallowed hard, feeling her eyes brim with tears as she became overwhelmed with the depths of her feeling.

"I love you," she whispered, as she fought to keep the emotion from consuming her.

Lily let her hands run slowly up from Helen's backside, up her sides, enjoying the feel of Helen's contours. She gripped Helen's face and brought their lips close. "I love you too."

She pressed her lips gently against Helen's. They took their time to build the kiss up; sensuously reacquainting themselves with the others taste and feel. Their hips started to move pushing against each other as the desire that that they had been unable to express for so many months started to engulf them.

Helen reached a hand down between then groaning softly as she realized how much Lily had missed her, she allowed her fingers to tease slowly before neither of them could take the slow pace any longer. Lily's back arched as she felt the exquisite sensation of Helen inside of her, they moved together their bodies creating a captivating dance as they flowed together, until finally their movement stilled as Lily's muscles trembled. Her hands grabbed at the thin mattress beneath her, her grip so tight she could feel the blood pulsing through her fingers as she thrust her hips towards Helen, her head snapped back and her mouth opened in a silent scream. The tension released from her body as she relaxed back onto the mattress gazing up at Helen with brown eyes, hazy from her climax and the love she felt.

"I've missed you so much," she smiled, reaching up to tuck a strand of hair behind Helen's ear. Helen planted a soft kiss on Lily's lips.

"I've missed you too."

Lily pulled Helen tight to her, they lay for a moment before Helen husked into Lily's ear, "So, reverse thrust?"

Lily's body shook with her chuckle. "I should probably be in the pilot seat for that," she grinned maneuvering them carefully in the small cot so that she was on top.

***

Lily woke early, smiling at the arms tightly wound around her body. She pulled Helen's hand up to her face and kissed each of her fingertips. Feeling movement behind her, she looked over her shoulder.

"Hey," she said quietly. "I should get back before Adrienne wakes up and wonders where I am." Helen sleepily shook her head and nuzzled closer against her warm body. "I have to," Lily said reluctantly, pulling Helen's arm from around her and sitting up. She stretched her back out, stiff from a combination of their love making and sleeping on the small bed in the same position all night.

"I'll see you at breakfast?" Helen asked.

Lily turned to look at the blonde woman, who was now propped up on her elbow, her hand reaching out to trace the length of Lily's spine with a fingertip.

"I will see you at breakfast," Lily stood up before she started something that she did not have the time to finish, if her absence was to go undetected. "I hope there's a lot because I worked up quite an appetite last night," Lily smiled pulling on her zoot suit and tugging on the zip.

Helen flopped back down onto the bed her arms tucked lazily behind her head as she grinned smugly, "Yes you did."

Lily gave a small chuckle before walking over and leaning down to take one of Helen's nipples in her mouth and nipping her playfully, she turned her head to look into Helen's eyes.

"I'll see you in a bit, I wove you," she smiled.

"I wove you too," Helen replied swatting Lily's ass as she turned.

Opening the door to their shared room, Lily breathed a small sigh of relief as she heard Adrienne snoring softly; she changed quickly and slipped between the covers. She lay with a huge smile on her face as she thought about Helen.

***

"So how long are your friends here for?" Matty asked as she and Helen took off in a test flight.

Helen looked out of the cockpit window unable to stop a smile appearing as she thought about Lily, "Another night."

Matty nodded thoughtfully, "You and Lily seem close."

A flicker of panic shot across Helen's face as she wondered whether they had been indiscreet. "Yeah, We were a pretty tight bunk in training. I would have washed out had it not been for her," she said dismissively, hoping that Matty's line of questioning would stop. "Awww hell," she muttered. "The flaps are stuck, I swear to God, those engineers hate us." She attempted to loosen the wing flaps, growling in frustration as they refused to budge.

She called back to the base, "Hey Betty, we've got a problem, our flaps have stuck. Are we okay to come back in?"

"Hey Hollywood, you're clear. Come on home," Betty responded, checking the flight line.

As they turned back towards the base, the right engine stalled, there was a splutter as the propeller slowed and then finally stopped.

"Well that's not good," Matty said dryly, looking out of her side window at the stilled propeller.

"Betty, we may have a bigger problem. We're lame," Helen shouted into her mouthpiece. "One of our engines just quit."

Matty looked back towards the base and the windsock on top of the tower, "Helen, we've got a crosswind, with the three sixty approach pattern. This isn't gonna be pretty."

"Base, this is Hollywood. Request emergency landing procedures."

"Roger that Hollywood," Betty responded, turning from her seat she picked up a phone and dialed to get the fire engines and ambulance onto the flight line.

Lily was with Adrienne talking to the male pilots about how to fly the B-26. Giving instructions on how they should make sure that they fly by the book, as the plane was not one for cowboy flying, the landing, and take-off were done at over one hundred kilometers an hour and if you didn't nail the speed by the book, you would pay a hefty price. Their discussion became distracted at the sound of sirens outside the hangar. Looks were exchanged then by group agreement, chairs were scraped back, and they moved outside to see what the problem was.

"Hey Lewis," one of the pilots yelled. "What's the deal?"

The surly looking officer turned, "Hollywood and Matty are in trouble. They've got an engine out and are coming in."

Adrienne heard Lily gasp. Together they ran forward pushing their way past the gathered male pilots so that they were at the front. They looked up and approaching the strip was a UC-78 with one propeller spinning.

"Please let her land safe," Lily whispered, her hands pressed against her mouth, tears threatening. "Please let her land safe."

She felt Adrienne's arm around her shoulder.

"She's the best there is, she'll be fine," Adrienne said, her eyes never moving from the crippled plane, silently offering up her own prayer for their safe landing.

The cockpit was ominously silent, neither woman spoke, sweat was beading across their forehead as they did everything they could to ensure a safe landing, there was no noise coming from the tower in their headsets, as the occupants waited for them to land. The silence across the airwaves was broken suddenly by a male voice from the tower, "This is why a woman's place is in the home."

Helen released an incredulous laugh at the comment and shook her head, "Whoever said that, when I land this thing, run and run fast." She continued to nurse the plane along, waiting until the final moment to release the landing gear to minimize the drag

"Hollywood, your landing gear is up," Betty yelled into her mic.

"It's okay tower, it's on its way down," she confirmed, checking the status as the wheels locked into position seconds before she set the plane down. The wheels touched the tarmac and bounced along, Helen slowed the plane to taxi speed, blowing out a burst of air before looking over at Matty and grinning, "Let's go park up and find out who the smart ass in the tower was and kick some butt."

Lily and Adrienne exhaled slowly, hugging each other in celebration as the plane touched down and limped its way back towards the stand.

Lewis let out a long breath, "I swear to God, she scares the crap out of me when she does that sort of stuff."

Confused at the comment Lily, spun around towards the officer, "How often does that happen?"

"One engine hardly ever, emergency landings where the whole base is on alert, usually once or twice a week," he ran a hand over his short hair before giving the taxiing plane another glance and shaking his head. "She's never crashed one yet though," he said proudly, turning and heading back into the office.

Lily watched his departure; then turned back ready to meet Helen the moment she set foot back on land.

"And we thought we were living dangerously with the B-26," Adrienne mused. Turning she realized that Lily had already set off.

***

"Is it always like that?" Lily asked, dragging her fingers up Helen's stomach and between her breasts.

Still fuggy minded from the climax that those fingers had just created, Helen looked quizzically at Lily. "Huh?"

"Today, the emergency landing, the grumpy officer on the flight line said it happens a lot."

"Lewis?" Helen shifted so she could look at Lily's face fully. "It can be," she said carefully. "They have so much work on and those UC-78, they're on the wire. We're flying them to see whether they have a couple hours left in them. So all sorts go wrong," she frowned as she found herself defending the ground crew that she was so usually critical of.

Lily snuggled her head under Helen's chin, "Yesterday, after Lucy's news I was grateful that at least I know where you are."

Helen smiled, "Me too."

Putting her arms securely against Helen, Lily closed her eyes tightly, "Now I'm not so sure, I know where you are, but I also now know how dangerous it is at least before I was worrying about everything."

Helen took a moment to process Lily's words, she narrowed her eyes trying to figure out the logic, "Okay you've got me, it was better that you were worrying about everything?"

Giving a small laugh, Lily realized how odd it had sounded, "I meant that before it was just my over active mind but I didn't have anything specific to worry about or any evidence and now, now I'm going to worry that every time you go up that someone's not done their job right."

"I love you," Helen laughed. "I am not going to get myself killed…I promise."

***

Lily snuck back into the room. Adrienne was still in her bed facing the wall opposite. She had just unzipped her zoot suit and let it drop to the floor when Adrienne's voice startled her.

"You need to stop it."

Lily looked confused as she quickly re-dressed, "Sorry?"

"You and Helen. You need to stop it?" Adrienne repeated turning around. "Because she won't and you should."

"I have no idea what you're talking about," Lily replied stiffly.

"Then where have you been sleeping the past two nights?" Adrienne asked gently, sitting up on her bed. "Credit me with some intelligence, Lily."

Frowning Lily started to repeat her denial but Adrienne held a hand up, "I can't begin to understand what's going on between you two, but you need to stop before people start talking."

Walking round the cot, Lily sat down on her bed and rested her arms on her knees, "I'll tell you what you need to understand, I was married to a man that stood up in front of our families, stood up in front of God and made all manner of promises. This same man took every opportunity to criticize and belittle me and just when I thought that he couldn't hurt me anymore I find that he had a mistress." Lily took a deep breath and looked towards the ceiling to stem the angry tears filling her eyes. "I was married to a man who made me feel that I was less than I should be." She leveled her eyes to Adrienne, "Helen makes me feel like I'm more than I ever dreamed I could be. So no. I won't end it because I can't end it, any more than she can."

Adrienne nodded slowly a wry smile appeared on her lips, "You remind me of someone."

"Who?"

"Me. When everyone told me to end it with Ben. Have you thought about what you're going to do afterwards?"

"No, we've not spoken about the future. I only know that she is part of mine."

Adrienne nodded thoughtfully, plucking at the hem of her pajama top, "I'm going to say this because I love you both. It is tough and it is hard to have to hide your love constantly and you need to know that." Frowning, she opened her eyes widely as she struggled to find the words to express herself, "The sneaking around that you're doing, the not being able to show too much emotion in case you give yourself away, that eats at you over time. We live in a world that is mixed up and crazy and that shows no sign of changing anytime soon. Apart from the fact that one half of the World is trying to kill the other. We live in a country that is messed up."

Lily looked surprised at the passion in Adrienne's speech, "Look Adrienne, I know…"

"No, you don't know," Adrienne interrupted sitting up. "I wear my wedding band on a chain around my neck because half the states in our country not only don't recognize my marriage but class it as illegal. My husband can fight for his country but only as long as he's in a unit 'with his own kind'. They let us fly their planes, but won't give us military status. Hell, the man in Sweetwater wouldn't serve you because your skin was too brown." She exhaled and blinked repeatedly, "It's hard Lily, really hard and you need to think about what you're going to do in the future, because this war won't last forever." Adrienne rose from her bed and planted a soft kiss on Lily's hair, "I can see how much love is there, but you need to see past the love and rainbows." With that, Adrienne picked up her wash bag and moved to the bathroom, leaving Lily sitting contemplating her words.

***

"Grits! Oh how I have missed thee and for breakfast no less," Adrienne grinned, placing her tray down on the table.

Helen laughed returning her smile, "You protest a lot about them, but I think secretly you are a lover of all things grits." Adrienne rolled her eyes in response. "So Liliana how 'bout you show me inside that bird of yours before you both disappear into the wild blue yonder again," Helen said trying to keep her tone light.

"I think I can arrange a tour for a small fee," Lily replied in a flirty tone.

Matty's eyes lit up, "Can I tag along? I'd love to see inside the bomber."

Both Helen and Lily tried not to let their disappointment show.

Adrienne gave out a small groan, "I was hoping you could take me up for a quick spin in one of the pursuit planes first thing, Matty. Then I could show you the bomber afterwards?"

"Sure. We can do that," Matty said, sipping her coffee.

Lily shot Adrienne a quick grateful glance, receiving a wink in reply.

***

They walked so close that their arms brushed against each other, every now and again Helen would flex her fingers subtly allowing them to intertwine briefly with Lily's.

"Adrienne knows about us," Lily announced as they approached the bomber. She turned to look at Helen whose eyes were obscured by her aviator sunglasses.

"How?" Helen asked surprised.

Lily smiled at her girlfriend, her blonde locks were being tossed around her face. Her loose fitting white shirt billowed against her skin as the wind made it look like the material was breathing, "She says the way you greeted me plus the fact that I haven't slept in the room with her since we arrived may have confirmed what she already suspected."

Helen nodded thoughtfully, "What did she say?"

Sighing Lily dug her hands into the pockets of her flight jacket, "You want the long or the abridged version?"

"Gimme the highlights," Helen smiled, sensing a reluctance in Lily.

"That the World isn't ready for us, that our country can't even decide to make us military and that we will have to hide our relationship and we should think about our future because if we're together it will be tough. I think that covers the gist."

Helen stopped and pulled on the arm of Lily's jacket, the leather squeaking at her touch, she took a deep breath, "The World, the World may never be ready for us Liliana, but what is important is that we are ready for us. Things around us will change. People grow, society evolves and while they haven't decided to make us military, did you think three years, two years or even this time last year, that you would be flying one of those?" she pointed across to the large silver bomber sitting in the stand the morning sun reflecting off its body. "We may not be able to be affectionate in public, but, what we do in private more than makes up for me holding your hand at a movie." Helen took a deep breath, "I know that it has been tough for Adrienne and Ben, but ask her about the times they are together and watch her face. Ask her whether she would rather live in a world with him or without him, because for all its faults this World and my World is perfect, provided that I share it with you."

Lily allowed her head to drop to the side and smiled broadly with soft brown eyes, "You Miss Richmond, know how to turn a girl to Jell-O."

"I try. Now show me your plane. I bet the wobble pump is huge on it," she grinned, looking at Lily's chest suggestively her dimples making her appear even more mischievous.

Helen climbed into the plane through the hatch under the wing. She was about to head off to the cockpit when Lily grabbed her hand spinning her round, she felt Lily tug her gently and soft lips press urgently against hers. The warmth of Lily's tongue parted her lips as hands worked the button and zip on her pants. She pulled away a look of shock on her face. "What are you doing?" she gasped, her cheeks flushed with arousal.

"Making up for not holding your hand in a movie," Lily growled against her lips.

Helen let out a small snigger that turned to a moan as Lily's fingers worked their way between her skin and the material of her underwear. Her knees buckled slightly as fingertips grazed against her. Rolling her eyes back into her head Helen leaned backwards until her back thudded against the thick soft insulation that lined the fuselage. Lily moved her lips down Helen's neck pressing against the sensitive spot behind her earlobe, she wound her arm around Helen's waist holding her in place as her fingers continued to stroke. The blonde gripped Lily's shoulders for support as she raised herself onto her tiptoes, her hips bucking as the rhythm of Lily's caresses increased until finally the muscles in her legs weakened and trembled as she peaked. Slowly she lowered herself back onto her heels and gulped in a lung full of air.

"So much better than holding hands at a movie," she grinned, taking Lily's face into her hands and peppering her with soft kisses.

They were sitting in the bomber's cockpit, Helen half listened as Lily took her through the instruments.

"Liliana."

Lily stopped mid-sentence her hand pointing towards one of the dials on the dashboard to look at Helen.

"I will understand if you don't want us because you no longer love me, it will devastate me, but in time I would be okay. I would never be okay if we don't give us a try because of fear of others reactions." She reached over taking Lily's hand in her own, "We have an obligation to leave this world a better place than we found it and if all we do is make one person see past intolerance and ignorance, then we will have done something worthwhile. I love you and you love me, everything else we'll figure out as we go."

Lily smiled and took Helen's fingers to her lips, "There you go with the Jell-O again."

"Well look what it got me last time; you can't blame a gal for trying," Helen smiled, cocking her head to the side.

***

Standing on the flight line Helen watched as the silver bomber prepared for take-off, the large plane sped along the runway before slowly starting to lift off and up into a climb. Thankful that her aviators were covering her tear-filled eyes. Helen chewed on her bottom lip as Lily flew into the distance.

***

Lily threw her duffle bag onto the bed that was tonight's sleeping place. Adrienne lay down and immediately started her ritual of comparing it to other beds from their trips.

"Does Ben make you happy?" Lily asked loosening the toggle on her bag and deliberately avoiding Adrienne's gaze.

"I see my comments have got you thinking," Adrienne smiled affectionately. "Why don't you ask me the question you really want to know?"

"Do you regret being with him?"

Adrienne sat up and looked steadily into Lily's eyes, "Not for one minute." She let her words sink in then slapped her thighs and stood up. "Do you suppose we can get something to eat here that isn't grits?" she asked, pausing by the door waiting on Lily to join her.

Chapter Fourteen

<u>August 1944 – Las Vegas Army Air Field, Las Vegas, Nevada</u>

Stopping the steady rhythm that she'd built up with the boot brush on her shoes, Lily pushed her cap back on her head; using the back of her hand she wiped sweat from her forehead. She had been grateful that for the largest part of the summer she had been travelling with Adrienne in the B-26 around bases and not subjected to the Las Vegas heat. However, it was now the end of August and she'd been back on base for a week and it felt like her lungs were burning; she was used to heat having grown up in Florida, but that was a humid heat. In the Nevada Desert, it felt like the heat seared her insides every time she inhaled.

Her mind played over the conversations she had had with Adrienne and Helen while in Dodge, her mind had started to divert towards the future, following the news in June that the bill to make WASP part of the military had been overturned in Washington and the recent events in Europe where Paris had been liberated. They didn't know what the future held in terms of being a WASP or how long the war would continue. The one thing that Lily was becoming more and more adamant about was that she wanted to be with Helen. Any doubt she may have had regarding that fact, had been confirmed by how she felt as she and Adrienne had taken off from Dodge. She pulled her cap back down, dipped the bristles of her brush into the tin, and worked the polish into the leather.

"Rita, do you ever think about what you're going to do?" she concentrated on the circular motions of the brush. "You know after all this is over," she looked up at the blonde woman.

Pushing her sunglasses up onto her forehead, Rita thought about the query, "I suppose, get married and have kids," she shrugged. "That's what everyone expects."

"Yeah, I guess it is," Lily gave her a small smile then resumed polishing her shoe.

***

December 1944

Marjorie quietly pulled clothes on top of her pajamas; she slipped her feet into her shoes, picked up her flashlight and headed out into the darkness. Walking towards the deserted flight line she was careful not to make any noise to alert anyone to her activities. Across the country, the women of Bay Four were making similar journeys.

Adrienne dressed in several layers before heading out into the cold night; she was on leave and staying on her parent's estate in Martha's Vineyard. As a last minute thought, she dragged the comforter from the bed and swaddled it around her shoulders. Clutching it closed with one hand, she struggled not to trip on the material as she walked out to the center of the gardens, allowing the large flashlight in her free hand to lead her way.

Lily padded silently across the bay.

"Where are you going?" a sleepy voice asked.

Turning Lily put her finger to her lips, "Sshhh, there's something I need to do Rita. Cover for me."

Rita nodded sleepily before dropping her head back down and resuming her sleep. Lily took a relieved breath, squeezed out of the bay's door and headed towards the flight line.

Lucy yawned widely and shook herself to try to wake herself up; the action did not appear to have any effect as she continued to yawn the entire way to the flight line.

Helen checked her watch; she gave a small nod to herself before lifting the flashlight she had in her hand and, pointing the light into the night's sky, started to flick the switch in a sequence that she had rehearsed throughout the day; her fingers struggling with the button through her thick gloves warding off the Kansas cold.

At exactly the same time, the other Bay Four women in their own locations were mirroring that same signal, this their agreed tribute to mark the anniversary of Adele's death. Each sent the message into the night's sky that they had repeated over her coffin that day in the funeral home.

Chapter Fifteen

19th December 1944

The winter evening sun was starting to set in the distance as Helen neared their destination.

"Tower, this is Army 344780. Permission to land?" the radio cackled while she waited for a response.

"Army 347780, this is tower. Can you confirm the highest rank on board?"

Helen turned to Stewie the engineer accompanying her on the trip to pick up a part for a bomber. Stewie shrugged in reply.

Being a WASP Helen had no rank; she quickly checked the engineer's rank insignia and called back to the tower, "Army 347780. Corporal. Over."

"Can you repeat?"

Frowning Helen repeated the message into the radio.

"Permission granted. Proceed to landing. Over."

Helen set the plane down and taxied to the position that the tower directed her to. She completed her flight checks quickly and shut the engines down. She and Stewie jumped out of the small UC-78 utility plane onto the tarmac.

Helen turned to close the door and looked quizzically at Stewie at the sound of approaching sirens. They were walking away from the plane towards the base when cars and Jeeps screeched to a halt around them halting their progress.

"Put your hands on your heads," a voice yelled from behind an open door of a Jeep.

Helen and Stewie exchanged worried glances before slowly raising their hands up complying with the order as far as their winter flying gear would allow.

"Is there a problem?" Stewie asked, his eyes scanning the number of guns currently trained on him and the small WASP pilot to his right.

"We have reason to believe that you are flying a stolen plane," the disembodied voice informed them as hands grabbed them from behind; their hands were roughly dragged from their heads and handcuffed behind their back.

The military policemen that cuffed Helen shouted over her head to the officer in charge. "This one's female, Sir."

"You sure?"

Helen gritted her teeth, her jaw tensing at the ridiculousness of the situation. "If he's not sure, I sure as hell am," she shouted in the direction of the query.

Two hours later after repeated questioning the military police weren't getting anywhere, both detainees were consistent with their stories. They had thrown Helen and Stewie into separate cells to wait while they called the Dodge base to check out their story. Helen folded up her heavy leather jacket into a makeshift pillow, lay down on the small bed, and waited for them to come back. Automatically, when not thinking about flying, Helen's mind would settle on her other favorite thing in life... Liliana.

Her lips curled into a smile as her mind conjured up an image of her lover. She hoped that their conversation during the summer had done enough to convince Lily that they had a future together, unable to discuss it openly it in their letters was proving frustrating, and with more and more victories announced on the radio, it started to feel like the war was going to be ending sooner rather than later. Greece, and Albania, had been reclaimed during the previous two months and Helen wondered whether their future may be closer than either she or Lily were prepared for. Her thoughts drifted to their impeding leave over Christmas, which she hoped would allow them to spend time to discuss what their future together would look like.

The door to the cell opened and a rather sheepish looking military policeman cleared his throat, "So we've spoken to Major Chiswell and it appeared that your story checks out. We're sorry and if it's any consolation he's just chewed our asses off for arresting you both."

Helen raised an unimpressed eyebrow at him, "Why on Earth did you think we'd stolen the plane?"

"Corporal is a low rank to be the highest on a plane. Tower thought it was either stolen or hijacked," the young officer shrugged inspecting the cell keys in great detail.

Standing Helen swept up her flight jacket. "So can we get our part and go now?" she asked walking out of the cell into the hall where Stewie was waiting on her, a look of relief on his face.

"Sure…we just need to complete some paperwork and you're both free to go. However, you may want to stay tonight and fly back tomorrow. There's a storm coming in."

Helen rolled her eyes and followed the man towards the office.

***

"Home, sweet, home," Stewie sang as Helen taxied the plane back into the base. "Never thought I'd be relieved to be back here."

Helen gave him a quick grin, "Me neither!" she switched off the engine and waved to Matty who was standing on the line waiting on her.

"Well if it isn't Bonny and Clyde!" Matty shouted as Stewie and Helen walked back from the plane. "Rumor has it that Chiswell asked them to keep you Hollywood but after only one night they said you were too much trouble."

Helen stuck her tongue out at her friend and thrust her parachute into her arms, pushing the her friend back onto her heels.

"Very funny Matty, tell me again about the rampaging cows that were out to get you?" Helen smirked referring to Matty's emergency landing of the previous month; where she had landed in a farmer's field, only to find it full of his dairy herd, which were rather inquisitive at the new addition to their grazing patch. Being a city girl Matty wasn't used to animals of this size and immediately took to her heels in panic, with the herd in tow, she had thrown herself over the fence and had landed at the farmer's feet much to his amusement.

"Funny, for a fugitive," Matty muttered as she followed Helen into the ready room.

"Gordon, Richmond the Major wants to see you both, his office ASAP," Lewis' voice filled the room.

Matty looked at Helen confused, "I get why he wants to see you, but what did I do?"

***

Lily landed in Romulus Base; she had been excited when she had seen the entry on the flight roster for a delivery of an AT-11 Kansan to the Michigan Base and had swapped with Rita for the duty. A trip to Romulus meant she could catch up with Adrienne, even if it was for only an hour or two before she made the return journey in a Bobcat.

Adrienne was waiting huddled in her winter flying gear for Lily to climb down from the plane, As she jumped down Lily noticed the look on her friend's face.

"Hey Red, what's up?" she asked hugging Adrienne tightly.

Adrienne blinked back tears and held out a piece of paper, "It's over."

"What do you mean, it's over?" Lily asked confused taking the paper, she looked down and started to read the orders that Adrienne had passed her.

Her eyes scanned the order. The words *'No longer needed,'* and *'Program to be inactivated immediately and all WASP be released immediately,'* leapt off the page at her. She looked back at Adrienne her mouth open in shock.

"It's over," she repeated, her tone full of resignation.

Adrienne nodded dumbly, choking back tears.

***

Helen and Matty walked back out of the major's office; trying desperately to mask the bubbling emotion of disbelief and disappointment that their service had ended. Lewis waved at them as they passed.

"Hey you two, hurry up! We've got a full schedule of flights planned today."

Shaking her head, Helen yelled back, "You're going to have to get someone else, we've been deactivated."

"What?" Lewis shouted. "Who the hell is going to fly these planes?" he asked gesturing around him.

"Not our problem," Matty managed to get out, her hand immediately going to her mouth to cover her trembling lip. "We're demobbed," she squeaked.

Helen put a comforting arm around her shoulder, "You'll have to get one of your pilots to take them up."

Looking around him at the empty hangar Lewis held his hands up, "Can you see them? 'Cause I sure as hell can't." He thumped his hands back down against his thighs and stormed off to speak to the major.

"So what now?" Matty asked as they walked back to the nurses' quarters, arm in arm.

Helen took a deep breath, "Now we get on with the rest of our lives."

***

"I'm sorry what do you mean I can't get back to Vegas?" Lily asked the base flight coordinator.

"We don't have a delivery going out there now for another couple of days and you can't fly yourself back as you're no longer authorized to fly military aircraft," he shrugged.

Lily huffed trying to control the anger that was rising in her, "So what am I supposed to do, all my stuff is in Vegas and I'm here?"

"You can either wait for the delivery flight and we'll let you ride along on that, or you make your own way back," he said uninterested, snapping closed the folder and turning away from the woman whose face was starting to flush with rage.

"Fine," Lily seethed and stormed out of the office, running into Adrienne.

"Whoa," Adrienne said taking in Lily's demeanor. "Not good news then?"

Lily took several breaths so that she didn't release her rage on her friend, "I can either pay my own way back to Vegas or wait two days to get a delivery flight back down."

Adrienne shook her head, "What a crock."

Laughing at her friend's description, Lily growled and shook her head, "Yes it is, so I guess I have to wait. Any ideas on how I can entertain myself for two days?"

Adrienne looped her arm through Lily's. "About a hundred and almost all of them are legal," she ginned, starting to run pulling Lily with her.

***

Helen hugged Matty. "You stay in touch," she demanded.

"I will! You too," Matty replied, fighting back tears as she picked up her case and stepped up onto the train.

Helen stood on the platform, rolling her neck trying to release the tension that had been there since the previous day when their orders had come through. She had tried to contact Lily by phone but the girl that had answered in Vegas said that she was on a delivery flight and would not disclose where. Helen had no idea where Lily was when demobbed.

The guard blew his whistle and the train's pistons started to move back, and forth, forcing the crank and connecting rod to move, the wheels started to turn slowly and the train belched into life with smoke billowing from the chimney up front. Matty pushed the window down on the door and stuck her head out, shouting over the noise of the departing train.

"Hey, Pocket Rocket. Happy landings!" she waved her hand madly then ducked back into the train.

Helen waved in response waiting until the train was in the distance before leaving the station.

***

Lily entered her bunkhouse, both Rita and Sadie's lockers were empty, and their beds stripped. She let her head fall forward in disappointment it would appear that her delayed return meant that she'd missed both their departures. A note signed by both of them had been placed neatly on her pillow.

Hey L

Sorry we couldn't hang around, but we got the opportunity to get a lift north by an officer going on leave…couldn't pass up the opportunity of a free ride (especially since the Army won't pay for our trip home!)

Keep in contact and best wishes for the future.

Rita and Sadie

P.S. Your friend Helen called the base…she left a message said you'd know what it meant…IWU?

***

Throwing her duffle bag over her shoulder, Lily took a meandering route to the main gate of the base. It felt odd to be walking through the flight line for the final time and to be dressed in civilian clothes. She said a silent goodbye to the planes sitting gleaming proudly in the winter sun, before checking her watch. The base commander generously had offered to pay a cab to take her to the station where she would catch a train to New York. She had tried to get hold of Helen when she had returned but had been told that the she had left Dodge and they didn't know where she headed. As Lily walked towards the guardhouse, the guard on duty saluted her.

"You don't need to salute me Dan," she said lifting her violin case. "I'm just a musician now."

"No Ma'am, you'll never *just* be anything," Dan smiled. "Your ride's here," he added noting her departure down on his clipboard.

"Thank you," Lily said smiling towards Dan as she walked around the guardhouse. "Take care of yourself, and your…" she stopped mid-sentence as she turned her head round. "Loved ones," she said absently, her eyes never leaving the figure leaning cross-legged against a red motorcycle.

Helen sat opposite the gate of the base, dressed in blue jeans and a white t-shirt, Aviators blocking out the Nevada sun.

"Thought you might need a ride," she shouted, standing up and indicating towards the bike.

Lily walked forward, dumped her belongings onto the dusty road in front of Helen, and pulled her into a hug.

"I do," she eyed the motorcycle over Helen's shoulder, "and the first thing we're doing is buying a car."

"What!" Helen protested, pulling from Lily's embrace. She bent down and picked up Lily's suitcase, "You don't love my 'cycle?" she asked, tying the case to the back of the bike.

"I love you and your 'cycle, what I don't love is how I can't feel my ass after twenty minutes," Lily grinned, happy to be with Helen again.

Helen threw her leg over the bike and settled onto the seat, "If you want I can feel your ass for you in twenty minutes, save you the bother?"

Lily laughed as she picked up her violin case and mounted the bike. "I will take you up on that offer," she whispered in Helen's ear, smiling at the shiver that went through the blonde-haired woman's body. She wrapped one arm around Helen's middle and relaxed her other arm with her violin case at her side.

Smiling, Helen started the engine, she was about to pull on the throttle when the familiar sound of a bomber drowned out the motorcycle's engine. They sat in silence watching as the bomber flew overhead towards the runway.

"Can you believe you flew those?" Helen asked her eyes still on the now empty sky.

Lily dropped her gaze to study Helen's profile. "Sometimes," she replied, squeezing Helen's waist affectionately.

Happy that Lily was as comfortable as she was going to get Helen tugged on the throttle. The bike kicked up a dust cloud around them before they set off down the open road.

"Happy landings?" Helen shrieked, over the roar of the engine.

Lily's smile grew her hair whipping around her face as she shouted her response.

"Happy landings."

Epilogue

<u>March 8th 2010 – Washington, DC</u>

Lily took a deep breath as she stared at her reflection in the mirror. She touched her fingertips to her face, now weathered with age. The journey to Washington had taken more out of her than she cared to admit to either herself or her granddaughter and the next forty-eight hours would be emotional. While it was lovely to catch up with friends, she would be forced to reminisce and knew that would only cause her to dwell on all that she had lost.

"Abuela, are you okay in there?"

"I'm okay Ellie, just trying to make this old face look presentable," Lily replied. With one final glance in the mirror, she steeled herself against the emotions the memories would bring. With a brisk nod, she turned and opened the bathroom door, "I'm ready when you are Kiddo."

"You sure you want to do this? We can always go down later," Ellie asked, her face full of concern.

Lily smiled wearily, "I'm sure let's go."

They exited the elevator and scanned the foyer for Joanne, who rose from her seat when she spotted them.

"All ready to go Mrs Rivera?" Joanne asked as she walked up.

"It's Lily," Lily corrected, narrowing her eyes at Joanne.

"Sorry," Joanne smirked. "Lily, would you like to go into the exhibition now or would you like to relax and have a drink before you go in?"

"You trying to get me drunk, flygirl?" Lily quipped, winking at Joanne. "I'd rather go in now and drink later."

They walked into the exhibition hall and started towards one of the boards, Lily looked at the class numbers on top of each board trying to locate their graduation class. When she reached the board, she scanned the photos before leaning closer to one.

"Would you look at me here, this is after I flew solo for the first time. They dunked me in the wishing well."

Ellie and Joanne moved forward to look at the black and white photo, they both smiled at the broad smiles on the faces of the women in the photo. Standing in the center of the photograph wearing her flight clothing, dripping with water and her hair plastered flat against her head, with a huge smile on her face, was the younger version of Lily; holding out her hands as if shaking excess water from them.

"You were pretty," Joanne observed.

Turning with a look of disdain on her face Lily raised her eyebrows, "I. Was not 'pretty'. I. Was. Hot!" she corrected waving a finger in the air, waggling her eyebrows at Joanne.

"Look, there's Grandma," Ellie pointed excitedly to another female in the picture.

Joanne moved her head forward to the figure that Ellie was pointing at, she looked in confusion between the two women standing beside her and the image of a fair-haired woman with dimples. Catching Joanne's look of bewilderment Ellie chuckled slightly, "Sorry, I forget that people don't know about our rainbow nation family as my mother calls it. This is Grandma Helen. I'm named after her."

"My wife," Lily said, a soft smile on her face, her eyes misty and distant as she looked at the face of Helen.

"Your...?"Joanne looked surprised, her eyes wide open, her mouth turned downwards as she nodded slowly, finding her assumptions about the former WASP being stripped away slowly. "Okay."

Lily turned and smiled, "What, you think your generation invented sex and sexuality? I'll have you know..."

Ellie pointed to the picture again eager to stop one of her Abuela's famous rants, "And there's Aunt Addie."

"Did someone say my name?"

They turned towards the voice; sitting in a wheelchair behind them was a smiling woman whose blue eyes twinkled with delight at seeing her old friend. "And it's Great Aunt Adrienne to you, young Helen," she corrected, holding her arms out for Ellie to enter.

Giving her great aunt a careful hug Ellie laughed, "I know but Grandma Helen said I was never to call you that, 'cause it pandered to your superiority complex."

Adrienne tossed her head back and laughed, the action causing her to start coughing. She placed the handkerchief bundled in her hand to her mouth and waved at the tall caramel-skinned woman in her sixties, who moved to her side to assist.

"I'm fine. Don't fuss," Adrienne frowned once she regained her composure. "Lily, it's good to see you, it's been too long my friend."

Lily gave her a sad smile, "Two years."

Adrienne sighed and nodded her eyes starting to fill with tears.

"That long?"

Both women drifted off reflecting on the last time they had seen each other and the time that had passed.

Joanne nodded a greeting to Jennifer who was standing behind Adrienne's wheelchair, holding onto the handles.

The tall woman with Adrienne studied the photograph they had been looking at. "Will Lucy be coming, Mom?" she asked, spotting the smiling woman in the photograph standing beside her sister Marjorie.

"She should be, Adele, she wrote to say her Peter Jnr was going to bring her. She likes to come to these things now Marjorie is gone," Adrienne nodded.

Joanne picked out Adrienne in the photograph, turning and giving the older version a quick glance over before comparing her to the stunning looking woman in the photo.

"Who's that?" she asked pointing to a small woman, standing with Adrienne's arms looped around her neck.

Smiling both Adrienne and Lily answered as one, "That's Stotty."

Adele placed a comforting hand onto her mother's shoulder, "I'm named after Stotty."

"That photo was taken in, what? The August?" Adrienne asked Lily who hesitated trying to calculate in her head before nodding in agreement. "And Adele died at the start of December."

Jennifer peered over the top of Adrienne to look at the photograph, "What happened?"

"Midair collision with another cadet," Lily answered looking at the smiling image of Adele. "She was a character and a half," she laughed.

Adrienne nodded. "She was twenty three when she died. So young," she said sadly.

Adele patted her mother's shoulder. "Why don't we see what other photos are here," she said brightly, trying to raise the mood.

They walked around the display with Adrienne and Lily telling stories of their training, they reached a photograph taken of them standing beside a B-26.

"You flew those?" Joanne asked in admiration, reading the panel beside it with the statistics of the bomber.

"We sure did," Adrienne grinned. "Some of us even had sex in it," she looked pointedly at Lily.

"Abuela!" Ellie gasped as the others laughed at the comment.

Lily gave a half shrug, unabashed at Adrienne's remark, "What! It was good sex. Your Grandma Helen never complained."

Ellie placed her fingers into her ears and started to hum, she cautiously removed one, "Has she stopped?"

Adrienne pulled on Ellie's arm, "At least you didn't have to sleep near them. They did it one night in the bay when they thought we were all asleep."

Lily looked shocked as in the almost seventy years since it had happened, Adrienne had never before let on that she had heard them.

"Ask Lucy, she was the one that heard them in the bay. When you're at it ask her about the noises from the room in Atlanta," she added ignoring Ellie's obvious discomfort.

"I might skip that discussion," Ellie replied shaking her head.

Adrienne laughed, "Lucy didn't know what she heard, thought it was just Helen having one of her nightmares. Hell she didn't even know what a lesbian was until that tennis player in the eighties. She just thought Lily and Helen lived together as friends."

Both Adrienne and Lily laughed loudly as they recalled the look on Lucy's face as realization as to the true nature of Lily and Helen's relationship hit her.

Wiping tears of laughter from her eyes, Adrienne continued, "She's one of nature's innocents our Lucy, God knows how she didn't work it out, they were so cute together. You know your Abuela slept through every reveille every morning, the only thing that woke her up was a smack on the head or when your Grandma had a nightmare."

Lily smiled wistfully, "She needed me, I could never sleep through that."

They continued taking in the display, Lily walking beside Adrienne's wheelchair, every now and again a hoot of laughter could be heard from the women as they repeated a memory. Joanne fell into step beside Ellie.

"So two grandmothers? You failed to mention that earlier."

Ellie gave a small smile, "I thought it would be more fun for you to find out this way. My mother is Lily's niece. Her father died three weeks before the end of the war, and her mother died the following year from cancer. She was four when her mother died and my uncle was two. Lily and Helen took them in and raised them, so they're the only grandmothers I've known from that side of the family."

"What happened to your Grandma Helen?" Joanne asked carefully, trying to make sure she was out of earshot of Lily.

Ellie swallowed hard, "She died two years ago, peacefully in her sleep." Her eyes filled with tears as she discussed her grandma.

"Only thing she ever did that was quiet," Lily added, walking up to them catching what Ellie had said. "She died a month after we got married, after sixty five years of being together and raising a family, I made an honest woman of her. Finally the world was ready for us." She squeezed Ellie's hand, "I think I'll have a little lay down before the dinner this evening."

Ellie nodded, "Okay, I'll take you upstairs."

"No, I'll be fine. You stay here and tell Richmond here about your grandma and how she almost got herself killed a half dozen times," Lily smiled at Joanne. "Ask about when she got arrested. Thank you for your assistance today," she switched her walking stick to her left hand and held out her right for Joanne to shake.

Joanne shook it. "Thank you," she replied and honestly meant it.

Lily gave her a brisk nod, winked at Ellie, then made off towards the exit, waving to Adrienne, Adele and Jennifer on her way.

"So what happened to them after the war?" Joanne asked, watching the elderly woman walk across the conference room.

"Ummm," Ellie said taking a deep breath. "They moved back to New York which is where Abuela was living before. She was a violinist in the Philharmonic Orchestra there, my cousin plays cello there at the moment," she added. "But Grandma couldn't get any jobs flying, they wouldn't hire a female pilot, so she drove a chequer cab for a while, but Abuela said that while she could fly like a dream and ride a motorcycle like a racer. She was a God-awful driver." Ellie laughed, recalling the times that her mom had told her about her grandma's driving prowess. "Then when they took in my Mom and Uncle, they moved to Florida for a while, when my great grandparents died they sold the family businesses there and moved to California and set up their own aerial firefighting company. My brother runs it now and that's where they stayed."

Ellie finished stopping in front of another image of her grandmothers, this one was a rare color photo. Taken sitting on long wooden benches outside a building, Lily was laying on the bench a book held loosely in her hands, her head resting on Helen's thighs, both of them were in their zoot suits, sleeves rolled up past their elbows, squinting in the sun, wide smiles on their faces.

"If I find someone that I love, and who loves me, the way they did. I'll be doing well," Ellie mused, her fingers tracing the outline of her grandma's face.

Joanne looked at the picture then towards the door, which Lily had just departed through before studying Ellie's features. "We all would," she said quietly to no-one in particular.

***

Ellie helped her grandmother into her uniform.

"So little one, how did your date go?" Lily asked, as she allowed Ellie to pull on her jacket.

"It wasn't a date, Abuela," Ellie blushed. "We just had drinks and talked."

"And?" Lily raised her eyebrows as far as they would go.

"Oh okay," Ellie huffed. "You were right. She's gay…satisfied?"

"Hah!" Lily clapped her hands together. "You going to see her again?"

"She'll be at the ceremony today," Ellie replied, being deliberately obtuse. "Now stand still and let me get you dressed."

"I swear this used to be tight on me, it used to cling to my curves," Lily grumbled. "However at that time, my curves were in the right places," she acknowledged, earning a snort from her granddaughter. Lily looked at Ellie, "She was so proud of you, you know."

Ellie looked up; she clenched her jaw determined not to cry, concentrating on fastening the brass buttons on the jacket.

"There," she said, picking some lint from her grandmother's shoulder and brushing the material. "She would be proud of you too in your uniform," she added, unshed tears glistening in her eyes.

Lily checked herself in the mirror. "Nope, she would be horny, never could resist me in uniform," she winked at her granddaughter. "Let's get this show on the road."

***

Adrienne sat proudly wearing her uniform, holding Lily and Lucy's hands as a wreath was laid on the Air Force Memorial to remember those WASP that died during service. The remaining Bay Four women paused at the end to give their own memorial for missing friends; they bowed their heads then together recited, "We live in the wind and the sand and our eyes are on the stars. Happy landings."

***

Joanne stood at the back of the room next to Jennifer, her back ramrod straight as she watched the nominated WASP walk up to the podium to accept the Congressional Gold Medal on behalf of the WASP.

She clapped wildly as the medal was awarded, ignoring the look of surprise on Jennifer's face. She glanced several times during the ceremony across to Ellie, each time reveling in the surprise at finding soft brown eyes staring back.

"Today is the day when the WASPs will make history once again," the female colonel told the gathered crowd. "If you spend any time at all talking to these wonderful women, you'll notice how humble and gracious and selfless they all are. Their motives for wanting to fly airplanes all those years ago wasn't for fame or glory or recognition. They simply had a passion to take what gifts they had and use them and they let no one get in their way."

Lily sat listening to the speech, her mind filled with a lifetime of memories; she looked down to her hands, sitting in her palm were two sets of polished silver wings.

***

Entry In May 2012 Airforce Magazine

An open letter by 1st Lt Joanne Parsons

April 7th 2012

I am privileged

Had you asked me a couple years ago, I would have admitted this readily and put it down to the luck and chance of being born to a woman, who was married to a man whose career choice meant that he was rich. I'm not bragging about this, as no part of that was my doing…but I benefited. I grew up in Beverly Hills (with the zip code from the show that no one admits to ever having watched) I went to good schools; my college choice didn't come down to scholarship opportunities. Like I said…

I am privileged

However that was two years ago, ask me today - and I know I'm lucky not with the family I was born into but the era I was born in.

After college I wanted to serve my country by doing what I loved, and there was no-one stopping me (apart from an overwrought mother).

I am privileged

I was born in an era when who you love is becoming less, and less, of an issue (I hope future generations will be even more privileged than mine) thankfully who you love now does not stop you serving your country. I can now be open and honest about the photograph of the dark-haired, brown-eyed woman dressed in scrubs that I keep with me at all times – her name is Ellie.

I am privileged

So why the change?

Well just over two years ago I was chosen to provide an escort to an elderly woman to a ceremony, not a prospect that I relished (children, animals and old people are not my forte) However, the woman I met was Lily Rivera and the event was the Congressional Gold Medal ceremony for the WASP.

If you're asking yourself the who? You wouldn't be alone! I did the same when I got my orders…so here's the History bit.

To free up male pilots during WW2 over 1000 women holding civilian pilot licenses and meeting the entry criteria, left their jobs from all walks of life to undergo the same training as male pilots, becoming the first women authorized to fly military aircraft. They delivered planes, flew utility, became target practice for gunners and taught male pilots that flying the B-26 could be done, and some gave their life for their country… and they did all of this as civilians.

It wasn't until the 1970's that the government recognized their contribution and provided them with military status. In 1944, the experiment ended and those women returned to their lives, many never talked about what they had done during the war, even their families didn't know.

Lily Rivera was twenty-five and a violinist in the NY Philharmonic Orchestra when she was accepted into the program. She graduated top cadet of her class and assigned to transit duties, she flew over nine-hundred hours in the WASP uniform by the time her service was completed. (When you consider that her service was a yearlong…that's a lot of flying) including showing the men a thing or two in the infamous 'Widowmaker.'

I am privileged

Lily and women like her fought prejudice, discrimination, and often, outright hostility. In doing so, they are the reason why when I chose to serve my country…the opportunity existed.

I am privileged

During her time as a WASP, Lily met the love of her life, Helen Richmond. Helen was a stunt pilot and occasional derby racer, who also rose to the call for female pilots. From the stories told, theirs was a love story worthy of an epic movie. Their relationship spanned decades that saw civil rights increase regardless of race, sex, or sexual orientation. They raised a family and ran a successful business, teaching their children, grandchildren, and great grandchildren to 'Leave the world a better place than they found it.' Their love did not even end with the death of Helen in 2008 at the age of ninety-two. I never had the opportunity to meet Helen, but I know that her legacy lives on in those that loved her.

I am privileged

I can honestly say that the time I spent with Lily both on that day in 2010, and beyond, opened my eyes and made me appreciate what I previously took for granted. She made me consider how I want the world to be when I leave it and how I would relish a love that would last a lifetime as she experienced. But, mostly, I am privileged to have met such an inspirational, funny, courageous and filthy-mouthed woman and I, as a strong independent privileged woman, salute her.

Liliana Rivera: 25 August 1918 - 31 March 2012

About the Author

HP Munro lives in Scotland with her wife and a dog called Boo.

You can connect with HP through:

Email - munrohp@gmail.com
Twitter - @munrohp

www.red-besom-books.com

Other Titles by Author

Coming Soon

Grace Falls

Dr Maddie Marinelli is looking for a fresh start; she's leaving behind the ghost of a failed relationship and looking forward to starting a new job and life in San Francisco...what she didn't count on was car trouble and the colorful residents of Grace Falls.

Alex Milne has spent most her adult life putting other people's needs first. She is busy raising her daughter in her hometown while running her business and the last thing she expects is to be attracted to Grace Falls' newest, albeit reluctant, resident.

Sometimes you don't know what it is you're looking for, until it comes along and finds you.

Coming In Spring 2014

Stars Collide

It's tough growing up in the spotlight and Freya Easter has had to do just that, being part of the Conor family, who are Hollywood acting royalty, has meant that every aspect of her family's life has been played out in the spotlight. Despite her own fame Freya has managed to keep one aspect of her life out of the public eye, however, a new job on hit show Front Line and a storyline that pairs her with the gorgeous Jordan Ellis, may mean that Freya's secret is about to come out.

In a world of glitz and glamor, Jordan Ellis has come to the conclusion that not all that glitters is gold. She has become disillusioned with relationships and is longing for a deeper connection, and is surprised when it comes in the form of the most unexpected package.

Whilst their on screen counterparts begin a romantic journey, Freya and Jordan also find themselves on a pathway towards each other.

Printed in Great Britain
by Amazon